Franklin Matthews

The New-Born Cuba

Franklin Matthews

The New-Born Cuba

ISBN/EAN: 9783337378295

Printed in Europe, USA, Canada, Australia, Japan

Cover: Foto ©Andreas Hilbeck / pixelio.de

More available books at **www.hansebooks.com**

THE
NEW-BORN CUBA

By

FRANKLIN MATTHEWS

ILLUSTRATED

NEW YORK AND LONDON
HARPER & BROTHERS PUBLISHERS
1899

TO

WILLIAM ALLEN WHITE

WORTHY REPRESENTATIVE

OF THE

BEST TENDENCIES IN AMERICAN JOURNALISM

AND AMERICAN LETTERS

PREFACE

THE old saying that to start right is half the battle never had a better opportunity for exemplification than in the first steps of the reconstruction of Cuba by the United States. The world never saw a similar situation. An attempt has been made in these pages to tell what certain of the problems involved were and how they were met. Most of the chapters of this book appeared in a series of articles printed in HARPER'S WEEKLY early in 1899, but it has seemed best to supplement them with others giving a fuller account of what took place in Cuba in the first sixty days of American occupation and control, when the twig was bent for future growth. Whether the grown tree shall bear the fruit of national independence or of colonial dependence or of complete political assimilation depends largely upon the development and conditions of the future. The twig certainly was trained to stand erect and to grow straight and true by the American army officials and others, so as to produce national independence. What some of the agencies were that were used to that end and who some of the leading men were that carried out with absolute fidelity and most faithful zeal the orders issued in accordance with the intervention resolutions of Congress may be learned in these chapters.

Cuba's future, it is safe to predict, will reveal and justify the wise and beneficent acts of the American officials during the most critical part of American occupation—namely, its beginning and early growth, or during its first sixty days.   Whatever may be the result of later complications, American occupation of Cuba assuredly was started right.

F. M.

New York, *August*, 1899.

CONTENTS

vii

ILLUSTRATIONS

ILLUSTRATIONS

ILLUSTRATIONS

ILLUSTRATIONS

THE NEW-BORN CUBA

THE NEW-BORN CUBA

CHAPTER I

HAVANA UNDER AMERICAN MILITARY RULE

WHATEVER shall be the final outcome of the military occupation of the island of Cuba by the United States — whether complete independence of the people of the island, or annexation in some form to the United States — the first sixty days of that occupation will always remain most interesting and important. During the first two months of the stay of the American army in the island, for the declared purpose of pacifying the country and establishing a stable government by the people of Cuba, a vast and extensive governmental machinery was set in operation. It involved enormous labor and great tact. It required patience, courage, and a shrewd business foresight.

In those two months the momentous task of reconstructing a foreign land was begun. It was a land cursed by centuries of misrule, whose chief characteristics were corruption, disease, and filth, and this misrule was practised upon a nervous, volatile people, polite, and in most respects gentle, and as keen mentally, from the most in-

A   I

tellectual and refined to the most ignorant and brutal, as probably exists anywhere in the world. Not until one examines minutely the work that was established in these first sixty days can he understand thoroughly the extent of the labor involved, and not until then can

A BATTERY OF THE SECOND U. S. ARTILLERY AT GUARD MOUNT, CAPTAIN-GENERAL'S PALACE

he appreciate the devotion to duty of our officials—a devotion that required the burning of lamps by hundreds of men night after night until long after midnight—and what it has meant, and will mean, for the island of Cuba.

UNDER AMERICAN MILITARY RULE

Interest in American military occupation of Cuba centred first of all and chiefly in Havana. The moment we stepped upon the wharf at the landing, one night early in February, 1899, we needed no visual proof to know that we were in Havana. An odor, which only such a city could produce, and a description of which need not be given, reached our nostrils. It came from a sewer which runs directly under the Custom-house, and which had been one of the most deadly agents of infection in the city. Then came a dash in a carriage through the narrow streets of the older part of the city, past warehouses, past the captain-general's palace, up one of the business streets of the town, with its glittering shops, and then we came to the attractive park in the centre of town, about two-thirds the size of Union Square in New York City, called Central Park, alongside of which the celebrated Prado runs, and around which centres the life of the city at night. Electric lights made the place very bright, and the garish colors of the buildings, accentuating the arcades and columns and arches and barred windows, with the lights of hundreds of cabs speeding in various directions, and the babel of voices from the crowded cafés, made a night-picture such as probably only Havana could show.

Two sentries in the uniform of the United States soldiers, stepping smartly down a side street, gave us our first glimpse of the meaning of American occupation of a foreign land, and then we stopped at our hotel just as the notes from a chorus in "La Traviata" rang out upon the air from an adjoining theatre. I had caught a glimpse of no less than three balls on my drive, and as I

stepped to the sidewalk and bumped my way into the
hotel, I realized that the walks in the central part of town
were crowded with pedestrians. The city seemed to have
the gayety of a Paris and the activity of a London. A
mere glance showed that it was frivolous and happy, and
that the scars of war, if there were any, were hidden.

The streets were intensely interesting to a new arrival.
They were lined with sidewalk cafés; throngs were passing up and down; one caught the sound of more English
than Spanish in the hum of conversation; hundreds of
men in the American army uniform were seen, and soon
the notes of a bugle in the camp of half a dozen companies of the Tenth Regular Infantry, encamped upon the
promenade of the Prado directly in front of our hotel,
told me that American occupation of Havana was not
semi-commercial, as it seemed at first, but strictly military. The voices of street fakirs filled the air; boot-
blacks were crying "shine" and "polish"; a man in a
doorway next to the great Tacon Theatre was shouting
through a monster megaphone, in English, the merits of
his "magnificent Trilby show, boys not admitted." A
crowd stood about the doors of the central fire station
on Central Park, the modern fire apparatus and American horses to draw it being a constant source of wonder-
ment and pride to the citizens.

That night was a busy one in the well-known café of
the Inglaterra Hotel. At one table were Captain Sigs-
bee and a party of friends; at another sat Robert P.
Porter, fresh from his interview with General Gomez, in
which he had won the famous old man over to the idea
of temporary occupation of the island by the Americans,

TENTH REGULAR INFANTRY, HAVANA'S TEMPORARY POLICE DEPART-
MENT, IN CAMP ON THE PRADO

and proudly exhibiting to his intimate friends a telegram of congratulation from the President and Secretary Hay over the success of his mission. Senator Proctor passed through with another party of friends, and there were generals and colonels and captains and lieutenants enough for a small army seated at the tables or passing in and out. Over in Central Park hundreds were seated in chairs, from which the city collects a revenue of ten cents

THE HOTEL INGLATERRA AND CENTRAL PARK

a sitting, listening to the music that came from the ball-rooms of two of the clubs that face upon the park. Newsboys were darting about, cabs were hurrying hither and thither ; and as one walked about, dozens of little wizen-faced children, scantily clad, but with the air of professional beggars stamped upon their manners, thrust their hands into one's face and asked for pennies. Every

7

kind of head-gear was in evidence, from the Derby and tall hats of perspiring Americans to the light straw hats of the natives and the helmets of the tourist in the tropics. Here and there professional beggars carried naked babies about, in the hope of catching pennies from Americans overladen with riches, and occasionally a woman in widow's weeds passed along, telling a story to the imagination of the horrors of reconcentration under the butcher Weyler. Ticket-speculators were selling admissions to the separate acts to the opera in the Theatre Payret, and snatches of conversation were heard of Americans planning to get an option on this or that public works, or arranging to enter into some business venture, provided there was assurance of a stable government. There were said to be no fewer than eight thousand Americans in town even at that time.

The first thing to impress an observant visitor to Havana as he went about the town was the fact that the streets were really clean. In the first week of February, when I first saw them, one month after American occupation began, I found them as clean as the streets of New York, especially under Tammany rule. Another thing that was a great surprise was to find that the water of the harbor seemed even cleaner than that of New York Harbor. I remember that I spoke especially of this to General Ludlow, the military governor of the city and suburbs. I said :

"General, I crossed the harbor this morning, and was surprised—"

"You expected to find the water of Havana Harbor," interrupted the general, "precisely like the Chicago River."

MAJOR-GENERAL WILLIAM LUDLOW, U. S. V., MILITARY GOVERNOR
OF THE CITY OF HAVANA

"Exactly!" I exclaimed.

"And you found it as clean, if not cleaner, than the water in New York Harbor," was his response. And it was true. Another thing to attract instant attention in the city was that our soldiers, who were doing police

A HAVANESE HAWKER

duty with loaded rifles temporarily, were respected everywhere and obeyed instantly. The duty was irksome to them, and they rebelled inwardly against it, but on all sides there were quiet and order and a full disposition by all the people to make the best of the new situation. Still another thing to arrest attention was the fact that the horses, and even the dogs, of the street were in good physical condition. By nine o'clock in the morning the streets were lively with drays that were ungainly and unwieldy, and that filled up almost the entire narrow highways in the business part of the town. The mules which drew the drays were wiry little animals, and looked as much out of place drawing those enormous carts as a boy does in his father's clothes. A bunch of sleigh-bells attached to the collar of each harness, and long thick tassels of bright colors depending from the necks and flanks of the mules, were fitting accompaniments to the gaudy red Tam o' Shanters of many of the Canary-Islanders who drove the carts. The combination of noise and color accomplished the object of the drivers, which was to attract attention to themselves, and fulfil that ardent desire, met everywhere in Cuba, to occupy the centre of the stage, so to speak. As the hot sun sent its beams down through the narrow streets, with sidewalks just wide enough to be simply a stepping-stone from a carriage to a shop, clerks and porters appeared at doorways, and began to stretch the awnings across the ropes and wires that ran from building to building, thus shading the highways, a sight common in many old tropical and semi-tropical cities. All about the open space near the Custom-house drays were drawn up in large numbers, and in every quarter business dealings were in full operation.

The only sign that there had been a war was the American and Cuban flags flying from hundreds of buildings, and American soldiers going about the streets on their sentry beats. In walking down to the water-front on my way to General Ludlow's headquarters I passed into a foul-smelling narrow highway within three minutes' walk of the centre of the town, and soon an armed

GENERAL LUDLOW'S HEADQUARTERS AND RESIDENCE

United States sentry, with his rifle at port arms, stopped me, and said:

"Americans cannot go through here, sir."

"Why not?" said the rapidly rising independent spirit of the American citizen.

"General's orders, that's all."

"Yellow fever?" was the inquiry.

"No, sir; simply because this is the one place in Havana where no American can possibly have any business."

I took one glance down the street, and saw that the general was right. The heart of the sentry softened, and he let me walk with him to the corner of the next block, and I have to say that if there is a viler place this side of Port Said I don't know where it may be found. The episode was a good illustration of what our military occupation of Havana meant, and it is mentioned for that reason.

During the first two months of our occupation there were few busier places on the Western Hemisphere than the headquarters of General Ludlow, down in the palace of the city governor on the water-front; a fine building in a beautiful location, opposite old Cabañas, and commanding a splendid view of the harbor and its narrow entrance. The corridors were thronged, one might say, with hundreds, all desirous of an interview with General Ludlow himself. There were army officers, syndicate-hunters, dozens of persons seeking passes to Morro Castle, scores of impoverished people asking for food, city officials, personal friends of the general, priests, and tourists. Every one seemed to understand that General Ludlow was struggling with the most difficult problem, not purely military in character, that had probably ever been given to a United States army officer, but each also seemed to think that it would be a welcome respite to an overworked official if the general would give up a few minutes of his time for a conversation on this and that topic, and especially on the political conditions in

AMERICAN VISITORS TO CABAÑAS FORTRESS

Cuba. It was necessary for the general to hide himself up a narrow winding staircase, with two sentries at the bottom, and an aide in an outer office, whose chief business it was to act the part of a private secretary and keep callers away from his superior.

A cursory examination of General Ludlow's task was sufficient to show that if he succeeded in his work of regenerating Havana he would leave for himself a monument that will last for all time. It was also sufficient to show that he had the work well in hand, and that if he was left alone he would accomplish it. He not only had to attend to his military duties as Governor of the city, but he had to feed the starving, to clean the city outside and inside, to take the responsibility of putting off for nearly a year the work of sewering the city, to disarm the volunteers of Havana, to study the problem of reform of taxation, and to keep the city municipal machinery in motion, so as not to permit the military occupation of the city to become offensive to the people. How well he was accomplishing this task will be seen in detail in other chapters of this story of reconstruction.

In common with a host of other American citizens, I had felt a sense of disappointment that General Fitzhugh Lee had not been placed in direct charge of affairs in Havana. Without any disparagement to General Lee, it is proper for me to remark that, after studying General Ludlow's work, I became convinced that no mistake was made in placing this reserved, keen, apparently unsympathetic army engineer, than whom there was probably no better equipped expert in sanitary matters in the United States, in charge of this momentous work. He was bearing the hardest kind of a "white man's burden," and if, in addition, he was playing for the stakes of lasting reputation in the esteem of his countrymen and in history, it was that laudable kind of ambition that springs from a lofty sense of duty, and a willingness to sacrifice health and life if necessary to accomplish it.

It was pleasant to note that the people of Havana were co-operating with General Ludlow to the fullest extent. There was friction here and there, of course, but there was no disposition not to obey his wishes in every respect. The people of Havana accepted the new order of things without murmur. There was no sign, as one went about the streets and attended places of public amusement and talked with merchants and other citizens, that they resented the domination of a so-called "conquering army." There was no drawing of skirts by women as they passed American soldiers, no lofty tone of superiority by men as they went about their daily tasks. And on the part of General Ludlow and General Brooke, the military Governor-General of the island, as well as every other military commander in Cuba, there was the manifest disposition to make the military occupation as light a burden as possible, and in no sense that of a conquering nation. Our army was everywhere playing the consistent part of a sincere ally and pacificator.

It is only fair, however, to say that there was one discordant element in this acceptance of the situation. It came from irresponsible, and sometimes from responsible, journals published in the city. The spirit of yellow

DRAWING-ROOM, GENERAL GORDON'S RESIDENCE

journalism seemed to have descended upon the town. There was a disposition constantly to forget that the island was under military rule, and to nag and peck at the military authorities. In some cases outrageous criticism and assaults were made upon our generals—assaults that would justify the immediate suppression of the publications; but it was a tribute to the patience and good sense of our generals that they ignored them publicly, although privately they chafed a good deal under them, and chose to regard them as mere mosquito or flea bites, the most common causes of personal irritation in the island.

Probably the most striking signs of American military occupation, outside of the actual presence of our soldiers, were the placards posted up in every café and drinking-place in the city to the effect that by order of General Ludlow positively no alcoholic liquors were to be sold to our soldiers. The order was obeyed almost literally, but occasionally a soldier could be seen under the influence of liquor—the only drunken persons to be seen on the streets, for the people of Cuba do not get drunk. Everywhere in Havana there were brilliant lithographs advertising various brands of American beer. It was a wonder that some enterprising agent had not plastered the sides of Morro Castle with these signs. One would think, from the number of them in town, that we were simply a nation of beer-guzzlers. One noted with satisfaction, to offset this, that in many of the shops there were signs, "English Spoken Here," and American bicycle-stores, type-writing establishments, haberdashery stores, were a pleasant relief to "Greater

New York Cafés," "St. Louis Cabinets," and "Chicago Retreats," that had sprung up on all sides. The American occupation of Havana came home to me with a jar one day when I was passing through busy Obispo Street, as I read this sign:

STOP, AMERICANS!

CHEWING-GUM SOLD HERE!

Ten Cents a Package!

It was not wise to take too seriously the sign "English Spoken Here." The interpreter frequently lived, or did business, half a block away, and sometimes he could not be found. When he did arrive, his English was likely to correspond to an advertisement that I saw at the entrance to a barber - shop. It read: "Very good works made here." Here is the advertisement of an "American restaurant," taken from its business card:

This first class of establishment offeir the public, rooues with every confort and convinience for accommodation of permaent anf trancient guest.

It will be observed that there is more trouble with spelling than with syntax in that sentence. Here is an extract from a circus handbill printed in "English":

Special collection of train dogs introducing Dommestical Dogs and ETC presented by Mr. Antoni Pubillones.

And so the American military occupation of Havana unfolded itself to the visitor. Americans were to be

CARLOS III. AVENUE, ON WHICH IS GENERAL GOMEZ'S HEADQUARTERS

seen everywhere. There were adventurers, tourists, business men, investors, men and women of every kind, from the United States, but actual crooks—John McCullagh, in charge of the formation of a modern police force for Havana, sent home the first arrivals of American crooks, and the word was passed to the others to stay away. Then there were the sights of the town to be looked after. The bullet-hole in the mirror of the Inglaterra Hotel, where the correspondent of an American newspaper was shot at just before the Spanish evacuation, and the famous "dead-line" at Cabañas fortress, were alike the source of great interest to Americans. The bootblack who sat down and smoked as he polished your shoes, and then rang a little call-bell three times to announce that he was through, and afterwards, to amuse you, puffed out his cheeks, bowed his arms far out in front of him, and jolted himself up and down on his bench, as he shouted "General Lee!"—it would have made the general himself laugh—did a thriving trade. The drilling of the new police by John McCullagh attracted hundreds to the Prado daily. There was guardmount to be seen every morning. One of the most beneficent results of our occupation was the fact—marvellous to be told of Havana!—that not an immoral book was on sale in any of the book-stores. Four wagon-loads of them had been seized and burned by American soldiers. At regular periods a long train of army wagons, laden with provisions, started out for a trip in the surrounding country to feed the starving, and in five army depots in town hundreds of the hungry were to be seen drawing rations until they could find means of subsist-

ence themselves. Every tobacco factory was running
in full blast, and there was not a cigar-maker in town
able to work who was not making at least four dollars
a day — a circumstance which accounted probably for
the crowded condition of the cafés in all parts of the
town. Now and then one caught a glimpse of a carriage with coachman and footman, and occasionally some
of the aristocratic ladies of the city were to be seen
shopping at night. On every side the American soldier
was in evidence, and it did the average American citizen good to note his uniform dignity and the respect in
which he was held. The buildings, every window barred
with thick iron rods, the interiors disclosing a lavish use
of marble, seemed to make the place a city of jails and
fortifications.

And as night fell with a sudden blanket of darkness,
and the lights on the streets in buildings, street lamps,
and in hundreds of cabs dashing about like so many fire-
flies, came out; as the throngs appeared on the streets,
and the sound of music reached the ear from the public
square—one of the most unattractive of all the plazas
in Cuba—and scores of masked women were seen riding
to a dozen balls, it was interesting to stand on some
balcony and watch the attractive and seductive life of
the place. The light on old Morro, across the entrance
of the harbor, shot its beams up the Prado, over the long
rows of Indian laurel-trees that line the promenade of
that famous street, and it was easy not to notice the
beggars, who, after all, the children eliminated, were not
more numerous than along Park Row in New York in
the summer-time at night, and it was difficult to realize

that the city had felt the horrors of war in the starvation of thousands in its streets and public places only a few months before. The city was brilliant, happy, and there was only an occasional odor here and there to remind one that it was not yet entirely clean.

'

CHAPTER II

T HE saying that Havana is not Cuba was never more true than in the first few months after the war with Spain had ended. The war left few scars in Havana and in the other cities of the island (not including Santiago), except as were revealed in graveyard records, and in the applicants at military stations for food. In the country the war spread a blanket of devastation. As one went over the island on railroad train or in volante or on horseback, there was evidence on every side that the war was one of torch and famine rather than of powder and shot. The island was simply desolate.

Outside of cities of impressive architecture, and of towns and villages of huddling hovels, the country, ex-cept for a few miles around the cities of Santa Clara and Pinar del Rio, was bare of men and beasts, and almost bare of birds. The traveller even saw few flowers. Fruit trees were cut down and destroyed as a war measure. The fertile ground was rank with vege-tation. Although the Spaniards had gone and the hor-rors of reconcentration were over, the people would not

28

return to the country in the first few months of American control. There were no huts there; no seed, and no tools with which to till the soil; no cattle, without which agricultural work cannot be done in Cuba; no food;

WAR'S RUIN AT COLISEO, TWENTY-TWO MILES FROM MATANZAS

and so they stayed in towns and villages, worked in tobacco-fields and on sugar-plantations adjacent to cities and towns, ate what they could get, and wondered what the future would bring forth.

If there was one sight more pitiful in Cuba than any other, it was the women in black. Frequent as they were in Havana, where perhaps in some remote part of the city they even ventured to hold out their hands to you as you passed—women of refined appearance, too— the women in widow's weeds were the commonest sight in the small towns and cities. It was hard to tell where they got their mourning garments. It is no exaggeration to say that of a dozen women on a street in any Cuban village nine were in mourning. And their faces, sad with grief and thin with hunger even months after the war had ceased!

But there was a look of hope in the eyes of most of the widows—a forlorn hope, however, in many cases. The maidens early in the year were becoming cheerful, and as one went through the streets he heard occasionally snatches of a song they sung. It was one song, one tune, almost invariably. It was the Cuban National Hymn. The significance of that? Truly it was something for the United States, engaged in the work of reconstruction, to find out; as truly as was the meaning of thousands upon thousands of Cuban flags flying from huts all over the island—flags that it took bread to buy.

And then there was a still brighter side to the picture —the laughter of children. I remember that three days after the reporters reached the scene of the Johnstown flood one of them began his story, "The dogs are barking again in Johnstown," meaning that normal conditions were returning. So I might say of Cuba, the children were laughing and playing again. One could hear their shouts everywhere. On the streets and open spaces it was "One Strike," "Foul," "Third base," "Slide," as they played baseball furiously, and used American terms exclusively. At night, in the plazas of the cities, they played the Cuban game for ring-around-a-rosy to the music of American military bands. It was one of the commonest sights in Matanzas to see an American soldier trailing through the streets with two or three children, perhaps one perched on his shoulders, trading

English for Spanish words. The Spanish soldiers struck the children. Some of them the Spaniards maimed out of pure wantonness. The American soldiers coddled them, played with them, and everywhere you went it

TYPICAL PEASANT'S HOUSE, OUTSKIRTS OF MATANZAS

was "Good-bye," meaning "How do you do?" from the lips of the children when they recognized you as an American, and your hand stole into your pockets for pennies instinctively.

Never shall I forget how I was stumbling at night about a gloomy street in Matanzas, looking for General James H. Wilson's palace—I had lost my way—when an urchin of eight loomed up right in front of me and halted me.

" Good-bye !" he said.

" Good-bye !" I replied.

" Good-night !" he said.

" Good-night !" I said.

Then taking off his cap, the lad swung it in the air, and cried, " Dree cheer for de red, white, and blue !"

Lukewarm as I had tried to be about annexation, I could have caught that boy in my arms and hugged him, had he not darted away in a burst of merriment.

ROYAL PALM-TREES AND BLOCK-HOUSE NEAR MATANZAS

As one went through the island and caught glimpses of block-houses surrounding every settlement, big and little, and as his eye lighted upon the enlarged graveyards in every village and town, some idea of the horrors of the kind of war that was practised in Cuba came to his mind. I must have seen seventy-five graveyards on my trip in the various provinces, and I remember only one that was not enlarged because of the famine of the war. Major-General James H. Wilson told me that the story of the horrors of reconcentration had been only partly told. It was far worse than the people of the United States had believed. The pen of a trained historian alone can do that story of death by famine and military wantonness justice. Competent judges asserted that the island was nearly 200,000 men short. In most of the provinces the birthrate was less than one-half of what it was before the war. The island was stripped of cattle. In Matanzas, a province chiefly given to the cattle-raising industry, there were 298,000 cattle, according to a census, in 1894. When the war ceased there were fewer than 9000 cattle in the province—a region that could support 1,000,000 cattle with ease.

And yet the sunshine of prosperity was breaking through the clouds. One could see in the distances, especially in the provinces of Pinar del Rio and Matanzas, the smoke of numerous charcoal-burners. These pillars of smoke had taken the place of the smoke of war. They suggested only by contrast the burning of towns and villages and plantations. At railroad stations children and women held out their hands in mute appeals for charity, but that was a vast improvement upon the scenes of burials by the hundreds and thousands because of starvation. Here and there, through the blanket of devastation spread by war, the crops were springing up. This

was especially true for a dozen miles around the city of
Santa Clara, almost exactly in the centre of the island,
and in the district immediately surrounding the town of
Pinar del Rio, the centre of the tobacco-growing in-

BURNED SUGAR-REFINERY AT CAMPO FLORIDO

dustry. Although railroad stations and bridges were
destroyed, and in many cases entire towns were burned,
and although the tangled wrecks of twisted iron and
charred timbers of sugar factories confronted one frequently, gaunt spectres of the war and companion pict-
ures in the scene of ruin to the enlarged graveyards,
here and there could be seen late in February the smoke
of returned business activity pouring from the chimney
of a sugar-central, preserved from destruction only by
bribing both Spaniards and Cubans, or by the vigilance
of an armed force raised to protect the central at enormous cost, in many cases of considerable bloodshed as

well. On many freight sidings carloads of sugar-cane could be seen, their destination being the grinding-mills. Fields of tobacco were spreading their beautiful green mantle in the western end of the island. It was estimated that about one-half of a normal crop was being raised of sugar and tobacco, upon which, especially sugar, the life of Cuba depends. Although it was dreary to see the great stretches of unoccupied fertile country, land as rich as can be found anywhere, it was a satisfaction to realize that the worst was over and that the upbuilding process had actually begun. The country was in a passive state. There was practically no crime and no disorder in the land. The condition of Cuba was that

SUGAR-REFINERY IN OPERATION LATE IN FEBRUARY

of a person restored to consciousness after being stunned, but with scarcely more than enough strength to totter about.

The irresistible conviction was soon forced upon the student of the situation in Cuba that what the island needed most was men and money. Involved in the problem of securing them was the larger problem of the political future of the country. The normal increase in the population cannot supply the island's need of men

THE CUBAN SOLDIER AS HE WAS AFTER THE WAR

for many, many years. Immigrants, such as can endure the climate and can work to advantage in it, must come probably from the Canary Islands, or from Italy, rather than from the Southern States of this country. The tide of needed immigration, however, cannot set towards Cuban shores until there is reasonable assurance of the protection of human life ; and capital, always timid, will not seek investment there until there is a full guarantee from destruction or from serious injury.

The passive state of Cuba was due in some degree to its commercial and political prostration, but to a greater degree probably to the military occupation there. In all the large cities the United States army was in control. In every small town and in every village the Cuban soldiers were in charge. Whatever may have been the actions of the Cuban soldiers in and about Santiago during the campaign there, little reasonable fault could be found with them after the Spaniards went home. They moved into the towns and villages, preserved the peace invariably, and brought about a condition of order. They worked in perfect harmony with our forces after these arrived, and their commanders detailed their men in accordance with suggestions from our generals and military governors. They worked without pay, and they got their food and clothing as best they could. They practised no tyranny, and showed no spirit of hostility to American occupation.

Many were the complaints because they did not throw down their arms and go to work when the island needed laborers sorely, but there was another side to that. They had been fighting for three years, with little food and clothing, in their own peculiar kind of warfare—a warfare that our rank and file could neither understand nor appreciate—and they were still under orders from their superiors. To throw down their arms would have been a form of desertion, and at a time when there was prospect of receiving a gift of money from the United States —money that was absolutely necessary to start most of them in life again. If there was any fault to be found with the Cuban army, it was with the mysterious increase of about 20,000 in its numbers, and the Cubans themselves showed that they were not lacking in humor as they referred to these so-called soldiers as the "veterans of 1899." As one saw these Cuban soldiers patrolling at railroad stations, doing guard duty at sugar factories, going through the country with American officers on hunts for bandits that swooped down into towns occasionally and stole horses, a sense of respect for them was uppermost, despite the sneers that one heard from

A TYPICAL CUBAN VILLAGE

many Americans who based their judgment upon the episodes around Santiago. I could not but think that perhaps the Cuban soldiers had been as much misunderstood as the Cuban people had been by many of our people, who referred to them with contempt as "Dagoes," and I recalled the words of Mr. E. G. Rathbone, our Director of Posts in Cuba, who had unusual opportunities for the observation of the masses there, and who said to me, with the privilege of quoting him :

"The people of the United States have a wrong impression of the Cubans. They are kind, gentle, tractable, and easy to get along with. By kindness you can do anything in the world with them. I have studied them closely, and that is my belief."

Whatever may have been their personal opinions as to the future of Cuba, not one of our generals swerved in the least from making it plain to the people that our occupation was to be only temporary. I know whereof I write, for I talked fully and freely with every one of our major-generals in the island, with one exception, but I am not at liberty to quote their words. Major-General Wilson, in Matanzas, publicly made a declaration to this effect, however, on several occasions. He held to the strict letter of the resolutions passed by Congress, which declared :

"That the United States hereby disclaims any disposition or intention to exercise sovereignty, jurisdiction, or control over said island, *except for the pacification thereof*, and asserts its determination, when that is accomplished, to leave the government and control of the island to its people."

"We are here as pacificators," General Wilson said, repeatedly, and it was in accordance with this idea that in the latter part of January, while making a tour through the province of Matanzas, he said, in an address to some school-children, that he hoped the boys would grow up to be good and smart men, and that some day one of them might become president of the republic of Cuba.

I know that Governor-General Brooke in the early part of his administration earnestly hoped, and bent every energy to the end, that an occupation of only a few months might be necessary, and it is no secret that he would have liked to bring the entire American army home from Cuba before the rainy season set in. I am not betraying any confidence when I say that he held the opinion that if Cuba should ever become part of the United States it must be through the open and declared request of the people of the island, with a unanimity of purpose and sentiment behind the request. I know that Major-General Bates held that the one way for the Cubans to secure self-government was to co-operate with our forces to the fullest in the absolute restoration of peace and tranquillity, so that the United States troops might be sent home at the earliest opportunity. I know that Major-General Lee felt that he was in Cuba simply as a soldier. I am positive that Major-General Ludlow, while desirous of carrying out his great task of cleaning up Havana—a task involving more than a year's labor, even with the utmost expedition—personally would have welcomed orders that would have taken our troops out of the island, on the proof that Cuba was able to take care of herself. The administration of Major-General Wood in Santiago indicated freely and openly that he was in accord with these views.

And yet the United States forces still remained in the island, and no one could tell when they would leave. Outwardly the island was pacified. The younger army officers made no secret of their desire to leave the place. There was not an officer of thought, however, who did not hold the opinion that if the United States troops should go home anarchy at once would break out.

MAXIMO GOMEZ

" We have pacified the island," said one colonel to me ; " now let us go home."

" Yes," said another colonel, "and if we should go home, our transports would be lighted out of the harbor, if they should sail at night, by the flames of anarchy ; but that is none of our business."

From a thorough study of the situation I became convinced that what the officers said about anarchy was true. Our major-generals knew it, and if they had spoken their minds freely they would probably have said

41

that unless the United States desired to stand before the
bar of the nations of the world convicted of leaving a
condition of affairs worse than the horrors of war that
existed in Cuba before they went there, it would be not
only one year, but two years, and probably three, before
our troops could leave the island. "Except for the pacification thereof," the resolutions of Congress read. The
administration was compelled to interpret that clause as
meaning the *permanent pacification thereof*, and in the
full meaning of that interpretation, no matter what the
real purposes of the administration were, lay the future
of the island of Cuba.

I went to Cuba with the earnest purpose of obtaining
any material that would be of service in controverting
expansionist ideas, and that would justify the advocacy
of a prompt relinquishment of the island to its own
people. This is what I found: Every person of the
pro-Spanish class, those who sympathized with Spain
and hoped she would defeat the Revolutionists, wanted
the United States to retain control of the island. Only
in such control did they see any hope of safety for
themselves and for their property. The merchants of
the island, almost without exception, wanted American
control, because only in that way did they see any assurance of stability in commerce, and any hope of the
full development of the business possibilities of the
island. The peasants and laborers, the men who lived
in huts in the country and in hovels in the cities, cared
only for peace. They wanted to be let alone. They had
been starved and harried and driven about. They are
ignorant, they do not know what free institutions mean,

but they wanted the kind of government that would leave them undisturbed by terror, and give them free-dom to work and toil, and that would fill no more grave-yards with their numbers.

It was only the members of the Cuban army and the members of the Cuban Military Assembly and their im-mediate sympathizers, so far as I could find, who wanted complete independence for the island. There were many earnest and honest men in the Cuban Assembly, now a thing of the past. Patriots, in the truest sense, could be found among them. They were not strictly a represent-ative body. One of them said to me—a man who had proved his courage and devotion by heroism that few men would have displayed:

"We want independence for a year, or a year and a half. By that time it will become evident that we can-not maintain a national equipment, and, as a natural course, we shall ask the United States to save us from ourselves."

On every hand it was admitted that the members of the Assembly were men who would like to become presi-dents, generals, governors, foreign ministers, and the in-timation was not lacking that the opportunity to profit, as the Spaniards had done, by means of the agency of governmental power was not missing among the hopes of a few of them. They were denounced by many as political adventurers, and in a sense they were, but there were many honest men among them who believed that Cuba could govern herself, and in that belief they were upheld by the pronounced attitude of General Gomez. Early in the year it was clear to every mind that Gomez was the key to the situation. The Assembly even recognized it. A foreigner, he had fought in two wars for Cuba, because he loved liberty and he hated Spain, which once he served. After he resigned, at the request of the Assembly, because he was not a Cuban and had no right to dictate to Cubans, he remained the key to the situation. I met him in Cienfuegos while he was on his tour of triumph through the island. He was ill, and could scarcely stand more than a few minutes, but there was that spirit of command in his eye and voice, and that moderation and conversation in his language, that impressed one as being characteristic of the statesman as well as of the crafty soldier. He was suspicious and reserved in manner, but as he talked with members of his staff in my presence on the duties of the citizen to the community, his voice grew louder and louder, and rang throughout the rooms of the club where he was stopping with the resonance of a commander on the field. He asked me not to quote what he said to me, but not in the class-room of the university have I ever heard more profound philosophy as to the duties of a man towards his fellow-man, or heard words that had a more sincere ring of personal disinterestedness, than those he uttered in an excited voice in that club-room. In an active experience of fifteen years as a newspaper man, I have never met a man who was so impressive at first sight as a statesman, in the broadest sense, and as a lover of liberty, as Maximo Gomez. Our government recognized the situation when it dealt with him as to the payment of the $3,000,000 gift to the Cuban army.

I should have liked to express a conviction that the

Cuban Assembly could set up a stable government, but it was my firm belief that that body took its first step towards final extinction on the day of General Garcia's funeral in Havana. In fact, its members seemed at that time to try to commit political suicide over the body of their former chief. They abandoned his corpse on the street and left him to be buried by the United States authorities because they could not have the place they wanted in the funeral procession. They said that General Brooke had insulted and slighted them. He did nothing of the kind, as I shall show in another chapter. He really knew nothing of what was going on. He sat in his carriage, and a man came to him and asked him if it was his desire that his staff should go with him, and General Brooke naturally said it was, and that was all there was about it so far as General Brooke was concerned. Some of the men who were at Garcia's death-bed were among those who abandoned the body. They made that worst of all scenes—a row at a funeral. They wanted, undoubtedly, the political distinction of being the preferred mourners in a great spectacular pageant in a city hostile to them, and when they thought they were slighted they acted like children.

"Why did you do it?" I asked one of the leaders that night, when all Havana was excited and it seemed as if the town would burst into a riot. "It will hurt you with our people. There is nothing Americans dislike more than a scene at a funeral," I added.

"We made a mistake," he said, with only a slight show of resentment, "but we showed one thing." His eyes kindled as he' spoke. "We showed that we controlled the Cuban army, for every soldier withdrew at our order."

The only response to that was a silent nod of assent. The Assembly delegate saw its meaning, and with spirit he added :

"You do not believe we are capable of governing ourselves. You surely will not misrepresent us to the American people. There is no one else to govern if we do not."

"I wish, for your own sakes," was the answer, "that you could have shown qualities of self-restraint. How can you govern without that ?"

"We are willing to give the United States complete control of every kind, except political annexation. You may annex us commercially—that is what we want ; but we also want independence—in name at least."

"In other words, you want the offices and the opportunities of office," was the reply, and he acquiesced.

My mind went back to a Cuban colonel whom I met in Santa Clara with Major John A. Logan, whom he was assisting in establishing a temporary rural police of Cuban soldiers. The young colonel spoke English fluently. With vehemence he declared that there were only two Americans on the island who understood the situation. One of them, he said, was Major Logan ; I have forgotten who the other man was. This Cuban colonel denounced General Bates openly because the general had kept Spanish officials in office. He said that it was all that he and his companions could do to prevent an uprising. General Bates had told him to his face, he declared, that he wanted trained men in office, and he

was not sure that the Cubans would be as satisfactory as those he had retained. So violent did he become in his denunciation that I turned to Major Logan and said:

"I think we are not going to have an easy time in pacifying this country. Haven't you found indications of a desire for revenge here and there?"

"Revenge, did you say?" inquired the colonel, as he sprang to his feet and pounded the table. "Revenge? Revenge? No! We want simple justice!"

I hope I do that man no wrong, but I want to say that if I were a former Spanish official and a personal enemy of that young man, I would not be willing to trust myself out of the sight of other men in his presence. He showed plainly that his ideas of patriotism at that time were limited by public office as to their horizon.

There could be no mistake about it, the war fever was still in the blood of that people, so frightfully wronged and outraged by Spain. I did not blame them for it. It was intensely natural and human; but it was there, and the United States must take account of it. And what is of more importance, perhaps, this country must also take account of the women in black and the enlarged graveyards. The meaning of the tens of thousands of Cuban flags flying from huts, I confess, I failed to understand fully. Whether they meant rejoicing because the Spaniards had gone, or a mere natural love of one's native land, or a simple gladness because war was over, or a deeper feeling of devotion to the country—a devotion that meant strife with us to secure full freedom from foreign domination—only the future can tell. Those who displayed them were invariably silent as to their meaning.

It was no secret that a large amount of what hostility there was to a long-time American occupation came from the women. The women suffered most in Cuba. Theirs is the burden of the present and the future. The limits of grief, especially a woman's grief, may not be bounded geometrically. Here are extracts from some notes taken by General Wilson in a tour through his province, which he permitted me to use :

SANTANILLA.—About 800 widows, girls, and helpless children left without male support.

JAGUEY GRANDE.—About 550 destitute widows, besides 850 destitute women and children.

LAS CABEZAS.—There are now about 300 widows and their families; total destitute, from 700 to 1000.

BOLONDRON.—About 450 women and children without male support.

CORRAL FALSO.—About 100 widows and 400 orphans.

And so the list might be extended to town after town. Remember, this was the situation in small towns, mere villages, and only in one province.

Here are some notes taken by General Wilson as to the conduct of the Spanish soldiers :

LAS CABEZAS.—After the people had planted and raised crops the Spanish soldiers would not permit them to gather them, but took from them, and also stole everything they had—cattle, cows, and chickens.

BOLONDRON.—Spanish soldiers stole everything in sight, and told council to pay for it.

JAGUEY GRANDE.—Eight hundred Spanish troops here for eighteen months; left 28th of November; went to Matanzas; they

robbed the people of everything they possessed—poultry, live-stock, vegetables, fruits—everything.

CUEVITAS.—Spanish troops left here on December 17. They stole everything they could find every night; even broke into houses.

CUMANAYAGUA.—About 800 to 1000 Spanish troops left here on December 11; they stole right and left — everything and everybody.

MACAGUA.—The Spanish soldiers behaved in the blackest and worst manner. When travelling by train and they saw a herd of cattle, the train would be stopped, such quantity as they needed for use would be killed, and the remainder ruthlessly shot and left lying along the track.

And that feature of Spanish conduct could be extended indefinitely. Let me make another quotation from these notes, which General Wilson jotted down roughly :

Nobody seems to have yet understood how far-reaching was the effort of General Weyler to starve the Cuban people. He took occasion to send to every town a garrison whose business it was to sweep in all the cattle and other live-stock, and con-sume it, as well as the garden products; and also to destroy the bananas in the field, leaving the people absolutely without any-thing to eat or the liberty to procure more by cultivation or purchase.

In explanation of the fact that no farm-houses are to be seen, General Betancourt says that while the custom of the people used to be to live in the country, the war resulted in the burning and destruction of all the houses, and the people were all forced into the towns.

To illustrate the causes for deep resentment on the part of the Cubans who were left, and the possible desire for revenge on Spanish sympathizers, let me relate an incident of an aggravated kind told to me by an American missionary, and vouched for by him as correct, as the result of personal investigation. Just before the reconcentration order went into effect in Santa Clara, a Spanish lieutenant and a detachment rode out into the country one morning. They passed a peasant who the lieutenant thought did not show him sufficient respect.

"Tie that man up!" said the lieutenant. After that was done he said: "Bring out his wife and his daughter there."

The soldiers did so. The girl was fourteen years old. Then, by orders, the soldiers began to hack at the man with their machetes. The woman fainted. They revived her; and then, as the missionary told it, "it was hack and faint, hack and faint, until the man was killed." The detachment went on, and the widow the next day came to town to ask permission to give her husband's body decent burial in town. The Spanish authorities were very sympathetic, and even gave her written permission to do as she wished. The lieutenant and detachment came back, just as the widow went for the body.

"What did they do with the body of that man killed here yesterday?" asked the officer.

"Here is his widow," said a man who was acting as her escort, "and she has written permission to give the body burial."

"That is the way they treat me, is it?" said the lieutenant. "Tie the woman up! Tie up her daughter!"

Looking at the woman closely, he said, with a refinement of cruelty that probably only a Spaniard could show: "There will soon be another Cuban to take that man's place. Kill her and her daughter!" and they did.

And so, to conclude, I was forced to believe that ninety per cent. of the people in the island of Cuba wanted annexation of some kind to this country; that the war fever was still in the blood of the soldiers; that there was a love of country which had not yet been fathomed; that the grief-stricken women had a strong feeling of resentment; that the Cuban Assembly and the party it represented, so far as there was one, had not capacity for self-government as we understand it. So it might be said that the real desire of the people of Cuba was for union with this country. That, bluntly, was what they wanted. The problem was, what we wanted to do about it. One of the foremost champions of the recent revolution said to me:

"I am now asking my people whether they would prefer freedom under the American flag with security, or freedom under the Cuban flag without security."

A former Spanish Senator, a man who accepted the new order of things, frankly said to me:

"Even if we were perfectly harmonious here, we could not establish a government for a long time. We are in a passive state. There is no co-ordination of forces yet. We must wait until some party with strength comes to the front, or your people must take us into your federation."

Whatever was to be the result, it was evident that American occupation was to last for some time. If there should arise a final determination by the people of this country to annex Cuba, it must be done through tact.

That would be a form of high statesmanship. Force will be resisted. The American government must at least be polite, even if it is not sincere. I do not advocate annexation, but of this I am certain: there will be no permanent peace in Cuba unless the island is under our protection, and Cuba will not be all that Cuba can be unless it is under our flag. If that should come about there will soon be no lack of men or money for the island. But it will bring its color-line discord and its sugar-tariff problems. In one sense, American annexation had already begun. Our money became the standard of currency in Cuba. Reports from Santiago said that American money had practically driven out Spanish money. During the first week of our management of the Havana custom-house only about $500 in $50,000 was paid in American money for duties. In less than six weeks these figures were reversed, and the prediction was made that in less than a year American money would practically be the only money in general use in the island.

As one goes through the island of Cuba nature presents to him one inspiring sight. It is the presence by thousands upon thousands of royal palm-trees. They are beautiful, majestic, useful, stalwart, commanding, and emblematic of integrity and lofty purpose. Why that tree was not used as a symbol on the flag of Cuba I cannot understand. I am sure that if Cuba had raised up among her people men as towering and as commanding as she has raised trees among her vegetation, no one need worry as to her future. But, alas! what country has ever done that?

CHAPTER III

TWO important events occurred practically within twenty-four hours in Havana in the early part of February that were so wide in their contrasts, and yet so typical of the temperament of the people, that their story should be told together in order to reveal their full significance. One was the funeral of General Calixto Garcia, and events immediately associated with it, and the other was the first Sunday of the first carnival under American rule. The funeral occurred on Saturday, February 11th, and the carnival was held the next day. The funeral was characterized by evidences of profound public mourning. A scene occurred also which I believe to have been of far-reaching importance, and it developed at once into an excitement such as I have never seen in any part of the United States. The carnival was characterized by such boisterousness and hilarity, and such a waste of flour at a time when thousands within the city and within easy reach of the city had no food except what was given out at public relief stations, that the American sentinels who paraded in solemn tread up and down the promenade of the Prado, and the hundreds of

59

Americans who came out to see the show, looked on in open-eyed amazement. Both events were picturesque.

The moment that the booming of the guns in salute announced the arrival of the remains of General Garcia, on an American man-of-war, thousands upon thousands of Cuban and American flags appeared at half-mast on flag-staffs and roofs and in arches and windows. In a twinkling it seemed as if the old pro-Spanish city of Havana had become a Cuban stronghold. It had been supposed that there was little sympathy there with the Cuban cause, and that although Spanish rule had ended, the people were still hostile to the idea of Cuban independence. The elaborate display of bunting intertwined with black, from the palatial residences of the rich and the hovels of the poor, seemed to indicate either a complete conversion of the people in patriotic sentiment, or a profound testimonial to the personal worth of General Garcia, or perhaps both. In an alleyway scarcely one hundred feet long, and lined with mere shanties, I counted no less than thirteen Cuban and American flags at half-mast—flags that must have varied in cost from twenty-five cents to five dollars.

The city was stirred tremendously by the arrival of the remains. The city authorities had made arrangements for a public funeral, and for the body to lie in state two days in the Governor-General's palace. Far into the night the crowds swarmed about the palace in the effort to view the body. It was placed in the room where the city council meets. The walls were lined with black with gilt spangles, and hundreds of artificial flower pieces, with purple and white and red ribbons and

THE PRADO, HAVANA'S GREAT SHOW STREET—THE SCENE OF THE CARNIVAL

rosettes attached, filled the adjacent rooms. Some of the best known residents and officials of the city and some of the recognized women leaders of the highest society sat in a room adjacent to the remains, while the people, in single file, streamed through, hour after hour. Out in the street the people fought madly for places in the line. Women of refinement were pushed about in the crowds, and their clothing trampled upon. The hoarse shouts of the American soldiers as they beat back the crowds were mingled with the cries of alarm from women and children. All wagon and carriage traffic was stopped within three blocks of the palace. Hundreds of the ladies of Havana, those who are seldom seen outside of their homes except at night, and then only in carriages on their way to some social or other function of importance, drove as near as they could, and then walked the rest of the way to the palace, where they had to fight for places in the line that was filing past the body, which was guarded by a detail of armed Cuban soldiers. It was a time of deep public mourning, and it was the disposition of the United States authorities to leave the manifestation of public grief and public sentiment in the complete control of the people of the city, so far as possible.

The arrangements for the funeral had been completed, practically, when General Brooke, as Military Governor of the island, received orders from Washington to give the remains burial honors fitting the rank of General Garcia. There was nothing left for General Brooke to do but to offer a soldier's hearse—an army caisson—and to attend with his staff, and with the other generals of the United States army near by and their staffs, and a proper escort, as representatives of the great American nation in military control of the island. It is worthy of special note that all our generals near Havana did attend

THE TROCHA HOTEL, VEDADO—GENERAL BROOKE'S HEADQUARTERS

personally, instead of sending representatives. The committee in charge of the event had arranged places for the hundreds of societies that wished to have places in the line, and, to all appearances, every detail had been looked after carefully. The procession was to move soon after one o'clock in the afternoon, on its way to the great Colon Cemetery, where the heroes of the *Maine* lie

buried, three miles out of town—a beautiful cemetery on a hill, from whose gates a splendid view of the Atlantic Ocean in the distance may be obtained. All business in the city was suspended. The societies, the military, the city officials and church dignitaries, went to their assigned places in the narrow streets, and thousands flocked to the plaza in the centre of town, known as Central

O'REILLY, PRINCIPAL BUSINESS STREET OF HAVANA

Park. There was a noticeable delay in starting the procession, but soon after two o'clock the dirges of the bands were heard and the horsemen clearing the streets came into view. Half a dozen companies of the Tenth

67

Regular infantry were drawn up on one side of the plaza, and their regimental band mingled its strains of mourning music with those that were in the procession.

The people stood silent in crowds. Every window and balcony was filled. There were long lines of civilians carrying banners and artificial flowers, with streamers, on which some sentiment of mourning and of honor to Garcia had been printed in gilt letters. What was the chief surprise to Americans was to see thousands of women and girls in the parade. They had numerous societies of their own. They were smart in their gowns. Some wore hats, some wore mantillas, some carried sunshades or fans, but the majority were bareheaded. They carried their banners high in the air, and held their artificial floral tributes up to full view. That part of the procession reminded one of the annual Sunday-school parade in Brooklyn. The procession moved at a very slow pace. There were scores of men in tall hats and evening dress; priests stepped along sedately with heads uncovered, and their white or black gowns trailing in the street; American cavalry and artillery clattered and rumbled along, with that marked spirit of strict attention to duty that characterizes the Regular soldier everywhere; American generals and their staffs rode or drove by; city officials and university professors were on foot; showy hearses with lackeys in gorgeous uniforms, and escorts burning torches, rolled by, filled with floral tributes; the coffin on the army caisson, and draped with the Cuban flag, made a severe and simple show, such as befitted the occasion; and then there were the volunteer firemen in their showy uniforms, followed by

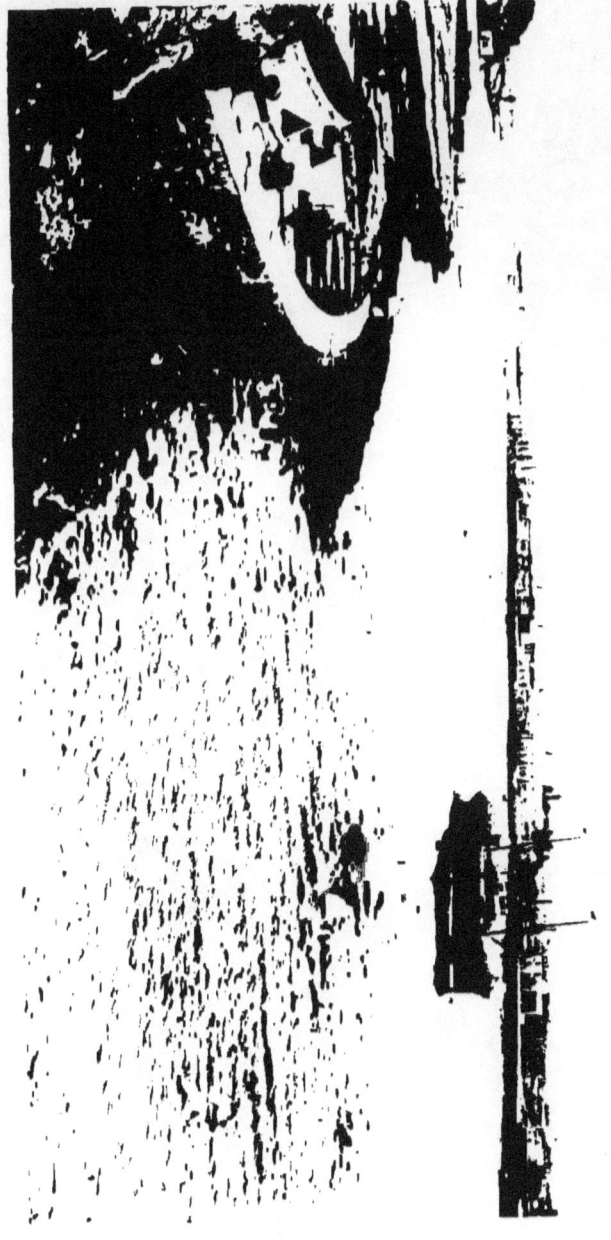

THE HARBOR SEEN FROM MORRO CASTLE

a long line of empty carriages at the rear of the procession. It was an imposing spectacle of public grief and respect to a dead chieftain on the part of a demonstrative and sentimental people.

To those of the spectators near the Central Park it became evident that there was something wrong. The procession had come to a halt, and soon files of Cuban soldiers with arms reversed were seen to be walking rapidly on either side of the carriages containing the American generals and their staffs, as if to overtake the caisson with the body, and to march beside it or near it. Then a young Cuban officer ran by, and in a few minutes the Cuban soldiers were seen coming back to the square, after which they disappeared. No more Cuban soldiers were seen in the parade at any time that afternoon. The withdrawal was a mystery to all the spectators, but the people were so taken up with the procession that almost no attention was paid to it' at the time. It was a fine show to see the civilians—men, women, and children —parading the streets. Intense interest marked the appearance of the cavalry escort — the Seventh Cavalry, Custer's old regiment—dusty and dirty from a long ride into town from Vedado, every man sitting his thick-coated and sweaty horse with the ease and unconcern of a cowboy, and yet maintaining strict and careful military alignment. The rumbling guns of two batteries of American light artillery fascinated the people who a few months before had been face to face with the horrors of war. The seven hearses, one of which was said to have cost $9000, loaded with flowers, and decorated with golden angels and crosses and other religious emblems, and accompanied by flunkies in scarlet and gold, some of the men burning torches, made a show that interested the people, who were used to seeing only one gorgeous hearse even at a grand funeral. The simplicity of the funeral car, the lack of ostentation on the part of the American military authorities, the appearance of General Fitzhugh Lee with his staff on horseback, all made a striking contrast with the showy volunteer firemen, who appeared next in line by the hundreds. Most of these firemen had been members of the volunteer soldiery, the bitterest enemies to the Cuban cause—enemies whom even the " Butcher " Weyler seemed to fear and to be unable to control. They marched behind Garcia's body, however, and with their heavy helmets, rubber boots, red shirts, and axes of every description and of forbidding shapes, accomplished the end which seems to be dearest to the heart of the Havana volunteer fireman—namely, securing unusual public attention. They strode with far-reaching steps, and refused to be hurried, although a gap between them and that part of the procession preceding them of nearly a quarter of a mile had been opened. Then came the empty carriages to bring back to town some of those who had walked. There had been so much to look at that it was not strange that the absence of the Cuban soldiers and certain civilians, known as members of the Cuban Military Assembly, had not been noticed generally. At the cemetery the man who was to have delivered the oration was absent, and, to add to the surprise, a squad of American soldiers fired the last salute and an American bugler blew taps. Then most of those present knew that something really was wrong.

CABAÑAS

Before those who had been in the funeral procession
had reached town again it became known that there had
been a scene at the funeral. Excitable Cuban officers
were gesticulating in *cafés* about town, and loud denun-
ciations of Governor-General Brooke were heard on all
sides. What had General Brooke done? asked many
Americans. The Cubans said that he had insulted the
Cuban Assembly; that he had permitted his cavalry to
drive them from their place in line; that he had been
brusque to their committee; that he had caused all Cubans who had any self-respect, and who remembered the
treatment of Garcia at Santiago, to leave the procession
and to withdraw from any participation in the funeral.
They declared that he was a monster, an ingrate, and
that if President McKinley did not call him home—well,
the President had better watch out. After much ado
the Americans got the story out of the Cuban delegates
who had withdrawn. They said that they had been assigned to follow directly behind the body of Garcia.
There were less than forty of them, but they represented
what government the Cuban revolutionary party had
been able to form. Havana was always hostile to them,
but to have been made the chief mourners in the parade
would have given them a political distinction which in
the eyes of the impressionable people would have had a
tremendous effect. They learned, they said, that General Brooke was to participate in the parade, and the
committee in charge had asked them if they would not
yield their place in the line to General Brooke as the
official representative of the great American people.
They said they would, but to General Brooke only, and

as a favor. When the procession was formed they fell
in behind General Brooke's carriage. They interpreted
the order to fall in behind General Brooke literally—behind his physical presence. They were ordered out of
there, they said, so as to give way to Brooke's staff, after
a committee had gone to the general and asked him if
he wished his staff to crowd them out of their places,
and he had most rudely said that his staff belonged with
him, and with him it should go. According to their
story they had swallowed this insult for the sake of
Garcia, at whose death-bed in Washington some of them
had stood. Then there came a troop of American cavalry, and they drove right up behind the staffs of American generals in the carriages and ordered the Cuban Assembly out of the way. The procession started, and the
members of the Assembly filed along on either side of
the cavalry, and attempted to drop in between the horsemen and the generals. The cavalrymen drove their
horses on the sidewalk, they said, and cut off this flank
movement, and so they not only withdrew, but ordered
every Cuban soldier out of the procession, and the Cuban soldiers, who numbered fewer than four hundred,
had obeyed them. The fact that the Cuban soldiers had
obeyed them to a man, they said, was at least some satisfaction, and they were proud of it.

That was the story they told, and that night about
nine o'clock it seemed to have confirmation. An evening newspaper got out an extra, printed only on one side
of the paper, purporting to give a full story of the row.
It denounced General Brooke fiercely. The newsboys
dashed into the *cafés*, flung their papers right and left,

and then collected their money afterwards. In a flash there were hundreds of groups on the sidewalks, in the centre of each of which was a man reading in a loud voice what the extra contained. In less than half an hour the town was in an uproar, and seemed to rock

COMPANY KITCHEN OF THE TENTH REGULAR INFANTRY ON THE PRADO

with excitement. The one refrain was that General Brooke must go. The Assembly itself met and ordered an investigation of General Brooke's conduct, with much presumption, and with the intention of ultimately sending a committee to Washington to tell the President that General Brooke's insults could not be tolerated. I have never seen a more excited populace. It seemed as if violence must break out on all sides. It made the

Americans angry to hear the President and their representatives in Cuba denounced. After inquiry they soon found that there was gross exaggeration in the stories. Then their wrath arose in sundry places. One American whose ardent loyalty challenged my admiration took a couple of the members of the Cuban Assembly to task in these words :

" How dare you insult the American people who made you free? Do you really want Brooke to go? Then send your committee to Washington and see what you'll get. Do you know what you did to-day? You abandoned on the street the body of your chief—you who were present, some of you at least, at his death-bed—and left it to the American army to give it decent burial. Shame on you! Suppose even that it was true that General Brooke did insult you! Why didn't you endure it for the sake of poor Garcia, and then make a row afterwards? You have committed political suicide to-day. Do you suppose that the American people will consent that the government of this island shall be turned over to you, who show such a lack of self-restraint, who act like children? Mark my word! The days of the Cuban Assembly are numbered."

And it was true. I had been favorably impressed with several of the delegates to the Assembly up to that time. Their high-sounding assertions of praise for Americans and profound convictions of their own ability for self-government had made a distinct impression upon me. I still think that many of them were honest, pureminded, and patriotic. But one could not escape the conviction after that Garcia episode that they were not

AT THE ANCHORAGE

capable of self-restraint, to say nothing of self-government ; and then, when other Cubans, men who had been ardent revolutionists, and whose sincerity could not be doubted, declared, as hundreds of them did, that the Cuban Assembly was chiefly a band of political adventurers out for the spoils and the honors of office, the conviction became irresistiblé that if self - government was to come for Cuba it must be through some other agency than that of the Cuban Assembly. The soundness of that conviction has since been demonstrated.

The charges against General Brooke were all untrue. At first I thought that perhaps he might have lacked tact—he has a soldier's bluntness—and that with a word he could have straightened out any difficulty. "If he had only been polite to us," said one of the Cuban leaders, "we should have forgiven all else. The Cuban asks politeness, whether there is sincerity in it or not." To give the facts in the matter, let me tell what General Brooke said to me about it, and although it was said in a conversation not intended for publication, I am sure that the general will not object if I use his words in writing on this subject.

"All arrangements," he said, "had been made for the funeral when I received orders to see that Garcia's remains should have funeral honors befitting his rank. There was nothing for me to do, unless I should overturn all the arrangements, but to offer a soldier's hearse—a caisson—and to notify the committee that I should attend the funeral with my staff. I made no request for any place in the line, and was quite content to go where I was assigned. Just before the procession started I met

young Garcia, and asked him, through my interest in
him, where his place and that of his relatives was in the
line. He said that it was quite some distance behind
that of myself and the other representatives of the
American army. I said to him : 'That is not right.
Your place to-day is directly behind your father's body.
That is your place by every right on such an occasion.
Send word to the committee that I am unwilling to have
you go elsewhere. It is my wish that you, not I, should
be next to your father's body.' That was the only positive direction I gave in reference to the funeral. It was
obeyed. I was sitting in my carriage, shielded from the
sun as much as possible, because I was not feeling well,
and General Chaffee was with me. A man who looked
as if he might be a committee-man came to the carriage,
and asked me if I wanted my escort to go directly behind
me. 'I have no escort,' I said. He asked me if it was
my wish that my staff should go with me, and I said it
was, because that was the proper place, and the man went
away. He did not tell me who he was or why he asked.
He gave me no hint at all of any difficulty, and I knew
nothing of any dissatisfaction until it was all over. I
saw the Cuban soldiers leaving the procession, but inasmuch as I was not in charge in any sense, and was only
a guest, I made no effort to find out the cause. It did
not occur to me to investigate the reason for any move
made in the procession, and why should it ?"

The cavalrymen behind General Brooke were an escort,
it was said, to General Lee, who, with his staff, rode last
in the assignment of the American officers, and did not
seem to bother himself about questions of precedence.

His appearance even at a funeral was the occasion of a demonstration such as stirred one's blood. He was not far behind the coffin, and he made an effort not to notice the cries and shouts of " Lee!" " Lee!" " Lee!" but the dignified and constrained short bows that he made finally simply endeared him the more to the populace.

DINING TENT OF THE TENTH REGULAR INFANTRY ON THE PRADO

It was a revelation to the newly arrived Americans of the wonderful hold of General Lee on the affections of the masses in Havana. The people could not restrain their shouts even at Garcia's funeral. No one else was cheered.

Of course the feeling against General Brooke ended in smoke. In less than four days the same Cuban Assembly passed a vote of thanks to him for his part in the Garcia funeral, and for the honors paid to Garcia. He also received letters that if printed would have caused surprise at the fickleness of that body which presumed to demand that it be allowed to govern the island of Cuba in the name of the people.

Thus ended an exciting and important incident in the unfolding of new events for Cuba. Writing several weeks later, as I recalled the funeral, three living figures stood out in memory. One was a girl about seventeen years old, marching alone in the procession. Her gown was of broad blue and white stripes. Her bodice was of red with a large white star on her chest. On her head was a Liberty cap made of the Cuban colors. She typified Cuban hopes and national aspirations. Another figure was that of a little boy, not more than eight years old. He was in the uniform of a Cuban officer, and he swung a deadly machete with a fierceness of mien that showed that the war fever was in the blood of the children, indicative of the condition of affairs to be expected in the future. The other figure was Fitzhugh Lee, the popular idol of the people, to whom, as a living embodiment of American interference in the war, the gratitude of a freed people went out.

Then came the carnival. The flags that had been at half-mast for Garcia were raised to tops of poles, and the emblems of mourning were removed bright and early. Havana, still greatly excited, did not seem to know whether there would be any carnival. The condition of the people was hysterical rather than joyous. The sky was overcast, and in the afternoon a few raindrops fell.

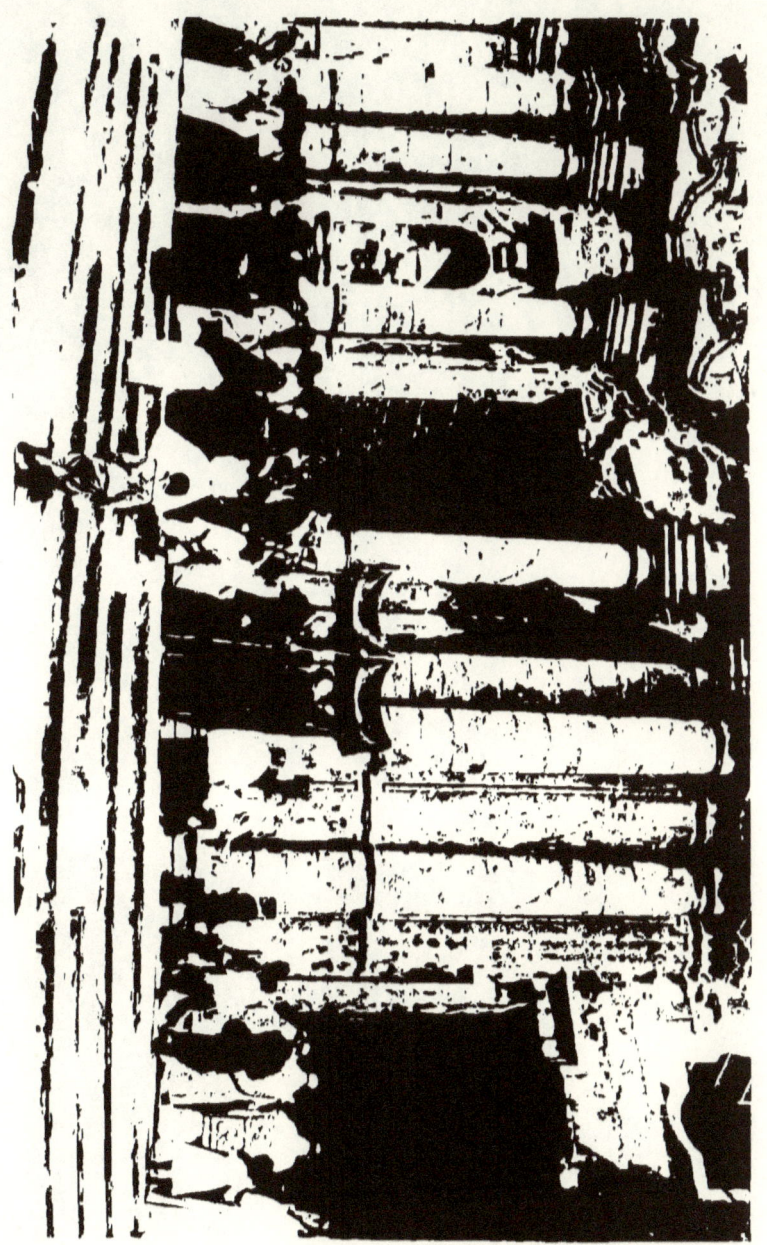

By three o'clock the only sign of a carnival was a long row of chairs for rent placed along the promenade of the Prado. About four o'clock a child of four, looking as if she might be Mrs. Tom Thumb over again, escorted by her proud father and dressed in a gown that had a long sweeping train, walked down the Prado promenade, flirting her fan vigorously and talking vivaciously as she bent her little head with its powdered hair from right to left. That was a sign that there was going to be some kind of a carnival. Then came a United States army wagon loaded with the witnesses to a murder committed the night before. An American army officer driving a tandem next appeared on the street. Soon a dog-cart containing two masked women drove down the Prado, and disappeared, as if ashamed at the lonely show it made. Then there came a wagon drawn by two mules in tandem. The wagon was full of laughing children. The chairs along the street were now filled, and the promenade was almost crowded. The American sentries looked on with curious interest as they kept up their slow, deliberate step of patrol. Soon private carriages began to appear. The bridles of the horses were decorated with red, white, and blue rosettes, the first significant hint of the new order of things in Havana. Smart Cuban horsemen on beautiful ponies appeared here and there, and then dashed away on side streets. It was evident that Havana wanted to have a carnival, and had sent out advance-scouts to see if any one was coming out.

The decision was favorable, and after half-past four o'clock the carriages were seen to be coming towards the famous street of Havana in throngs. All the balconies were crowded, and in front of the Sport Club and the United States Club and a saloon down at the foot of the street, where the drivers and riders turned, there were groups of men and boys, whose expressions told that there was mischief afoot. A girl in white drove a beau-

GUARD-MOUNT OF TENTH REGULAR INFANTRY ON THE PRADO

tiful high-stepper all alone. A spirited team of bays, driven by a woman, who was proud of her skill, but whose husband sat on a back seat ready to seize the reins, made a fine figure dashing up and down. Here and there little streamers of paper trailed out behind in tangled confusion as the carriages sped along. The dignified people of the town were out in vehicles that had been stored away since the war began, and entire families in this way made the circuit of the Prado several times. All the women and girls had their hair powdered and wore their prettiest summer gowns. The men sat with them as if they were out simply to protect the gentler sex. There was no disorder, and it looked as if the affair was to be simply a driving and riding show. The smart horseback riding of the young Cuban men was a pretty spectacle of itself. Occasionally a bonbon would be thrown from a balcony, and there were recognitions and bows on all sides. It was a very sedate affair. The war had sobered Havana.

But at five o'clock the street had become almost furious with the whirl of carriages and horsemen. The horses were steaming and flecked with foam. Some of the men who were riding in victorias began to bend over to look after certain mysterious packages in their vehicles. One of them gave a peculiar look as he rounded the end of the Prado, and forthwith twenty young men arose from their chairs in front of a saloon and brown-paper missiles were hurled at the man in the carriage. They went straight to the mark, broke over him, and a great white cloud filled the air, and shouts of laughter were heard hundreds of yards away. The bombardment had begun. It was mimic war. The clouds of flying flour were the smoke of battle. A commotion arose in front of the Sport Club. Hundreds ran towards it. Half a dozen young horsemen were seen to be approaching. They halted; then they spurred their horses on at racing speed, bent low in their saddles, and were pelted with flour as they rushed by like the wind. Another bombardment broke out at the United States Club. Havana was itself again. The floating particles of flour filled the air and whitened the clothes of the spectators. The dignified families drove off the street to avoid trouble. The bombardments increased, and soon the entire street was filled with a shrieking, laughing populace enjoying the sight of horsemen and carriages tearing madly up and down, and men on horseback and in carriages covered from head to foot with splashes of flour. The flying ribbons swirled in confusion behind the carriages, and daring children dashed out to catch them, only to be rescued by soldiers or pedestrians from danger and death, as the excited horses rushed by, practically beyond control. Volley after volley, single shot after single shot, went whirling through the air, and now and then the hurlers of the ammunition had to wait for the atmosphere to clear so as to see the flying targets. Men in the carriages began to stand up and pelt one another as they raced side by side. It was no carnival of flowers, such as Nice presents, nor of floats, such as New Orleans exhibits with pride. It was a carnival of the most boisterous kind of hilarity, with confetti and bonbons soon exhausted, and with packages of flour as the only missiles in a city where there were thousands of persons who would have starved except for the care and generosity of the American government. And the strangest part of it all was to see the American army sentinels marching sedately up and down with their rifles on their shoulders, for the first time part of a unique show in a foreign land.

At 5.15 o'clock the fun ran riot. The horses were becoming tired. They and their drivers and riders had become transformed into white apparitions. Even the leaves of the trees became powdered, and then the people, their sides aching with laughter, began to go home.

MERCEDES CHURCH, BUILT 1746

Raindrops pattered down upon the throng, electric lights began to splutter, the long beams of the Morro Castle light shot up the Prado and out to sea, and then, as the noise and confusion lessened, the strains of a band were heard. The music came from a stately building at the foot of the Prado, and the players, dressed in white uniforms, were in the corridor behind stout iron bars, but close to the street, and in full view of the pedestrians. It was the convict band in the state-prison that was playing, and its members were in high feather as they realized that they too were part of the show. No music was ever gayer than that which they played, and as its strains floated out upon the street, and as little Mrs. Tom Thumb swished her way along, and all the other pedestrians turned to go home, and the drivers and riders began to thin out, with the flickering lights dancing upon the heads and faces of pinched and starving people and ghost-like participants in the activities of the hilarious carnival of half an hour, the Americans who had been out to see the show shook their heads in amazement, while the imperturbable sentries resumed their duty of keeping the peace in a foreign land. Garcia had been buried only twenty-four hours, the fever of riot had been in the blood of the masses, but the carnival had come, and Havana had forgotten all about bloodshed and mutiny, and in the evening came out to see the children play ring-around-a-rosy in the public square, to the music of a local band, and beneath the shadow of the statue of Queen Isabella, since removed.

Havana grave and gay! Havana mutinous and hilarious! Havana always hysterical!

CHAPTER IV

P ROBABLY the greatest surprise that thousands
of persons found, when they flocked to Havana in
the first sixty days of American military control,
was clean streets. I have said that they were as clean
as those of New York City under Tammany control. On
bright sunshiny days they seemed even cleaner than New
York streets. On rainy days they were not so clean as
the streets of New York in wet weather. The reason
was that there is no foundation for the paving-stones in
the streets of Havana. When hard traffic jolts over the
square, ungainly paving-stones of the city on a rainy day,
the black mud, poisoned with the filth and disease germs
of decades and even centuries, exudes between the stones,
and the streets become black with dirt, just a trifle black-
er and thicker than the black mud of lower New York
streets when street-cleaning becomes largely a matter of
politics—that is, part of the game of getting money out
of a public treasury without giving an equivalent. The
rain over and the sun shining, Havana's streets under
American military rule were as clean as those of any
city in the United States.

94

PUBLIC WORKS—STREET-CLEANING

When the Americans took actual charge of the city, however, the streets were filthy. Dead animals abounded, garbage was encountered everywhere, gutters were foul, and open mouths of sewers running into the ocean

STREET-CLEANING FORCE—CORNER OF PRADO AND NEPTUNE STREET

or into the harbor were reeking. Nauseating odors filled the air, and the condition of the public buildings was such that the American army officers practically refused to occupy them. To illustrate the frightful condition of the public buildings, let me say that in one of the rooms of the Fuerza Castle, occupied by the civil guard, and in the group of public buildings of which the captain-general's palace was the chief, the bodies of no less than fifteen dead cats and dogs were found. These animals had not died of starvation. They had strayed into this room in their search for food, and had died of the foul

atmosphere. A candle would not burn in the place.
Thirty-two cart-loads of dirt were taken from the palace
of the governor of Havana province. The condition of
the captain - general's palace was such that General
Brooke would not occupy it, and he went out to a suburb
called Vedado, where he and his staff and office help occupied the building in which the Evacuation Commissioners held their sessions.

Major-General Francis V. Greene, who was in charge
of Havana when the Spanish forces evacuated, began the
preliminary work of cleaning the town; and General

FACTORIA STREET, UNDER REPAIR

Ludlow, who succeeded him, with larger opportunity and
a wider scope, carried it on so that within thirty days,
and even less, Havana became clean in outward appearance. General Ludlow was charged, in the order assign-

ing him to duty in Havana, with caring for the collection and disbursement of the city revenues, with forming a police force, with providing a sanitation scheme, and also with the general government of the place, under regulations provided by the President. It was in obedience to these instructions that the general burned the midnight oil night after night. His duties were defined clearly. He formed a commission to investigate the matter of city revenue; he took up the work of forming a police force, which was well under way during General Greene's *régime*, under the guidance of John McCullagh, former chief of police in New York City ; he divided the sanitation work into two classes, one that had to do with matters out-of-doors, and the other that had to do with work inside buildings in the city, one of the departments being known as the department of public works, and the other the department of public health ; he established food-depots to feed the starving, and then he carried on the military routine connected with his office.

Lieutenant-Colonel W. M. Black, of the engineer corps of the volunteer army, was in charge of the public works department when General Ludlow came, and it was through the work of his department that Havana was made clean to the eye in a few weeks. Colonel Black first organized his work thoroughly. He formed various bureaus. One had to do with the cleaning and repairing of streets and with the collection of garbage ; another bureau had to do with the matter of sewers and water distribution, everything pertaining to public works underground ; a third bureau was for the inspection of buildings, similar to such bureaus in most of our large cities ;

a fourth had charge of temporary public work ; a fifth looked after public property ; and a sixth was responsible for the harbor, with the work of dredging, repairing and constructing wharves, the care of buoys and fixed beacons, as its especial duty.

ZULETA AND TROCADERO STREETS — STREET·CLEANING FORCE GOING
TO WORK

The work of cleaning the streets was placed in charge of Captain W. L. Geary, son of one of Pennsylvania's famous governors. Captain Geary is a resident of Seattle, Washington. He really began the work on December 2, 1898, and advanced with his carts and laborers as the Spaniards gradually evacuated the town. He is a quiet, methodical, determined officer, with excellent executive ability, and he went about his work in a systematic way. A careful inspection of the city and suburbs had been made. What this meant is illustrated by the following official report on the condition of Casa Blanca,

A

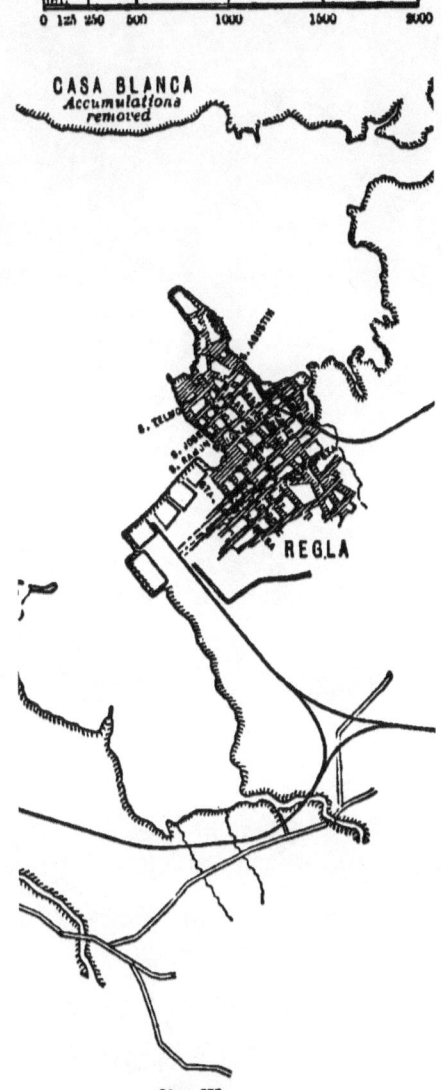

SCALE OF METRES

0 125 250 500 1000 1500 2000

CASA BLANCA
*Accumulations
removed*

REGLA

Map III

SHOWING THE

STREET CLEANING

FOR WEEK ENDING

March 4th, 1899

Streets cleaned daily
Streets cleaned three times per week
Streets cleaned once per week
* Dumps

the little fishing-village at the end of Cabañas fortress, and directly across the harbor from the captain-general's palace :

The streets are very narrow, overgrown with grass, and it is evident that they have never been repaired. Some are on a level with the bay, and others six or eight yards above it. There is absolutely no water-supply nor any drainage. The filthy waters are thrown into the streets or into the bay. The same may be said of every kind of garbage or organic matter. Everything is thrown into the streets, and in every place large quantities may be found. The coal deposited there (there are large coal-docks on that side of the harbor) soils the streets and houses near by. The vaults of Cabañas drain near the town, and while the Spanish troops were there the bad smell was terrible. It is not so bad now, because there are no soldiers there.

Almost all the houses are of wood. In the remains of some demolished buildings the Chinese have formed, with the aid of boards and rags, some miserable huts, in which a large number of them live. In one of these filthy huts I counted seventy of them. All these huts are in bad condition, without light or ventilation, and the streets serve for all private uses. Some families of reconcentrados live in a similar way. Some houses are separated by an alley, in which are placed boxes, barrels, and everything that is not useful in the houses, especially if the building is a store. On the shore are great deposits of garbage from the vessels.

Then followed in the report ten recommendations to remedy the situation. These recommendations involved the demolition of the Chinese habitations of rags and boards, the cleaning of streets, construction of gutters, purification of dwellings. The physician who made the report, a Cuban, who wrote in English, closed with these words : "It is necessary to clean the town, for it is a constant danger of infection for vessels in the bay."

Captain Geary laid out the city in districts, got the

LIEUTENANT-COLONEL WILLIAM M. BLACK, U. S. A., CHIEF
OF THE DEPARTMENT OF PUBLIC WORKS

names of as many men who needed work as he could, appointed superintendents and foremen, hired carts, obtained brooms and shovels, and started in. Early in Feb-

ruary, when the work was well under way, the report of
what had been accomplished in the previous week showed
that 575,000 lineal feet of streets had been cleaned, that
983 cart-loads of sweepings had been taken away, that
585 square feet of paved streets had been repaired, that
2750 square feet of macadamized streets were being repaired, and that 13 scow-loads of street refuse had been
taken out to sea and dumped. In that week 650 men
were at work on the streets, and the pay for the lowest
of them was 83⅓ cents. A great deal of work was done
at night, because of the narrow streets and because of the
climate. Some of the cleaners were sickly, because they
had lacked food. These were put at the easiest kind of
work, and day by day most of them showed physical
improvement.

Colonel Black's report, made to General Ludlow under
the date of February 16, 1899, gave this résumé of the
work done in January under Captain Geary :

An investigation showed that the surface of the streets of Havana was fairly clean, through the efforts of Captain Geary, who
had removed 2500 cart-loads of dirt. Captain Geary's force was
largely increased. The entire city and suburbs were redistricted,
and an inspector was appointed for each district, with from 100
to 150 laborers, in gangs of 10 to 15 men each, under a foreman.

Each gang has a definite length of street assigned to it. In
general the equipment of each gang comprises 5 water-sprinkling
cans, 3 hoes, 12 brooms, 2 rakes, and 10 shovels, and, for the
broader streets, 4 wheelbarrows. Carts follow the gangs and take
up and remove the sweepings to the dump-boat. Owing to the
narrow streets and the great amount of traffic, the use of the bag
system was found to be inadvisable. Later it is proposed to sub-

divide the districts and assign a definite piece of street to each man. Under the organization, at the end of the month, with a force consisting of 8 inspectors, 38 foremen, 663 laborers, and 63 carts, 150,000 feet of street were cleaned daily, 200,000 feet three

FLORIDA STREET BEFORE AMERICAN OCCUPATION

times per week, 100,000 feet twice per week, and 35,186 feet once per week, covering the entire city. The total number of running feet cleaned per week was 1,735,186. The cost of cleaning for the month was $16,930 18. The sweepings were carried to sea and dumped.

Within a month Colonel Black's pay-roll for all his departments—the chief of which, so far as the number of

employés was concerned, was the street-cleaning department—carried more than 2000 names. In the matter of
street repairs Colonel Black made this summary :

Great difficulty was experienced in getting a supply of stone
for macadamizing. No new paving-blocks were on hand. Owing
to the absence of a complete system of street grades, and also to
the certainty that the pavements would have to be torn up at an
early date to permit the construction of a sewer system, the work
of street repair was confined to filling bad holes or breaks in the
pavements. During the month about 3000 square yards of re-
paving and about 23,000 square yards of macadamizing was done.
In preparation for replacing the street pavements, it will be necessary to prepare grade sheets for the entire city street system.

When it came to the question of sewers, General Ludlow and Colonel Black were face to face with the biggest
problem in Havana. It has been the general impression
that there are no sewers in Havana. That is a mistake.
There are nearly ten miles of them, some public and
some private. Some of them open into the harbor, like
the one that runs under the Custom-house, and others
into the ocean. The ends of these sewers, in some cases
for a distance of a hundred yards, are open, and although
there is a good flow in them, they are a source of infection because they are open. Havana is a place not pre-
senting any difficult engineering problems in sewering.
There is an easy pitch to most of the streets, and the city
runs along the ocean on one side and borders on a blind
harbor, but close to the ocean, on the other side. Near
the mouth of the harbor, and along the ocean-front, the
sewers left no noticeable deposits or odors.

The great problem was how, when, and by whom the sewers should be established. It was conceded that they must be built. The city was full of men who were looking for just such contracts. Colonel Waring had been down there, and had reported that it would cost from $10,000,000 to $12,000,000 to do the work properly, and it was said in Havana that a company of his friends was organized to take hold of the work. Michael Dady, the

MERCADERAS STREET, LOOKING EAST FROM
EMPEDRADO

well-known Brooklyn contractor and spoils politician, had a contract for something like $15,000,000 to do the same work on a different plan. There was a good deal of mystery about Colonel Dady's contract. The fact was that the City Council of Havana, before the war, had approved Colonel Dady's plan without authorizing a direct contract. Thereafter steps were taken gradually whereby the city became committed to Colonel Dady's plan, and before the place was evacuated by the Spaniards the council authorized the contract to be signed. Then came the change in control of affairs, with the understanding that existing laws and obligations were to be respected by the United States authorities while in temporary control. When the sovereignty of a country changes, the new rulers may abrogate not only contracts that have been authorized, but those that are in force. It was a delicate question, however, in view of the proclaimed purpose of the United States to act merely as a pacificator, whether it would have the right to throw aside Colonel Dady's contract. As a conquering nation this country could do as it pleased ; as a pacifying nation it might revoke the contract on the ground of high military necessity, and because the contract did not conform to good public policy. I know nothing about the engineering merits of the scheme of Colonel Dady, but I am warranted in saying that practically every man in Havana, who had looked into the matter and was competent to judge, whether he was engineer or lawyer, believed that Dady had at least an equity in his authorized contract. This opinion was shared by some of the highest military authorities. There was not so unanimous an opinion as to the wisdom of following out his plan, and, indeed, it was my belief, after talking with the experts, that some other plan was preferred by the officials.

Colonel Waring had urged that work be begun at once. There was delay in Washington. Some of the authorities had said that sewers could be put in in sixty days. A well-known brigadier-general said to me that he had told General Ludlow that he would produce a contractor who would guarantee to put sewers in the town in that time. It was simply ridiculous. There were no maps showing grades and distances; there was no general scheme as to size of main sewers, and their branches and the disposition of them; there was no sewer-pipe to be had in Cuba for drains, and to have decided upon the sizes and amount would have taken time, to say nothing of the difficulty of getting sufficient quantities from the United States in short order; there were no plumbers' supplies in Havana; most important of all, there were not a sufficient number of plumbers in Havana to do even a small part of the kind of work involved, and it would have been almost impossible to have secured them from the United States, with the danger of losing their lives from exposure to deadly germs; there were no laborers to be had to dig up the streets, the island being short, it was estimated, nearly 200,000 laboring men; it would have been necessary to organize a great force of laborers in the United States and to transport them to Havana. All this preliminary work, the formation of a scheme involving a vast study of details, the drawing of plans, the preparation and the award of contracts, the importation of men and materials, could not have been done in less than sixty days after the United States took hold of affairs, to say nothing of the litigation over the Dady contract that might have followed, and by that time it would have been too late to begin.

Probably the most important reason for General Ludlow's decision to put the matter off for a year, even at the risk of a serious yellow-fever epidemic, was the fact that to establish a complete system of sewers in Havana in a short time would simply paralyze the business of the town just when the place needed all its strength for recuperation. The streets in the business part of Havana are so narrow that vehicles are allowed to go only one

MONSERRATE AND O'REILLY STREETS—STATUE OF GENERAL TACON

way in them. There are no sidewalks in these streets in the sense that Americans know them. To put down a sewer in such a street means to block it up completely with piles of dirt. It will be necessary to do this a block at a time in Havana if the business interests are to be conserved. To stop all street traffic in the business part of the town ; to expose its people to the possibility of a frightful death-rate, just after a war, because of the germs released from the ground; to make haste in a matter that required the utmost deliberation and study so that no mistakes should be made in a work intended to last for centuries, were things for which General Ludlow would not take the responsibility.

Speaking from the standpoint of a layman in this matter of sewering Havana, and after looking over the ground, I was convinced that General Ludlow took exactly the right step. It required courage of the highest order. Everywhere there were predictions that there would be a frightful death-rate in the summer in Havana, and General Ludlow chose to face that contingency. It took courage to stand off syndicate-hunters with pulls in Washington. The passage of the clause in the army bill forbidding the award of franchises in Cuba by our government probably took a load off the general's shoulders. A thorough, well-developed system of sewering the town is now being drawn up, based on scientific principles, and when it is ready the responsibility will fall upon the authorities in Washington of saying whether that plan or some other plan shall be adopted.

Meantime General Ludlow went about the work of justifying his decision. He ordered a plant whereby a disinfectant is prepared from salt water by electricity, and he made arrangements to have the streets sprinkled constantly. He ordered the erection of a $35,000 plant for the burning of the garbage. He set native Cubans at work cleaning out the open ends of sewers. With immunes to do the work, he had public buildings, jails, and hospitals and the like, as well as Morro Castle and Cabañas fortress, Principe Castle, and the Punta, made wholesome, and other buildings put in order for barracks for the troops, who were then encamped in the very places where thousands of reconcentrados starved and died. He kept improving the street-cleaning system, and then he took hold of the matter of harbor improvement. Even at the end of the first month of American control in Havana, General Ludlow had the great satisfaction of seeing the death-rate for the month lowered exactly one-half, compared with the corresponding month of the previous year and before war came. As late as the middle of June there were no infectious or contagious diseases in the city. That of itself was an amazing showing. There doubtless will be serious sickness in Havana in 1899, and there may be an epidemic; but I am convinced that when the records are all in, it will be found that General Ludlow not only did a brave thing in refusing to tear up Havana's streets at a critical time, but that he did a wise thing, and he will be justified in the end. He is face to face at this writing with a grave responsibility, and he is meeting it without flinching. What shall be done ultimately about Havana's sewer system I cannot say, but this much I am justified in saying—that no system will be adopted or put in operation in Havana, during General Ludlow's term of office there as military governor, which does not commend itself to his engineering sense of fitness and right.

The matter of purifying Havana Harbor is one in which nature will help greatly. With the present sewers put in a fairly good sanitary condition, there was really only one other source of pollution of Havana Harbor. It is known as "Slaughter House Creek," a little stream of water up at the head of the harbor, where slaughtering was done in the city, and by means of which the offal was carried into the harbor. Of course one of the first things done in cleaning up the town was to regulate this matter of slaughtering animals. Then arrangements were made to dredge the mouth of Slaughter House Creek for several hundred yards. Dr. Guiteras, the national yellow - fever expert, has been quoted as saying that the harbor in Havana was not responsible for the

HOW THE "NORTHERS" CLEAN OUT HAVANA HARBOR—BEACH BETWEEN MORRO CASTLE AND CABAÑAS, SHOWING CLEAN CORAL AND SAND

spread of yellow-fever. I was surprised to find the water cleaner in appearance than that in the Hudson River opposite New York City. The sewage, as was pointed out by Colonel Waring, that runs into the harbor can readily be cared for by the mere process of solution.

Havana's harbor has been called dead because no streams empty into it. No current runs from it into the

ocean. That is true, but it does not follow that the harbor is never cleaned by nature. I saw no less than three storms—"northers," they are called—drive millions upon millions of gallons of sea-water into the harbor, until it must have been scoured thoroughly with pure salt water, one of the best of disinfectants. One storm had such fury that the spray broke clear over Morro Castle light. It drenched General Ludlow's palace. It made traffic in the bay dangerous. White-caps broke at the foot of old Cabañas. The harbor was scoured clear to its upper end, and when the wind went down and allowed the water which had been piled up in the harbor to escape, thousands of tons of matter in solution were swept out into the ocean. Put in a sewer system with most of the sewers running direct into the ocean, have the matter that runs into the bay from the sewers made into a solution by the liberal use of the fine supply of water that Havana has — the only thing in the way of public works that was praiseworthy — and dig out the poisoned mud at the mouth of Slaughter House Creek, and even a layman can understand that Havana Harbor can be made wholesome, and that no vast system of canal and channel cutting to create an artificial movement of water in the harbor is absolutely necessary. It will be hard to convince contractors of this, however.

The American officials found the water department of the city in fair condition. Havana has a modern plant in the matter of water-supply. The water is obtained from a series of springs in the Cerro district of the city. Reservoirs and conduits were put on a modern basis in 1894. Part of the aqueduct is an open ditch in some places.

The part of the aqueduct crossing the Almendares River was not in good condition, but radical defects were soon remedied. The greatest defect in the water-supply was in the distribution. More of it escaped or was stolen

THE CORNER OF O'REILLY AND COMPOSTELLA STREETS

than was paid for, and that aspect of the case led to an investigation, which resulted to the great pecuniary advantage of the city.

Although the water department was the best cared for of all the public works of the city under Spanish rule, it is a fact that Colonel Black did not see any one who had been in charge of the city's public works for an entire month. There seemed to be no office like that of a city engineer, as we understand it in the States. Here is what Colonel Black had to say in respect to that phase of Spanish official life in his report to General Ludlow on February 16th:

There was a very small city engineers' force for municipal work. By your direction I assumed charge of that organization. It was constituted as follows: One engineer, director of the aqueduct works, two architects, two assistants, ten draughtsmen and clerks, a few gardeners for the parks, and a small force of watchmen for the aqueduct. There were no instruments of any kind, no maps of the sewer systems, no map showing street grades or pavements, and in general practically nothing in the way of the records and data deemed essential in such an office, excepting drawings showing the aqueduct and water-mains. The Engineer Director was reported to be sick, and I saw nothing of him during the month. The office hours were from 2 to 4 P.M. Nothing in the way of public work was being done, and back pay was due the entire force. The duties of the various men were somewhat indefinite, without a proper assignment of work and responsibility.

The remaining branch of the engineer work of the department, the care of the harbor of Havana and its wharves, was in charge of the Engineer Director of the Obras del Puerto. This organization was also placed under my orders by you. I found it to be efficient, with quite a good plant, consisting of one tug, three dredges, seven scows, two pile-drivers, and small boats and appliances. It was idle for lack of funds.

Such was the story of the start in the direction of saving human life and increasing the value of property by simple cleanliness. When a sewer system is decided upon, and the streets are dug up, it is to be expected that an increase in the death-rate will follow, because of the release of fever germs from the soil where they have lain for generations. After asphalt pavements are put down—asphalt is one of the natural products of Cuba—and after the people have learned not only how to keep the streets clean, but also have learned something of sanitation, and have educated themselves into abhorring bad smells, there should be no reason why the city should not be healthful. But before that comes about we shall learn, through General Ludlow's decision to delay the institution of sewers and to stick to ordinary cleanliness temporarily, what the people and the authorities of Havana could have done in saving life if they had used these same simple methods, without going into any scheme of permanent sanitation.

CHAPTER V

SANITATION IN HAVANA

NOT less important than cleaning the streets, purifying the harbor and sewers, protecting the water-supply, and putting all public works in proper order in Havana, was the task of cleaning the city from the inside, the work of purifying the buildings of every grade in the town. Inside thousands of dwellings were "black holes" in a frightful condition. The walls of hundreds, if not thousands, of buildings were the abiding-places of germs of yellow-fever and other infectious diseases. A building without an offensive odor in it, whether the home of a wealthy citizen, the business place of a rich merchant, a so-called first-class hotel, a factory, or even some churches, was a still rarer thing than honesty in dealings at the Custom-house. Whether a sewer system and street pavements should be put down at once or delayed for another year, it was obvious to the American authorities that the buildings must be cleaned, as a primary necessity in keeping down the death-rate, in endeavoring to prevent yellow-fever from reaching American shores, and in preserving the health of American soldiers.

General Greene, the first military governor of the city

after the Spanish evacuation, at once set about having the buildings cleaned, as he had set about having the streets cleaned and the public works put in order. The man placed in charge of this work was Major John G. Davis, a Chicago physician of large practice and wide reputation. Major Davis really became the health-officer of Havana. General Ludlow, who relieved General Greene, gave him the heartiest support. Major Davis is one of those military officers who do things. He has the energy of an eager business man. I could not find any tendency on his part to shut down his desk at a certain hour every day; to pay undue attention to the matter of rank or red-tape when there were lives to be saved; to spend time in the exercise of petty jealousies lest full and proper credit and due promotion should not be given to him for his work. His sole care seemed to be to get the town in a more healthful condition and let everything else go. He worked constantly and never seemed to tire, and he had the satisfaction of seeing the death-rate for the month of January, the first full month of his work, cut almost exactly in half, compared with the January of the previous year. In January, 1898, the deaths in Havana numbered, according to the imperfect accounts of the Spanish authorities, 1801; in 1899, under the accurate system of records made by the Americans, the deaths were 900. Month by month up to the beginning of summer the records showed a still decreasing death-rate.

A house-to-house medical inspection in the city was necessary. For this purpose Major Davis employed 114 physicians, most of them Cubans and residents of the city. The town was divided into districts, and a certain territory apportioned to each inspector. It took time to organize the force, to prepare report blanks, and the like; but during the first week in February the buildings of the city were being inspected at the rate of 1200

MAJOR JOHN G. DAVIS, U. S. V.,
DEPARTMENT OF SANITATION

a day. This inspection was no informal hit-or-miss affair. It meant an examination into every room, every court, and every yard of every building in town, whether that building was occupied or owned by rich or poor or high or low. It meant an inspection of every cesspool and the condition of the water-supply in every building.

For each inspection a report had to be made out, show-ing the street and number of the building, name of the owner and occupants, dimensions of the building, and the purposes for which it was used; number of families and persons, adults and children, in it; whether there was any sickness in the place, and if so, of what nature; what was done with the household waste of every kind; number of cesspools, or "black holes," and their con-dition; the condition of drainage; the disposition of gar-bage; whether there was need of vaccination of residents; and whether there was or ever had been any infectious disease in the building. There were some other ques-tions of minor importance.

This system of inspection and reports amounted really to a health census of the town. It contained data of the highest importance for various municipal purposes, espe-cially matters pertaining to the destitute and sick. It was necessary to examine every report carefully. Eleven clerks were kept busy sending out notices to owners and occupants of the houses inspected, ordering them to do certain things towards putting the places in a good sanitary condition. Whitewashing was ordered nearly everywhere. Thousands of cesspools were ordered to be cleaned and improved. Directions were given to put all garbage where it could be collected by the wagons under the Street - cleaning Department. Where it could be done, modern water-closets were ordered to be installed. Liberal use of paint was prescribed in thousands of places.

The examining physicians had not only to inspect, but to reinspect. They adopted a system of doing this, and

householders who neglected to comply with their orders
were notified that they would be arrested and fined.
Major Davis encountered little opposition from the people in his work. Here and there one heard of complaints
against this or that inspector, and assertions, largely by
persons who kept their homes clean and who had means,
that it was an outrage not to respect the privacy of

THE PRESIDIO, NOW THE CITY PENITENTIARY

homes. But all such persons, and those who sympathized with them, forgot that the city was under military rule, and that the health of the place demanded
that all should be treated alike in this grapple with disease in its hiding-places. Some of the householders
asked for time in which to make repairs and to clean
up, and it was usually given to them. In most cases

the time limit for thorough cleaning was set at thirty days.

Now it was not easy to secure material or men to clean places. In the first days of American occupation large quantities of lime and disinfectants, used by the military authorities in cleaning public buildings, had to be brought from the United States on hurry orders. There was not enough paint in the city with which to obey the orders by Major Davis's men. It had to be sent for, and brushes with which to do the work had also to be imported. There was a great scarcity of workmen, such as painters and plumbers and carpenters, and even day-laborers could not be hired, for there was none in good health not at work. The price of labor rose, and for all these reasons it was absolutely essential that time should be given for the needed changes. Still, there was work that could be done in almost every place, and instantly the effect was felt in the reduced death-rate.

This inspection work was only part of the duty that fell to the lot of Major Davis as chief health-officer. One of his first tasks was to inspect the streets, so that an efficient basis for street-cleaning could be established. Every street in town was examined. Reports of their condition went to the Department of Public Works under Colonel Black. It was a big undertaking. Then there was the matter of caring for the destitute sick. The inspection reports revealed their condition and addresses. A dozen physicians were employed in caring for these persons.

Another duty was the task of analyzing the milk of the dairies in town, and of that which was brought into

OLD MILITARY PRISON, PLAZA DE ARMAS

town. One of the sights in Havana was a dairy. The cows were kept in buildings such as are used for residences or stores, and were in plain sight. They stood in a stall constantly, and never had any grazing or exercise. The stables were usually in bad sanitary condition, and a danger to health for the entire neighborhood. The manure was not cared for on sanitary principles. Dr. Davis told me that, judging from the reports he had received already, he thought there must have been at least 1000 cows kept in these close quarters in the city for dairy purposes. He declared that it was his intention to drive every one of these dairies out of town.

Dr. Davis had to care for the municipal hospitals, and to see that they were supplied with medicines and proper medical help. He established five houses of assistance, where those needing medicine could have their wants prescribed for. He also designated certain drug-stores in various parts of the city where prescriptions would be put up at government expense for those who had no money to purchase such necessaries. He looked after the medical condition of the orphans, and co-operated with those who had charge of feeding the poor. By means of this system begging lepers were banished from the streets, and one of the most loathsome sights of the place in the early days of American occupation was soon gone.

Although the work of cleaning the public buildings came under the care of Colonel Black of the Public Works Department, Major Davis had to pass upon it and inspect it. There were no less than eighteen of these large buildings being cleaned during the month of

January. All the barracks in town, all the palaces of officials, all the public offices, were undergoing a thorough cleansing. Even Morro Castle and Cabañas fortress were closed to visitors on this account. All the rough work was done by Cubans who were supposed to be immune to yellow-fever. The buildings were "rough cleaned" by them and large quantities of quick-lime and a solution of chloride of lime were used. Then came coats of paint or whitewash, with repairs to wood-work, and a thorough disinfection by the sanitary department. The Spaniards left the public buildings in a frightful condition. They stripped the places of everything that could be sold, including plumbing, gas-fixtures, wash-stands, doors to closets, bath-tubs, and furniture, and seemed to take delight in making the places as dirty as possible. A curious discovery was made in one of the public buildings at the foot of Zulueta Street. It was a barracks, and had a new floor. It was thought wise to pry up a board or two. To the astonishment of the officials, the entire space between the floor beams was filled with old grape-shot and cannon-balls. There must have been from twenty to thirty tons in the place. The floor was literally ballasted, and no one could guess the reason, unless it might be a steal of some kind requiring that the old stuff should be hidden.

Major Davis had the medical care of the American soldiers in Havana to look after, as well as to prepare estimates for his department, supervise the work of his clerks, and co-operate with other departments in ordering supplies from the United States for the preservation of the health of the community. One of these orders was for a large number of odorless excavators for the cleaning of the terrible " black holes " in the town.

In justification of his hopes of reducing the number of yellow-fever cases to a large extent, Dr. Davis allowed me to make this extract from a letter written on February 6th to him by Dr. Manuel Delfin, an expert of high repute in yellow-fever cases :

From now on I feel assured that if the cleaning the streets is kept up, and that of the houses is continued, obliging the owners to put in water and modern water-closets, and, above all, the streets are sprinkled with electrozone, that also could be employed in the cleaning and disinfection of houses and public buildings, I feel assured that the coming summer will appear in our history as the foremark of the endless series that the future has for a new era in civilization.

Although it was not strictly sanitary in character, the work of feeding the poor of the city contributed in large degree to the improved healthful conditions of the city, and it will not be out of place to tell the story of that work here. This task was under the direction of Captain E. St. John Greble, a volunteer officer from Philadelphia, whose tact, unlimited patience, and sympathetic temperament made him peculiarly fitted to the undertaking. It brought him in direct contact with the sad and pitiful side of life in Havana. During January and February no less than 20,000 persons were being fed by the United States government through army agencies, and in the first week in February Captain Greble said to me that he believed that there were no persons in town suffering from a lack of food. He had no doubt that in the early work of his bureau he and his officers had been imposed upon here and there, but it was no time for complete investigation. Wherever a hungry face, or what seemed to be a hungry face, was seen, immediate aid was given, and Captain Greble had to take chances as to impostors. He had to provide for the orphan children, many of whom were being cared for by Catholic Sisters in public institutions, and many of whom had no homes, nor even distant relatives. Scores of them had slept on the streets and had begged their food. Their condition was such that even a strong man could not notice it without a shudder.

Then there were the widows of Spanish officers in the Casa de las Viudas—Home of the Widows—left behind in Cuba without support of any kind. They were refined and highly educated, many of them, and too proud to ask for charity. They were timid about seeking assistance from the United States government, because their husbands had been Spanish officers. In making a public appeal in their behalf, General Ludlow referred to these widows as a " unique and pitiful legacy " of Spanish rule. Mrs. Ludlow generously offered to take charge of the work of applying any assistance that might be sent to Havana on their behalf.

Captain Greble reached Havana on December 15, 1898, and at once took hold of the work of feeding the destitute. As soon as the Spanish forces left the city he began to put a system in operation. He established five military depots, where food was given to the poor on presentation of orders duly signed by the authorities. The station that attracted most attention from visitors was at the head of the Prado, where several companies of the Tenth Regular Infantry were encamped. A large tent faced the street, and about it was built a fence with a sort of shelf on top. The fence seemed to be thronged all the time. It was there that one saw to the best ad-

CAPTAIN E. ST. J. GREBLE, U. S. V.,
DEPARTMENT OF FOOD-SUPPLIES

vantage what the war meant to the people of Havana. Many refined persons plainly showed their humiliation as they carried away food to their homes. Tears stood in their eyes; a look of pitiful humiliation was on their faces, mingled with one of gratitude. Some were hardly able to walk. Many brought boys with them to carry away their rations. Many were old and feeble, and the patience with which they stood about awaiting their turns to be served touched the American spectators who had strolled up to see one of the sights of the town. It was not an infrequent sight to see pieces of coin slipped into the hands of applicants, or placed upon the board shelf where they might be picked up. From morning till night the detail of soldiers dealt out the rations, and although it was a dreary task, Uncle Sam's boys did their best to throw some cheer into it by attempts at humor in their talk, and occasionally by cutting up some caper that made the wretched people go away with a smile. Those smiles seemed to satisfy the soldier boys keenly.

I spent some time at this tent watching the soldiers fill the bags of the applicants. Rarely less than five rations were given in any one case. Five rations consisted usually of three one-quarter-pound cans of bacon, four pounds of flour, five ounces of coffee, eight ounces of sugar, three ounces of salt, five ounces of rice, one-fifth of an ounce of pepper, a little vinegar and soap thrown in. For the sick the rations included corn-starch, condensed milk, deviled ham, canned soup, and dried apples in addition to the regulation rations.

In the first days of feeding the poor, Captain Greble received hundreds of applicants at his office, where clerks made out requisitions for food. So far as he could, Captain Greble personally questioned the applicant, and listened to his or her story. Gradually a system was evolved and put in operation, whereby committees from the Cuban Patriotic League, the Junta Patriotica, were established in every ward in the city, subsidiary to the five relief stations, and through these every house was visited and all worthy persons were provided for. The needy soon found out where to apply, and the districts were so small in territory that there was little likelihood that any hungry person was overlooked. In this way something like 20,000 rations a day were distributed, the supplies

DESTITUTE CUBANS DRAWING RATIONS FROM THE
RELIEF STATION ON THE PRADO
Photograph by C. E. Doty and S. R. Fox

amounting to food for as much as thirty days in some cases. From six to ten days' supply was the average amount given out. Ladies long identified with charitable work, and pastors of churches also, assisted in recommending deserving cases to Captain Greble and his men, and in that way distress from hunger was soon relieved in the city. Here is a blank form, made out for me by Captain Greble, which will reveal something of the system involved, and the thoroughness and care with which this important work was done :

HAVANA, *February* 7, 1899.

Name, Adriana de San Juan, widow.
Address, Teniente Rey, No. 56.

Adults .... { *Males, No*................
{ *Females, No.* 1

Children, total No.. 6
Ages, males, 2, 7.
Ages, females, 3, 5, 8, 13.   —

Total in family................................... 7

Remarks—Destitute and sick with fever.   Four children sick. Two in bed.   Investigated.

Officer in Charge of Station at Campo de Marte.   *Issue* 70 rations, 7 persons, for 10 days.

E. S. J. GREBLE,
Capt. and A. A. General.

The case of the Spanish widows, to which General Ludlow referred in his appeal, was peculiarly sad.   They were housed in a large institution, built partly by convict labor and partly by military labor.   The inmates were supported in part by the government of the island, and in part by contributions from the salaries of Spanish officers.   Some of the widows were very old, having spent most of their lives in Cuba.   Some were born in Cuba, but most of them were from Spain.   They were a mournful reminder of war and its penalties, and they were recognized as part of the Spanish military outfit in Cuba. The Spanish troops sailed away, and simply abandoned them to the vicissitudes of a new order of things.   Their pensions had not been paid for more than a year and a half, and with the revenues from the salaries of Spanish officers cut off entirely, they were in a deplorable plight. There were seventy women of various ages in the home, and ninety girls and fifty boys. They were almost without friends, and suffered keenly before they allowed their condition to become known to the American authorities. Some were able to do such work as teaching, but there was none to be had.

Other public institutions called for immediate attention. There was the Casa de Beneficencia, upon which several hundred persons were dependent. This institution has property estimated to be worth something like $1,250,000, but its income was cut off. Captain Greble sold it 5000 rations at eight cents each, to be paid for when the institution should again be in receipt of its income. The Sisters of the Good Shepherd and the Sisters of the Heart of Our Lord were caring for many orphans, and Captain Greble went to their assistance as quickly as he could. His first care had been, of course, the feeding of the absolutely destitute on the streets. These were provided with shelter as well as food, in barracks which were made clean. Some of these destitute persons were aged, but a good many were orphans. Arrangements were made to place most of the orphans found on the streets in asylums, the government paying ten dollars a month for their maintenance, with the understanding that they were to receive instruction in some trade in addition to other schooling.

Soon after Captain Greble began to get his city work organized he also turned his attention to the suburbs.

Reports of starving people in the country reached him. He sent out an officer, who looked the situation over, put himself in touch with the officials of the places and the women leaders in charitable work, and then had sent in reports as to about the number of rations that would be needed for a given time. Blank forms of requisition were left to be filled up, and the first wagon-train with food to sustain these people was sent out early in February. It was a pleasing sight to see these heavily laden wagons starting on this errand. There were twenty wagons, each drawn by four mules, and each having one non-commissioned officer and four privates to deal out the food. The wagons made a noise as they rumbled through the streets like an enormous circus outfit coming into a stone-paved city at night. The train seemed to be fully a quarter of a mile long, and it left town with signs of public approval on all sides. In a few days all the needy within reasonable wagon travel of Havana had been supplied with food for at least ten days. The work was to be kept up until there was no longer occasion for it.

In all this work of relieving the destitute there were bound to be some unworthy cases. When the machinery was organized thoroughly Captain Greble began to look for these. He began to study the requisitions, and here and there he was able to find a case where there was imposition. The day before I left town he had discovered a flagrant case of fraud. A woman of refined appearance had simply been filling up her place with rations secured by misrepresentation. It may have been fear that the food would be cut off some day, or it may have been just an ordinary desire to steal, that caused her to do as she did, but the result was that she was arrested promptly and placed in jail, to be dealt with by the courts.

Thus not only was the city cleaned inside and outside, but the people were built up in health. There was no complaint, from those whose suffering had been relieved, of the military occupation of Cuba by the United States.

WITHIN THE TENTH U. S. INFANTRY'S RELIEF STATION
ON THE PRADO

Although in no way connected with the military occu-pation of Cuba, the branch of the Marine Hospital Ser-vice established in Havana contributes largely to the protection of this country from infection, and therefore is part of the general system of health restoration there. As far back as 1878 this government established an office in Havana, under the National Board of Health, to study yellow-fever, and to protect this country from it. In

1883 this work was transferred to the Marine Hospital Service, under the Treasury Department. Its work is to inspect vessels and passengers coming to this country. Dr. W. F. Brunner was in charge of the work until July, 1899. He was one of the last to leave Havana when the war came, and he was one of the first to return. He played an important part in the visit of Americans to Havana. It was essential that all visitors should appear at his office. Unless the visitor had been vaccinated and had "good marks" to show, he could not leave the island for the United States until vaccinated and the vaccination had begun to "take." The day before one left he had to go to Dr. Brunner's office and get a bill of good health. No steamship line may sell a ticket to this country without such a certificate. One of the office assistants goes to each vessel, and leaves it just as the anchor is pulled up. He takes a final look at all the passengers before they sail.

This office is one of the busiest places in Havana. A dozen cabs are to be seen in front of it at almost any hour of the day. The authorities have given orders for a disinfecting-vessel to be stationed at Havana under the Marine Hospital Service. Passengers and sailors, baggage and other goods, can be disinfected thoroughly by such means before sailing. When Havana really becomes clean, and when all these precautions which have been adopted are in working order, doubtless, not only will Havana and other parts of Cuba be freed from the dreadful scourge of yellow-fever, but the southern part of the United States will no longer suffer from that form of epidemic.

CHAPTER VI

AN HONEST CUSTOMS SERVICE IN CUBA

ONLY a few days had elapsed after the Spanish evacuation of Havana, and after the United States army officials had taken charge of the government in all its branches, when the merchants of the city began to realize that the strangest thing in all the world had happened. The Custom-house was being run honestly. Even money collected in overcharges was being refunded, and the fortunes of war could have brought about nothing so unexpected. It was almost impossible to believe that honesty ruled there. Tests had to be made. A blackmailer made one of the first of these tests. Corrupt officials still in the service made another test. It took the form of a strike, but it was nipped in the bud in a flash. Merchants who preferred evil ways to those of honesty tried to force a return in part to former crooked paths. A show of firmness and the turning of the light upon them sent them scurrying away. Attack after attack was made in the dark to reveal weak spots in the system of honesty, and every man left in Havana of the gang of thieves, blackmailers, pilferers, and plunder-sharers that had infested the Havana Custom-house turned away discouraged and forlorn.

The last refuge of such men, the dissemination of plausible lies, seemed to have no effect. Alas for the stupidity of American officials! Would they never learn the lesson that they could not become rich by being honest in custom-house dealings! And such a chance as they had!

The astonishment of the people of Havana over the new situation centred upon two men. The first man

COLONEL T. H. BLISS, U. S. A.,
COLLECTOR OF CUSTOMS, HAVANA

was Colonel Tasker H. Bliss, Collector of the Port of Havana, and in charge of all the other custom-houses in the island, reporting directly to the Secretary of War.

The other man was Walter A. Donaldson, special Deputy Collector of the Port, of many years' experience in custom-house matters in various parts of the United States, familiar with the Spanish language and Spanish customs, able to guide his chief, Colonel Bliss, who had never had experience in collecting revenue from customs duties, through devious ways hedged about with technicalities. Colonel Bliss, as might have been expected from an efficient officer of the army, had an idea that the way to collect was to collect. He set himself about finding out what he had to collect, and then about doing it in the most direct and straightforward way. He had another quality, found always in the best type of American army officers—true courtesy and regard for the rights and feelings of others. In Mr. Donaldson, who had had more than twenty years' experience in such work, a large part of it being in New York City, and who had already reorganized the customs service in the province of Santiago, he had a most efficient and loyal assistant, a thorough believer in the methods of civil service reform, a man who held that the public service of the country should be administered solely for the benefit of the people, and not for the political fortune of some party hack, and whose ideas regarding public office and politics had a rock-bottom basis of common all-around honesty. Between them they arranged it that there could be no stealing except by collusion with the collector.

These two men not only had to put in force a new schedule of duties and straighten out its problems and puzzles, but they had to begin work with a force re-

duced by one-third, owing to desertions for fear of losing Spanish pensions, and used only to the corrupt
methods of the past—a force fearful lest its members
should lose their places; almost incapable of any initia-
tive of its own. There were no blanks and rules for
management of details. Records left behind were value-
less. There was not even a pay-roll, and there was
nothing to do but to plunge right in and evolve a new
order of things, little by little, out of the confusion that
resulted.

What the Custom-house in Havana was under Spanish rule need not be told at length. Every one knows
that it was the place from which corrupt captain-generals and other high officials were supposed to obtain
the largest share of their stolen wealth, some of which
undoubtedly went to Spain for division with other men.
If there was any strictly honest transaction within
its walls it was the exception, not the rule. The place
had a withering influence upon morality in business life.
It was unclean, in more ways than one, from top to bottom. Mr. Robert P. Porter, who drew up the new tariff,
said of the so-called tariff which was in force that it
"was made by Spaniards for Spain, in the interests
of the Spanish. On any other theory it was inexpli-
cable."

What the tariff receipts meant for Spanish officials in
Cuba may be inferred from the following letter, written
to the Collector of Customs by General Castellanos on
the very last day of his term as captain-general of the
island, and found later in the Custom-house:

THE STREET HAWKER

HONEST CUSTOMS SERVICE IN CUBA

El Gobernador-General,
Capitan-General
de la

Particular.   Isla de Cuba.

Sr. Dn. Anibal Arriete :

MI DISTINGUIDO AMIGO,—Pueden Vds. seguir cobrando en esa Aduana hasta las siete de la noche. Para recibir lo recaudado hoy estará la pagaderia abierta hasta las diez.

Cualquier hora es buena para venir Vd. a verme, pues hoy no pienso salir de casa.   De Vd. affmo amigo S.S.,

ADOLFO J. CASTELLANOS.

HABANA, 31 *Diciembre*, '98.

This translation was furnished to me by the customs officials in Havana:

The Governor-General,
Captain-General
of the

Private.   Island of Cuba.

Mr. Anibal Arriete :

MY DISTINGUISHED FRIEND,—Your people can keep on collecting in the Custom-house until seven o'clock in the evening. In order to receive to-day's collection the Treasury will be open until ten.

You may come to see me at any time, as I do not intend to go out of the house to-day.   Sincerely your friend,

ADOLFO J. CASTELLANOS.

HAVANA, *December* 31, 1898.

That letter seems to be of some historical importance. I have no knowledge that General Castellanos and his "distinguished friend," Señor Don Anibal Arriete, the last Spanish Collector of Customs in Havana, were cor-

rupt, and I do not so charge ; but it is unnecessary to
call attention to the construction that would be placed
upon that letter of General Castellanos, with its direction
to "see me," in any country where a Latin race does not
rule. What the construction must be in countries where
officials are expected to steal as a matter of course, can
also be conjectured. The original, which would seem to
be of vital interest to the reputation of General Castellanos, can be produced at any time, and it is only fair
to remark that the general opinion in Havana regarding
Castellanos seems to be that he was the most "reason-
ably honest" of all the captain-generals they had had in
a long time.

It was in such an atmosphere and under such conditions that Colonel Bliss took hold of his work. He
kept the old force at work so far as possible. He opened
a new bureau of audit at once. With the advice of Mr.
Donaldson he established an entry division, a liquidating
division, an exporting division, and several minor divi-
sions and departments, one of which was a bureau of statistics. He placed the bookkeepers in a different room
from the cashiers; he set up gates in the place so that
the clerical force should not come in contact with the
merchants and their agents, who overran the place. He
opened the doors of his own office, so as to be accessible
to every man who could have any business with him.
He set up checks and balances to prevent stealing. He
started in to collect the duties in the very first case that
came up. He worked from eight o'clock in the morning
until twelve o'clock at night. He and Mr. Donaldson
saw every merchant who came to them. With their own

hands, more than once, they went over the routine of passing a consignment of goods through the custom-house. They drilled the clerks—and it was such a task! —and they saw that the money received was counted

WALTER A. DONALDSON,
DEPUTY-COLLECTOR OF CUSTOMS

every night and locked up with half a dozen big keys in an antiquated safe, but with a squad of soldiers near by to guard it night and day.

The first rule, one might say, that Colonel Bliss and Mr. Donaldson set up, was that no man should be discharged without cause, and no man should be hired without merit and especial fitness for the work. It was real civil service reform, and there was the right kind of "starch" in it. This was shown by probably the most interesting episode that took place under the new management within the first six weeks. An official in the cashier's department came to Colonel Bliss one day in a state of great perturbation, and wanted to know if it was true that he was to lose his place, or if any man who had a "pull" could bring about his discharge. He protested that he was doing his full duty, and was serving the United States honestly. Colonel Bliss told the man that he was secure in his place so long as he was efficient and honest. Then the colonel asked why the man, whose name I do not use, by request, had come to him. The employé handed the colonel a letter without signature, which he said came from the editor of a small afternoon newspaper, and of which this is a translation :

O'REILLY, 38, *February* 1, 1899.

DEAR FRIEND,—I have been waiting for you in my house, as you suggested, but I have not seen you. They are making the appointments at this moment. Though you are well supplied with money, you would not be pleased to lose your job. Let it be known that neither would I. I expect you this evening up to five o'clock. ———

Colonel Bliss questioned his employé closely. The latter was sure that a man named Robert, the editor in question, had written the letter. It was a case of blackmail, he said, and he would not submit. Colonel Bliss was puzzled. He decided to send for Mr. Robert. A polite note from the collector himself soon hurried Mr. Robert jauntily to the doors of the Custom-house. It was evident that he thought he was going to "do business" with the collector himself. Truly the Americans were not so bad, after all. The glitter in the eye of Colonel Bliss alarmed him a little, and so when Colonel Bliss asked him if he wrote the letter in question, he answered no, as a matter of course. He had to feel his way as to why the collector had sent for him. He had not the faintest idea that he had done anything worthy of censure. Colonel Bliss asked him if he was sure that he had not written the letter, and followed this up by what experts, and especially army experts, would call "chucking a bluff," and by pretending that he had the man cornered; and Mr. Robert surrendered. "Yes, I wrote that letter," he said, defiantly. He then said that the employé had been paying him tribute for years, and he had a right to a share of the man's salary. Colonel Bliss sat there amazed. Robert did not seem to have the vaguest idea that he had done wrong. Colonel Bliss could stand it no longer. The man wanted to explain further.

"Not another word!" thundered Colonel Bliss, and then he called in witnesses and denounced the man; told him that he would prosecute him or punish him in some form; pictured the contempt which Americans have for a blackmailer; summoned many of the employés, and proclaimed then and there that no man could cause their dismissal without just reason, and that they were to be accountable to no person for their places except himself. Then he dismissed Robert in scorn.

To his still greater amazement, Colonel Bliss received this letter from Robert half an hour later:

THE NEW-BORN CUBA

O'REILLY, 38, *February* 1, 1899.

SIR,—I pray you not to blame me for my note; it was not anonymous, because it was united with my card, and because that gentleman well knows that it belonged to me. This gentleman is indebted to me for some money, and if you want to get a good information in this matter, I have no objection to be submitted before him to a cross-examination.

Some years ago I used to publish all the proceedings of the cash, and Mr. —— came to me imploring my silence. He promised spontaneously to pay twelve subscriptions every month for the time he could keep his employment, and that is the amount I claim from him; because he is indebted to me for three or four months. Passing to any other question, it would be wise, when you make your complaint against me to General Brooke, to tell him that there is no Cuban in Cuba who may claim more distinction with respect to the United States, as I can prove by all my publications since the year 1884—the last one I enclose to you.

Yours respectfully,

ESTABAN A. ROBERT.

The next day Colonel Bliss was surprised again by finding two letters enclosed in a copy of Robert's newspaper, *La Tarde*, and lying on his desk. One letter was to the collector, and said:

COLONEL BLISS,—I take the liberty to enclose an open letter to Mr. —— for your perusal.

I remain,   Yours respectfully,

ESTABAN A. ROBERT.

The other letter read:

DEAR FRIEND EDUARDO,—What a devil of idea you had to show to Mr. Bliss my last letter! The consequence of it all is that I have had to tell him everything, because I am not a man

148

to lie. Mr. Bliss knows already that you offered me spontaneously twelve subscriptions. It is more than seven years ago, and payment had been declined.

Remember, if you are inclined to do it, that on San Ignacio Street you offered to pay me the amount of twelve subscriptions should I not write a word about the cash, because there was injury for you making those matters public. It was for you not to have uttered a word to anybody, because it is understood that there may be underneath this affair something deserving to be silenced. You ought to have in your pocket at least 200 letters in the same terms, and you only produced my last one, because it was not safe for you in other days to do the same thing, because there was danger impending.

ESTABAN A. ROBERT.

The case of Mr. Robert was attended to, and it had its effect, as did another incident that occurred about the same time. An agent of one of the largest importing-houses in the city forced himself through the gate and undertook to take charge of affairs at a certain clerk's desk, just as the agent had done frequently before. He represented a merchant who had had a big " pull." The clerk remonstrated, and sharp words followed. There was an exchange of blows, and soon Colonel Bliss had a complaint from the merchant that his agent had been assaulted grievously in the Custom-house by a certain clerk. Colonel Bliss investigated it, and found that the agent had been very offensive in manner, had broken the new rules wilfully, and had actually struck the first blow. He called in the clerk, commended him before others, and gave notice publicly that he would stand by his employés constantly. It was a matter of amazement

to Colonel Bliss that in view of past associations the
clerk had the courage to strike the agent at all. The
merchant was notified that that agent could no longer
do business for him in the Custom-house.

The management of the new system did not devolve
so much upon the "avistas," or appraisers, as in the

HAVANA—CUSTOM-HOUSE WHARVES AND LANDING-STAGE
Photograph by E. C. Rost

Spanish régime, but still it was concerning them that
the most critical situation in the control by Americans
occurred. In the old days the "vistas," as they were
called, were what in slang parlance would be termed
"the whole thing." They received very small salaries;
they made an enormous amount of money. A merchant
importing flour went down to the docks, "saw" a certain
vista, had the cargo passed as cement, paid the duty on

the spot, got an order for the release of his flour, and the vista "saw" his superior officers, and the share in the bribe that the merchant had paid for his "smuggling" did not stop until some of the money finally reached Spain. There were many advantages in this kind of an arrangement, not the least of which was that a merchant got his goods promptly.

It was not long before the vistas were in revolt. Collector Bliss and Mr. Donaldson found a strike of vistas on their hands one morning down on the Custom-house landing. Mr. Donaldson strolled down there, apparently unconcerned, asked what the trouble was, peremptorily discharged some of the ringleaders, and called for the resignations of several others, and the strike was over in less than ten minutes.

Not so easy to manage, however, was the next strike, that of the merchants. It is probable that they were inspired as to their action by some of the vistas whose sources of revenue had been curtailed. Word reached Colonel Bliss and Mr. Donaldson one morning that the merchants were refusing to apply for their goods, and would not do so until there was a return to the old system of doing business directly with the vistas. It was inconvenient, the merchants said, to take a paper and go from one clerk to another, at least five, and get various signatures before one could get a release of his goods. The old way was much the better. Probably then and there occurred the most critical day of Colonel Bliss's régime. He knew it, and Mr. Donaldson knew it. Colonel Bliss, with confidence in Mr. Donaldson's ability to deal with such a crisis, told him to see what he could do in the matter. The custom - house wharf could only hold so much freight; there was no system of bonded warehouses; the commerce of the port could not be tied up.

Colonel Bliss could have taken drastic measures. He could have hired buildings, locked the importations up, and told the merchants that they could get their goods at his convenience. It would have been a wholesome lesson, but it would have left sores. He told Mr. Donaldson to use tact, and the latter did use it. He strolled down upon the dock smoking a cigar. " Going to be a fiesta to-day?" he inquired, as he noted with apparent surprise that no work was going on, and that the merchants were standing around doing nothing. No fiesta? What was the trouble? Oh yes, he could understand. Probably some little hitch owing to lack of familiarity with the way of doing business. He asked for the entry blank of a merchant, offered to show him how to get his goods out, started half a dozen other men on the road in the same way, asked that a committee of half a dozen merchants be appointed to examine into the details of the new system with its checks and balances, and received the promise that that afternoon they would go into details with him; got this man and that man stirred up, and soon had all the employés engaged in work, and that strike was over, to the amazement of the strikers. That afternoon Mr. Donaldson took several entries and went through them with a committee, and then he asked them to make suggestions. Wherever it was possible to modify little things, such as placing more clerks in the cashier's department, it was done, and a permanent

AMERICAN CONSULATE

understanding was reached that at a certain hour each day Mr. Donaldson would show the workings of the Custom-house to all who had a right to inspect them.

But there was to be still more trouble with the merchants. They complained of needless delay in some schedules, and they thought that in certain lines they should be permitted to do business with the appraiser, liquidate the duties then and there, and get their goods at once. There was too much running around to this and that clerk. Colonel Bliss invited the representative merchants of the city to meet Mr. Donaldson in conference. I had the pleasure of attending the meeting. There were about twenty-five merchants present, some of whom were millionaires. Mr. Donaldson chose to speak in English and have his words translated. He told them that the first idea of the new management, after protecting itself by modern business methods, was to help the merchants in their business, to regard them as customers of the custom - house. Recognizing this fact, Colonel Bliss had already established an order that ninety per cent. of any cargo could be taken away at once upon arrival, the duties to be adjudicated later. Mr. Donaldson was willing to answer any question, to explain the reason for any step, and would be glad to consider suggestions of any kind.

But before this was done, he wanted to say that there were three or four vacancies among the vistas. Would the merchants be kind enough to recommend good men for the places, so that Colonel Bliss could appoint them? Then Mr. Donaldson started his callers off for a conversational gallop. They talked and gesticulated, and finally, after they had wandered over the entire range of custom-house business, Mr. Donaldson said :

"As I understand it, gentlemen, you would like to return to the system of liquidating your entries right beside the appraisers down-stairs?"

They protested that they were satisfied with the new system in the main, but they thought that in certain schedules—hardware was one—they could make better time by the former system.

Mr. Donaldson repeated their remarks, and asked if he understood them correctly. Then he paused, and, with great deliberation, said, in a quiet but most serious tone :

"Gentlemen, do I understand that you want to return to the old system of fines as well?"

A shriek of concerted and long-sustained noes went up from that room that could have been heard half-way across the harbor. Mr. Donaldson had them on the run. He followed up his advantage by asking :

"Do I understand that most of you would prefer to return to the old" (marked emphasis on the word, with a significant look) "system of doing business in the Custom-house?"

Another shriek went up. "Americano! Americano! Americano!" was the cry. Donaldson had won.

One of the most puzzling problems with which Colonel Bliss had to deal was the flag for Cubans engaged in their own coastwise trade. The flag of the United States could not be used on such vessels, and neither could the Cuban flag. The Spanish flag was banished forever. To meet the situation the President ordered that a blue flag with a white jack should be used for such vessels. Owners were required to take an oath renouncing allegiance to all former governments. Some of the skippers of the vessels thought they had a right to fly the United States flag. It took a long time to convince them that the only flag they could fly would be that blue field with a white patch on one corner, and that the forces of the United States would be used, if necessary, to protect them from being considered pirates or as belonging to a fictitious nation. That flag is the only flag of Cuban sovereignty or semi-sovereignty which the United States, up to this writing, has recognized, and, so far as this country is concerned officially, that is the present Cuban flag. It was impossible to find all the owners of these small vessels so that they might renounce their former allegiance, and Colonel Bliss, in order not to impair commerce, had recourse to the issue of temporary permits for each voyage. The other collectors on the island soon got to understand the new order of affairs, and Colonel Bliss had rounded another sharp corner.

This matter of coastwise commerce brought another question, that of an "open door." Colonel Bliss and Mr. Donaldson, as well as Mr. Porter, saw that if Cuba would be rehabilitated the ports must be open to ships of all nations. There were not enough ships under the American flag to deal with its commerce as if the island were our own possession. Had it not been for the open-door policy, the mines at Santiago could not have started up, and commerce at most of the ports of the island would have stood still. In a report, as far back as December 1, 1898, to General Wood at Santiago, Mr. Donaldson said:

It is to be remarked that the policy of non-discrimination in intercourse extended to the vessels of all nations, in the matter of entering and clearing at this port, as well as at the various other ports within this province, has greatly facilitated the re-establishment of commercial relations.

The same policy has been extended since then to all ports, and the " open door " has been of immense value in the restoration of the island. It is unnecessary to point out the lesson involved.

The story of the first sixty days in the collection of customs duties by the United States under Colonel Bliss could be extended at great length. The incident of the payment of the first refund would make a long story of itself. Word was passed that it was really going to happen. The merchant interested, and nearly all of his employés, gathered to receive the money. The report of what was going on spread, and soon the corridors of the Custom-house were jammed to see money that was paid into a custom-house through a wrong valuation actually paid back. It was received with cheers, and the sensation lasted fully a week, and existed two months later, to some extent. Oh, what queer people those American officials were, to be honest like that !

Then there was the matter of readjustment of salaries and the difficulty of making out a pay-roll. The employés did not use fixed names. One day a man would use his father's name, and the next day his mother's. Gradually Colonel Bliss got their signatures, and as long as they remained in the Custom-house the names they signed were to be their official names. That the read-justment of salaries was imperative may be judged from the fact that the head of one division received $2000 a year, while the head of another, equally important, received only $600. Then there was the matter of renovating the building, cleaning the sewer that ran under the building directly under the collector's office, and that

THE CUSTOM-HOUSE

occasionally drove him from his work. This, with the daily routine of signing permits, reports, listening to complaints and suggestions, settling disputes as to valuations, supervising the business of other ports, planning for bonded warehouses, drilling the force of clerks, occasionally descending upon the vistas to see if their appraisement had been honest, locking up the cash and transferring it to the officer designated by the authorities—all these and a score of other things kept Colonel Bliss and Mr. Donaldson busy.

So far as the new tariff was concerned, its operation had had little effect upon prices at the time of my visit. Large stocks had been imported under the old corrupt system, just before the Spaniards left. The competitive spirit as it is known in the United States does not obtain in business in Cuba to a great extent. Importations from Spain had not lessened materially, nor had those from this country increased to a marked extent. The people of Cuba are used to Spanish goods put up in Spanish ways, and it will take a long time for them to get used to new preparations. In time lower prices are bound to come and American goods will gradually displace certain importations from Spain, purchased simply because they are Spanish preparations. The official in Washington most directly concerned with the preparation of the Cuban tariff declared to me that there was no thought of exploiting the protection system. The plan was to secure about $15,000,000 in revenue, and to reduce the Spanish rates fully 60 per cent. In actual operation the reduction ranged from 30 to 60 per cent.

One great lesson to be learned from American administration of customs in Cuba is that of integrity in business affairs and the value of honesty in public office. This administration also furnished an object-lesson in the sacredness of public trusts. The Spanish officials simply could not understand why Colonel Bliss kept a force of men on duty until after eight o'clock one night to rectify a discrepancy of six cents. That was some more American foolishness.

Another great lesson—and perhaps the most important—related to the civil service reform side of the American management. It would simply have been impossible to conduct business had the old idea of loot in public place by spoils politicians been put in force in Havana. Doubtless many Cubans, who had their eyes on the Custom-house as a field for loot, as it existed under the Spanish régime, were disappointed at the new state of affairs. It was well for this country that it had this necessary reform in actual existence when it went into what might be called the colonial experiment. Mr. Donaldson pointed out to me that England had to learn the value of such a system after she began her colonial work, and at fearful cost.

When the American military occupation of Cuba ends, probably some attention will be called to the faithful service of civilians during the trials of this reconstruction period. More than one civilian from the States died heroically in the public service in Cuba, Puerto Rico, and the Philippines, as Mr. Donaldson pointed out in a speech at a dinner in Havana, and there was no pension, no salute at the grave ; and for those who continued to face danger there was no advancement in rank and no increased pay from time to time. Truly there was a civilian side to the military occupation of the island of Cuba.

Meanwhile Havana rubbed her eyes and marvelled at the sight of honesty in the Custom-house. That was really the only complaint to be made against the new management and against the hard-worked, patient, straightforward army officer that supervised it.

L

CHAPTER VII

THE condition of the postal system of a country is always an indication of the standing of that country, not only in commerce, but in civilization. The most highly advanced countries have the most complete postal systems. The method of handling the mails might be called the barometer of progress in any country. Up to the time of the American occupation of Cuba there was a very low barometer in this respect, and it told its own story of the meaning of Spanish rule. Like the other branches of government service, the Cuban mail service was honeycombed with corruption. It seemed to retrogade, rather than to advance. American occupation changed all that, and it was done in less than sixty days. Within that time the foundation was laid for a postal system such as never could have been evolved under Spanish rule, and such as might not have been established by the Cubans themselves within perhaps a century. The new system was thoroughly modern, and Cuba will always feel the great benefit of American progress in this most important phase of modern life.

The man who was sent to Cuba to establish this postal system was Estes G. Rathbone, formerly Fourth Assistant Postmaster - General under the administration of Benjamin Harrison. His home is in Hamilton, Ohio, where he has been known as a successful banker and man of affairs. He had served the Federal government repeatedly, having been a special agent of the

MAJOR E. G. RATHBONE,
DIRECTOR OF POSTS

Treasury Department from 1874 to 1882. For two years after that he was the chief of the special examiner's department of the Pension Bureau, having under him a force of five hundred and thirty-one men. In 1889 he became chief of the post-office inspectors, and two years later was made Fourth Assistant Postmaster - General, where he had charge of the appointment of certain post-masters, of the bond and commission division of the department, as well as of the inspectors. He became thoroughly expert in postal matters. In addition to this, he had served his adopted State of Ohio in the State Senate, and consequently was well equipped in matters pertaining to public life.

Mr. Rathbone was in business at home on December 21, 1898, when he was appointed Director of Posts of Cuba. He really became Postmaster-General of Cuba, and he was sent to the island to reorganize and assume control of the postal service. The elements of merit and fitness were exemplified in his appointment. Another evidence of wisdom relating to his appointment was the fact that the officials at Washington gave him unlimited authority, and in no way hampered him with orders or unwise suggestions. He was put in sole control, and was left to work out the problem confronting him in his own way. Night after night he worked, until he was fagged out, and for nearly thirty days he was at his office in the morning so early that it was necessary for him to strike a match to find the key-hole. Even the zealous army officers, with the prospect of promotion, advanced pay, honorable mention, and retirement on a reasonable pension, could not show a greater devotion to duty than this.

Mr. Rathbone took charge of the Cuban postal service at noon on January 1, 1899. He brought with him to Havana only three men—a private secretary and two men as clerks or assistants, who had never been inside a post-office except to get their mail, and who had been designated at Washington to help Mr. Rathbone. How they were appointed Mr. Rathbone did not tell me, nor did he have any fault to find, so far as I could learn, with their efficiency after they had been broken in to their work. He also brought with him a supply of United States stamps, surcharged for the needs of Cuba, and a lot of mail-bags and a few other equipments. Mr. Rathbone's first work was to appoint a temporary postmaster of Havana, whose name was E. R. Juncosa, an old employé in the service there, and then he began to look into the condition of affairs.

Mr. Rathbone found that the Spaniards had simply looted the postal system, as they had practically looted the Custom-house and every other department of government on the island. They did not leave a penny, a stamp, or even any official paper. There were no records of any value that would serve as a guide, or as information to their system of doing business. Up to January 1st the postal and the telegraph system of the island had been under the same management. They were separated at once, and the signal corps of the army, under Colonel Dunwoody, assumed charge of the telegraphs of the island. Mr. Rathbone notified all the postmasters he could reach by telegraph to remain at their posts, and he guaranteed that their salaries would be paid. This was joyful news to them, for they had not received any salary from the Spanish authorities for ten months. Most of them had stuck to their places because they were afraid to leave them, and also in the hope that they would some day get part of their back salaries. Most of them remained in office at Director Rathbone's request.

The next thing that the director did was to place his new stamps on sale in Havana. Then he gave notice that letters and other mail-matter could be sent through the island without postage-stamps for fifteen days, the postage to be collected from the persons to whom the mail-matter was delivered. During those fifteen days the director scattered the new stamps all over the island. There had been an American post-office at Santiago since the surrender, and that simplified the situation in a large city remote from Havana. Messages were sent to the old postmasters, strengthening their resolves to remain in office, and when the fifteen days had expired the island was practically supplied with stamps. It required a tremendous lot of work to bring this about. The same rates of postage as existed before the Spaniards evacuated the island were continued. So far as the people were concerned, the only change was a new kind of stamps.

The old system of routine was kept up; the clerks were retained, and no change in method was made for some time. Director Rathbone had to study out the situation. He found that there had been some mysterious way of doing business in the post-office department. The Spaniards were reluctant to give details. Very few of them probably understood the system in all its details. In Mr. Rathbone's own language, "They were very peculiar, to say the least; they seemed to have a system of covering their tracks behind them."

Under the Spanish system, Mr. Rathbone found that the letter-carriers received their pay by charging from three to five cents, and sometimes more, for every letter

UNITED STATES MAIL-CART

they delivered. It took only a day or two to have that system abolished in Havana, much to the relief of the merchants. The carriers were put on salaries equivalent to that which they were supposed to earn by the assessment method they were permitted to use under the former régime. This plan of collecting from the persons to whom mail-matter was delivered was allowed to remain, for a few weeks, in other places than Havana.

The carriers under the Spanish system not only charged for the delivery of mail-matter, but they rifled letters freely, and made money by stealing stamps from mail-matter and selling them. The letters and other grades of mail-matter would be forwarded without stamps, and the carriers at the other end of the routes would collect not only for delivery, but for the stamps that had been stolen. It was impossible for Mr. Rathbone to learn whether there was any thorough record kept of the collections for unstamped mail-matter. There was simply an unparalleled looseness in the conduct of post-office business, and every man seemed to have license to steal wherever he could. Even newspapers would be stolen from bundles and sold for whatever could be got for them.

Another form of corruption was evident when the salary lists were examined. There was no scale of salaries. In one city a postmaster would receive twice the salary that the postmaster of a larger city received. Salaries seemed to be arranged on the " pull " plan, with the possibilities of division with the appointing power afterward. Places that under the liberal payment of the United States would rate at $1500 a year were worth frequently as much as $3000 a year. There seemed to be no bond for the faithful performance of duty, and favoritism and corruption were evident at every turn.

Director Rathbone gathered all the information he could about every phase of the workings of the department, and finally decided that the former system needed complete eradication. It was useless, in his judgment, to try to make over the system that was then in vogue. He decided that the only thing to do was to set up a new system upon the most approved American methods. He wrote to the department authorities in Washington that such a course was necessary, and it is noteworthy that he did not ask for permission to make a new start. He simply said that he intended to put the new system in operation on February 10th if there was no objection. He wrote on January 24th. As soon as his letter reached Washington, and had been placed before the Postmaster-General, a cable message was sent to him approving his decision, and on the date set Director Rathbone began the Americanizing of the postal affairs of the island.

Ten bureaus were established, and most of them put in operation. They were the bureaus of finance, appointments, postal accounts, transportation, translation, postal money-orders, special agents, registry, disbursements, advisory counsel—all organized with inexperienced men; but in a few days the department was fully one hundred per cent. more efficient than had been the Spanish management of the system. The first definite step in the reconstruction of the postal affairs in the island, on February 10th, was to consolidate the "military postal stations" with the post-offices in the places where the military stations were situated. The military stations had been used solely for the United States troops. Wherever consolidation took place the military postal agent was made postmaster, and the Cuban postmaster was appointed his assistant, if he was willing to accept the place. The object of this move was to man the chief offices on the island with Americans, with the object of the more thoroughly Americanizing the entire system. It was the first important step in that work.

There was a registry system under Spanish rule, but it was hopelessly defective and complicated, and the American system of checks was necessary to secure safety for registered matter. The new system was put in force in the Havana office on February 19th, and arrangements were soon being perfected to extend it rapidly throughout the island. But more important than the registry system was that for money-orders. The Spaniards had had no such system. Some such plan was necessary for the transmission of money in Cuba. There was no thorough banking system in the island, and the use of checks and other forms of paper for the payment of sums due was unknown there. Facilities for the exchange and transmission of money to various parts of the island were practically of the most meagre kind.

The rule in Cuba seemed to have been always to keep your hands on your own money, and so be sure that it was yours. Spanish merchants in Havana were always their own bankers. They kept their money locked up in their safes rather than put it in any depository. When they did lend money, the custom was not to take a

mortgage or some form of collateral, but to buy outright the stock or material upon which they loaned
money, with the written understanding that the man
who borrowed the money could have his property back
upon the payment of a sum of money large enough for
principal and interest combined. It was necessary, therefore, for the development of business, that some sort of
money-order system should be established, and Director Rathbone decided that only the best—the American
system—should be put in operation. On February 17th
he opened the first office in Havana, and made it the exchange office. At the same time another exchange office
was opened in Tampa, Florida, and thus the first step
was taken towards adopting this important system of
exchange of money. It met with instant success. The
people were using it more and more every day, and
within two weeks it could be seen that the system would
become popular. The people of Cuba were distrustful
of banks and of one another, but there seemed to be confidence in the United States, and Director Rathbone
almost immediately had the satisfaction of seeing a
most important part of his work fairly well established
and in good working order, so far as it went. It was his
purpose to extend the system as fast as he could.

In order the more thoroughly to Americanize the
postal system, it was decided to fit up a new post-office
in the city of Havana. The old post-office had been
used for at least one hundred and fifty years. Like all
public buildings in the city, its sanitary condition was
frightful. In Mr. Rathbone's opinion its condition was
the "worst of any building in Havana." That distinc-

CENTRAL PARK AND HOTEL INGLATERRA

tion, however, could be claimed for half a dozen death-
traps and disease-spreaders. The man who would undertake to say which was the worst building, from a sanitary
stand-point, in Havana, when the Americans took control of affairs, would have to be an expert in germ prop-

THE PRESENT POST-OFFICE BUILDING

agation such as the world never saw. His sense of smell,
in a comparative sense, would be ruined in half an
hour.

The old post-office was condemned by the sanitary authorities, and some of the other public buildings were
not, and that would seem to bear out Mr. Rathbone's assertion of foulness approaching distinction for his office.
The Cuartel de la Fuerza, at the foot of O'Reilly Street,
was selected for a new office for local and general purposes in the city, and soon it was being transformed into

an American post-office. It was remodelled and furnished entirely on American lines. The furniture and fittings were strictly American, and all the appliances were such as are used in post-offices in the United States. It was thought that this would be most efficacious in the eradication of nearly everything Spanish in the management of the Havana office and the general post-office system. The new post-office in Havana is down near the water-front, close to the former palace of the captain-general, and not in the centre of the city. It is on the edge of the business part of the city. Sub-stations and stamp agencies were also established in the city, and modern letter-boxes were placed in the other cities and large towns of the island. It seemed as hard to get letters into the cumbersome and ungainly mail-boxes of the Spaniards as it was to get them out, and that involved a bit of skilful manipulation with a tremendous key.

In dealing with the postmasters of the island, Mr. Rathbone found that it was practically impossible to put them under bonds, as is done in the United States, and he adopted the expedient which has been urged for adoption in this country—that of compelling the postmasters to purchase their supplies outright. If a postmaster has to pay for his stamps in advance, it has been argued that he will be all the more careful of them. Compelling the Cuban postmasters to pay for their supplies was something of a hardship, but in some way they managed to raise the money, and after a time the system was in fairly good working order.

Mr. Rathbone made an arrangement with nearly all the railroads to carry the mails free of charge in the second - class cars. On every train one could find the postal agent in these cars. In some of the cars a place had been enclosed in the centre, where the mail agent did his work. In many of the cars, however, he turned over a seat and spread his letters out and sorted them as they came in to him at the stations. It was a crude way of doing business, but the mails were distributed correctly, and it answered the purpose very well. Under the terms or concessions by which the railroads were built, they were compelled to carry the mails free of charge. Two of the railroads in the island were claiming compensation for carrying the mails under the new condition of affairs, but it caused no delay in the mails, and the matter was left for adjudication. In addition to maintaining a railway mail service, there was a steamship service surrounding the island. Director Rathbone looked into the contracts for this work very carefully. When it is known that he saved $102,000 in two of these contracts alone, it is not difficult to imagine where some of the profits of being connected with the mail service were found for some of the higher Spanish officials.

In addition to looking out for the routine of the department work, Mr. Rathbone was planning constantly to improve the service. There was some complaint, as was to be expected, over a lack of prompt delivery of letters here and there. It was impossible to put promptness into the work of clerks who were keyed down to the inevitable mañana of the island. Gradually the American idea of clearing desks and tables was being instilled into the office help all over the island, and day by day the complaints of delayed mails grew less frequent. Mr.

Rathbone had very little to complain of in the way of insubordination. The post-office workers were glad to have employment where they were sure of getting their pay. It was a novelty for them.

Mr. Rathbone found that to put his system in operation he required money from the States, but he said he had not had to call on Washington for much money. He was using the ordinary revenues of the system to support his work. He said that he had had full support from the military authorities, and that his relations with all the generals had been most cordial. There was no tendency, he declared, by the military authorities, or the authorities in the Postal Department in Washington, to dictate to him or to interfere with his work even in a remote degree. He also made the confident prediction that the service would be made self-sustaining, or "practically so," within the first year of its existence. The cheapness of transporting the mails, and the saving he had effected in that respect, together with the practice of economy and ordinary honesty in business matters, he thought, would accomplish wonders in that line.

Even if the department were not self-sustaining, any one could see what a postal system such as that which Mr. Rathbone started would do for the island of Cuba. He declared to me that his one thought and aim, like those of the military authorities, was so to equip the service with which he was connected that when the time should come to turn it over to the Cubans themselves, it would be absolutely modern and in perfect running order. He wanted, he said, to leave the work in such shape that he could be proud of it, and the Cubans would re-

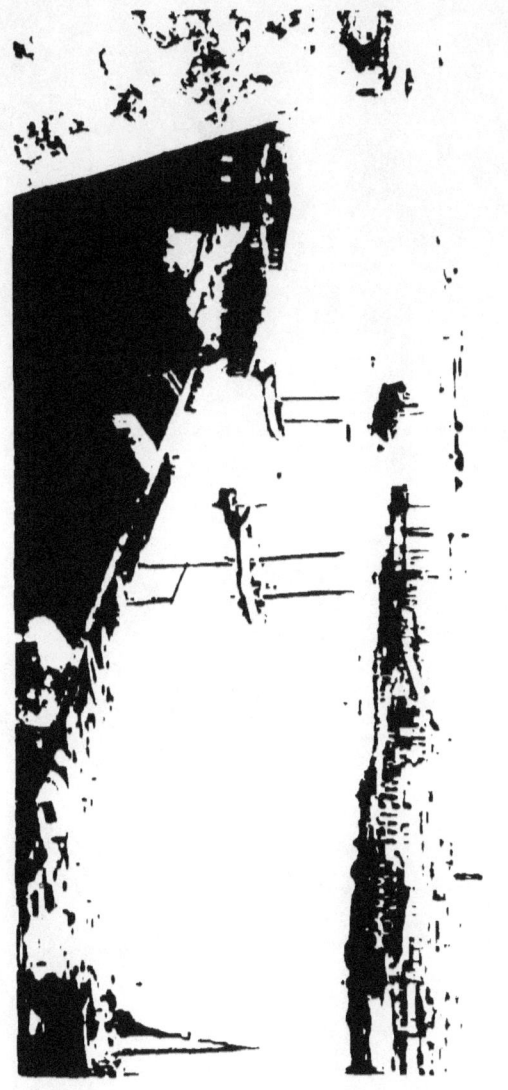

HAVANA HARBOR FROM MORRO CASTLE

joice over American occupation because it had proved a
blessing to them, and because it had brought about re-
forms which they could probably never have brought
about themselves unaided by the wisdom and active co-
operation of American officials.

It was worth while noting that Mr. Rathbone, like the
other American officials in Cuba, was following practical
civil service reform ideas. He was using the help he
found in the offices, and he was discharging no one except for cause, such as inefficiency and dishonesty. At
the time of my visit he owned that he had found it necessary to seclude himself from callers to some extent, in
order to get through with his work. There were quite a
few stranded Americans in the country, and, with the
true idea of the American when he gets out of money or
out of a job, they were turning to the government to get
places. The stranded Americans, none of whom had
experience in postal matters, with possibly one or two
exceptions, were flocking to him to get work. They had
no idea that special training was required in post-office
work, especially in Cuba. They wanted work. He was
an American, and they were Americans, and a good
many of them could not understand why they could not
have jobs right away. They were beginning to exercise
their "pulls" at home, and he was having something of
a task in standing them off. But the great changes which
he brought about in less than two months revealed not
only his success in this respect, but also told their own
story of his efficiency and fidelity.

One thing that Mr. Rathbone said to me ought to be
spread before the people of the United States, and I have

his permission to quote him. He came in contact with the real people of Cuba probably to a greater extent than any of the government officials that the United States sent to the island. He met men of every degree. He had to travel among them, and to seek out their wants in connection with his department. His intercourse was with the masses rather than with former officials or military men. In the language of the politicians of our country, he had to get right down among the plain people, and it is doubtful if any American sent down there had better opportunities to become acquainted with them. This is what he said to me for publication, as coming from him as the result of his experiences, and it is well worth the sober second thought of those who assert that the Cubans are a worthless people, half civilized, and unworthy of all that the United States has undertaken or has had to undertake in their behalf because of the Weyler atrocities and the destruction of the *Maine :*

"The people of the United States have a wrong impression of the Cubans. They are kind, gentle, tractable, and easy to get along with. By kindness you can do anything in the world with them. I have studied them closely, and that is my belief. The Cubans are naturally lethargic. They live in a climate that is enervating. They do not step off quite as quickly as Americans do, and they are inclined to put off until to-morrow everything they can, and are not as prompt as Americans. I think, however, that Cuba has advanced very much in the last fifty days."

CHAPTER VIII

IN the orders assigning General Ludlow to become the military governor of the city of Havana and its suburbs there was a direction that he should cause an investigation to be made as to the income and expenses of the city, and also as to the methods of taxation employed. The object was not only to obtain accurate and necessary information for the proper administration of the affairs of a large city under American military control, but also to correct such evils of grave importance as might be discovered. There was little doubt that such evils did exist.

In accordance with his instructions, General Ludlow issued an order, almost as soon as he reached Havana, establishing what was called a Finance Commission. The order was dated January 14th. A commission of six members was appointed to find out the exact condition of the city treasury—to learn the exact sources of revenue of the city; how this revenue was collected, accounted for, and where it was deposited; to learn the full disposition of the money collected, how it was spent, by whom, and on what authority; to learn particulars of the bonded debt and other obligations of the city, and for what purposes these obligations were incurred ; to learn how advances were secured and loans made, and to secure any other information of importance regarding the city's finances.

The commission was to make an exhaustive and thorough study into matters of the municipal revenue, with the hope of finding better ways of distributing the burden arising from them, and to stop corrupt practices wherever they existed. It was a task involving a vast amount of research, and it needed the supervision and study of clear-headed men. For the chairman of this commission General Ludlow selected Mr. Ernest L. Conant, a New York lawyer, just entering upon middle age, a man whose legal attainments had attracted wide attention in our law-schools. He had been a teacher in the Harvard Law School, and when he left the theoretical for the practical side of the law he did so against the earnest protests of President Eliot and other men, who knew his worth as an instructor and as a deep student. Mr. Conant had been called to Havana when the Evacuation Commission was in session in the fall of 1898. His legal work was of great value to the American commissioners, and when that work was over he remained in the city to look after certain American interests of large importance.

General Ludlow immediately decided to make use of Mr. Conant's ability. Mr. Conant informed him that he represented certain corporate interests in Havana, but General Ludlow said he saw no reason why, as a man of honor, he could not maintain business relations with the administration of the city and look after his private clients as well, inasmuch as his private business had no connection whatever with the matter of city finance and taxation. With the distinct understanding that if at any time questions relating to the interests he represented should become a matter for decision by the administration they should be passed upon strictly on their merits and without regard to Mr. Conant's association with them, he consented to head the commission to study and report upon the city's finances.

Associated with Mr. Conant were Mr. Leopoldo Cancio, Samuel M. Jarvis, Manuel Villanova, I. N. Casanova, and George W. Hyatt, most of whom had long been residents of Havana, were familiar with the business methods of the place, and occupied a recognized place of the highest integrity in the community. The instructions to the commission were to do the work thoroughly, and to report as soon as the work could be accomplished. General Ludlow gave the commission the fullest authority to examine documents and records and to question any one who might have knowledge of the affairs they were investigating. He set aside for them the office-room and workshop of former Captain-General Weyler, and they were instructed to sit as frequently as they could.

The commission soon found that there had not been any statement or report prepared regularly of the exact amount of money collected by the city or of its exact expenses. A budget had been prepared each year, showing estimates of the amount of money required to run the city, but it was never the custom to report how near the expenses, as estimated in the budget, were satisfied

by the actual collections and disbursements. Mr. Conant repeatedly called for a statement as to city expenditures, but the officials said there was none, and that it
could not be compiled. Mr. Conant thought it could
be compiled, and he told the city officials so. They said
it would take an immense amount of research and labor,
and the mañana pretext was called into use for delay.
Mr. Conant expected that and was prepared for it, and
the way he solved the problem was a passing illustration
of what happens when so-called Anglo-Saxon methods
come in conflict with Latin methods in the matter of
government. Mr. Conant had several interviews with
the chief book-keeper of the city.

Mr. Conant has a manner of reserve, but of great force.
He always speaks in a low tone, never gets excited, but
has a persistence that is developed in consecutive and
logical steps, and that refuses to be thwarted by anything
except the impossible. The amount of work involved in
the preparation of statements did not bother Mr. Conant
at all. It was possible to have the work done, and therefore Mr. Conant, in his quiet, determined way, that had a
strength of steel in it, said that it should be done forthwith.

Mr. Conant recalled to the book-keeper that the office
force had had practically nothing to do for several months,
except to report at the office, remain there during so-called
office hours, and then go home. " You have had a good
long rest," he said, "and it is only right that you should
bear a little of the burden and heat of the day. I myself
work from seven o'clock in the morning to midnight frequently. Suppose you have your clerks report at eight

PEOPLE BURNED IN SAN LAZARO STREET

o'clock in the morning, with the understanding that they remain as long as seems necessary." A hint that if the office help could not perform the work that was wanted it would be necessary for the commission to find men who could do it was sufficient to transform the office into a hive of excited activity. Mr. Conant set a time when he wanted the report of expenses for the year that had passed transcribed, visited the office several times during the day, smoothed out the wrinkles here and there, dropped a word or two, which were galvanic in their action upon the officials, and, lo and behold! the impossible, according to the officials, had been accomplished, and according to the time limit set.

It was a commendable piece of work, and Mr. Conant told the officials so, and, to prove his sincerity and his appreciation of it, said that inasmuch as they had prepared a table for one year, he then desired them to go back and prepare one for each of the nine years preceding. That was such a droll American way, the former Spanish officials thought, of doing unheard-of and really unnecessary business; but their shrugs and gestures and dismayed looks availed them nothing, and so the work went on, and promptly too. In this way tables of receipts and expenditures were prepared for ten years back, and the commission had something on which to begin work.

The committee's sessions were consumed with the examination of the figures and the questioning of witnesses. A complete record was kept of the proceedings, for submission to the American authorities and their inspection. The hearings were not public.

Every side of municipal finance was considered. All

the city contracts were examined and passed upon. Grants and concessions, made for whatever reason, were examined, and all their ramifications followed up. Many cases of favoritism were disclosed ; situations where there was opportunity for fraud were laid bare. There was need occasionally for great tact in the investigation ; and Mr. Conant, as chairman of the commission, was daily in consultation with General Ludlow. He was one of the few callers upon General Ludlow who practically had free admission to the general's presence at any time. He became practically the consulting counsel or city attorney of the American administration. It was found that the taxes were collected in several ways. Part of them were collected by the Spanish Bank, under an agreement by which certain loans were made to the city. The chief of these loans was one of $7,000,000 for the building of the excellent water-works system of the city. Other taxes were collected in a more or less loose way by contract and a percentage system. There was great looseness in the disbursements, as was to be expected. All sorts of licenses and imposts were exacted wherever it was possible to place them, and there was evasion and deception in returns. The revenue from water consumption was nearly $300,000 a year, and the tax on meat consumption was said to be as high as $675,000 a year. Certain contracts were found to be not in accordance with good public policy, and it was soon seen that some of them ought to be abrogated for good and sufficient cause. The purpose of the inquiry was not so much to punish as to correct abuses, although if it was found necessary it was decided that there would be no hesitation about punishment. The idea was to reform thoroughly the money administration of the city, and put it on as satisfactory a basis as that of the honest administration of the Custom-house under American military control.

It soon became apparent that there were great frauds in the management and collection of water rents. Gradually they piled up to such an extent that there was need of immediate correction in a wholesale way. It was found that there were thousands of persons getting their water free, through favoritism and corruption. The way this was stopped forms a fine illustration of what American thoroughness coupled with intelligence and tact can do. There are in Havana something like thirty-nine barrios, or wards, each having an alcalde of its own —an official with powers something like a mayor of the district. These alcaldes had control of the collection of water rents. They could give free water to persons for a consideration, and it was believed, with good reason, that they shared their plunder with other persons higher in authority. It was all part of the great stealing game that had been going on in Havana for decades. All public business and a large amount of private business in Cuba were keyed to the idea of plunder. Somebody robbed you, and you robbed somebody else to get even, and so the game went on, until the burden rested finally upon the one least able to bear it—the poor man who toiled for almost nothing, and was a slave to a base commercial system.

Mr. Conant had a long conversation with General Ludlow one day, and a plan was adopted to stop the water frauds in a flash, and to detect those who were committing them. The new police force had been formed, but was not in active service. One day General Menocal, the chief of police, received directions to place his entire force of something like eight hundred men at the disposition of the Finance Commission at a certain hour, without knowing what it was for. That morning Mr.

PERFECTO LACOSTE,
NEW MAYOR OF HAVANA

Conant, with a force of twelve clerks, descended upon the Spanish Bank and began an exhaustive examination of its books. By noon this force had copied the names of seven thousand persons who were using the water of the city without paying for it. These names were classified by districts and streets, and a certain number was apportioned to each policeman. It took an immense amount of work, but it was done thoroughly.

The plan was to send a policeman to each house and catch the person using the city water. It was feared, however, that if the alcaldes should find out what was going on they would send out runners and warn those committing the frauds, and thus the work of catching these persons in the act might be rendered futile to some extent. It was planned at first to arrest every one of the alcaldes, but Mr. Conant and his associates evolved a more clever plan, one that showed great tact.

It was decided to send a carriage with a messenger and a written invitation to each of the alcaldes, summoning them at once to attend a meeting of the Finance Commission to consult about the water - supply of the city, and to suggest to the commission any changes in the business methods that might seem desirable. The alcaldes took the bait. Some of them had never been in the Governor-General's palace, and they thought it a great honor to be invited there specially and to come in style. The carriages and messengers dashed away about one o'clock, and before two o'clock the alcaldes began to arrive. By half-past two o'clock more than thirty had arrived, and had received a warm welcome. As soon as the alcaldes were safely cornered the police were started out in their work, and they caught more than seven thousand persons actually stealing water. Of course it would have been impossible to arrest them all, and so their names were taken, and instructions were given that they must pay henceforth.

Meantime the alcaldes began to get restless. They did

not know exactly why they were summoned, and upon the pretext of waiting for belated arrivals a desirable delay was made before opening the proceedings of the conference. Finally, about three o'clock, Mr. Conant began to speak. He wanted information as to how they had conducted the water business in their respective wards. They were very reluctant to speak at first, but finally some of them admitted that there might be frauds here and there, but each one insisted that the frauds were in some other man's bailiwick. Every man present was sure that his own skirts were clear. Mr. Conant was glad to hear such convincing testimony, of course, but he wanted to know how it was possible to commit any frauds. Gradually they loosened up, and by four o'clock they were quite voluble. For an hour the conversation was animated on all sides. The full history of the water operations was gone into, and the commissioners declared that they were happy to get accurate and full information. Would the alcaldes continue to tell what had been done, and what they thought should be done? By five o'clock the tongues of the voluble alcaldes had become completely unloosed, and the commissioners quit talking. They preserved a grave face, although it was somewhat trying to do so, and the alcaldes ran the meeting. They were intensely excited, and even accusations came thick and fast. Of suggestions there was no limit. By six o'clock it was impossible to stop them, and it would have been hard to predict when the meeting would come to an end naturally. The commissioners were in high fettle, but concealed it most skilfully. Finally word came that the work of the police was done, and, with a gravity

ERNEST LEE CONANT
Chairman Havana Finance Commission

that only a true humorist could appreciate, the alcaldes were dismissed, with the great thanks of the commission for their valuable services, and they went home. They had been under a delightful duress all the afternoon and had not suspected it. They were told that, inasmuch as the conference could not complete its work that day, they might be summoned another day, and they left, pleased at the great consideration that had been shown to them. The Americans were not so bad, after all, and their politeness was especially worthy of all praise. That conference saved the city of Havana not less than $100,-ooo. The full report of the commission's doing disclosed many abuses, and as result there will be a reasonable system of local taxation set in operation, one that will be free from the burden of fraud and robbery, and at the same time that will be adequate to the financial needs of the city.

Although not directly allied to the subject of taxation, the introduction of modern banking methods in Cuba was a subject of great financial importance to the business interests of the island, and it will not be out of place here to refer to it. One of the first acts of the administration, after the American occupation of Cuba had become necessary, was to appoint the North American Trust Company of New York City the fiscal agent of the United States in Cuba. It resulted, first of all, in the establishment of a modern bank in Havana. There were banks in the city, but not such as are known in the United States and European countries generally. Their business was an exchange business chiefly. It had to do largely with the buying and selling of exchange on American and European money centres. There was no deposit system as we know it. The banks would take deposits, but they preferred not to encourage that branch of the business, simply because it was not the general custom. Checks were used against money deposited in a modified way, but it was an unusual method of doing business, and had little vogue in a community used to all kinds of stealing. It was for that reason that the large merchants kept their gold in safes in their business houses. They were fairly sure of having their own money by that means.

This method of retaining direct control of their funds probably explains one remarkable fact. There were no large failures in Havana as the result of the war and its complete prostration of business. The shrewd men of property and large moneyed interests discounted practically the serious state of affairs that they saw was coming, and husbanded their resources in such a way that they escaped a great crash, such as might have been expected from the complete stagnation of commerce, the inability to make collections, or to get good security for loans. It is a great tribute to the business sagacity of the merchants and moneyed men of the city that they were able to weather the storm as they did, and it showed a clever adaptation of means to ends in a community where the money side of exchange of commerce was managed so crudely.

There has been a general impression that there has always been great risk in investments in Cuba. Mr. Alfred H. Swayne, the Assistant General Manager of the North American Trust Company in Cuba, said to me that there was great error in this respect. Investments in Cuba, he said, were safe enough, and had always been safe enough if managed properly. Although there had been for decades a condition of uncertainty as to land titles, and although in many cases it required as much as 20 per cent. of the purchase price to have a

FELIX YZNAGA,
SECRETARY TO THE MUNICIPALITY

transfer of land recorded, there were other ways of securing loans than by giving and receiving mortgages. In the old way, when a man loaned money on any commodity the lender became the actual owner of the property until the money loaned was paid. Of course, in the hands of unscrupulous men, such loans were frequently used in oppression and fraud. Nevertheless, in a well-established form of business a general respect for the methods adopted was absolutely necessary, and the element of fraud in this line was not large. A favorite form of collateral was railroad stock. The railroads in Cuba had no bonds, but the stock was large and well distributed, and it was not difficult to secure it for the purpose of loan-making.

The North American Trust Company established a modern bank of exchange and discount. It also began to receive accounts subject to check. The merchants were slow to adopt such a serious change in their business methods, but not a day passed in the early part of the year when accounts were not opened. There was some difficulty at first in making out deposit slips, because it was necessary to keep two distinct accounts for every man. One was an account in Spanish gold, to which all Cuban money deposited was reduced, and another was in American currency. What is known as the Spanish five-dollar gold piece, the centen, had a value of $4 89 in American money at the time of my visit. The value of exchange was fixed by brokers who were accustomed to seek business in that form of buying and selling.

Another improvement in banking methods, early established by the trust company, was to open safe-deposit vaults—something that hitherto had been unknown in Cuba. There was under contemplation, at the time of my visit, the establishment of a savings-bank department. One wonders how the island ever got along under the old régime. It did retard business life, and in certain lines crippled it, but the merchants got on somehow, at the expense of that confidence and satisfactory means of exchange of commodities so necessary to the existence of modern business life.

With reduced rates of transportation on railroads already in sight—because Spanish robbery and taxation equal almost to reprisal have been removed—and with modern facilities of exchange already established in the island, it would seem that the business outlook for Cuba must brighten at once, even while the people are waiting to know what kind of a permanent government is to be established. If it shall really be a stable government, vouched for by the American people as represented by the national administration, capital is bound to go to Cuba with a rush, and the laborers to put that capital into full play will follow, and the result must be, it would seem, according to ordinary reasoning, that the island in good time will become, what many of the Cubans are fond of calling it, "a cup of gold."

Gold is a talismanic word in Cuba. With all its troubles Cuba never wavered in its devotion to the gold standard. An artificial premium was put upon gold to keep it from going to Spain. A great transformation in its money system early in the year was coming over the island. The American invasion of peace had practically established a new standard, the American gold standard—not the artificial and slightly varying Spanish gold standard. Our money was in free circulation all over the island in February last. Merchants, ticket-sellers on the railroads, and cashiers in other places knew just what to do when American money was given to them in payment for value received. There would be invariably a lot of figuring on a pad—figuring that I could never pretend to comprehend—but one always received his change accurately in Spanish or American money, as the case might be. The people preferred American money, not so much because it was gold-standard money as because it had an absolutely fixed value. It became the standard, and Spanish gold was adjusted to it day by day. It was driving Spanish money out of general use rapidly.

With honest taxation and the honest collection of taxes, with a modern and firm banking method upon the basis of the American gold standard, with the introduction of honesty in official methods, with the purification of the cities, with the consequent investment of large capital, it seems entirely reasonable to say that the recovery of Cuba from the disaster of war must be certain, and even more fruitful than is customary when the ways of peace have superseded those of the sword and the torch.

CHAPTER IX

THE peace protocol between the United States and
Spain had been signed only a few days when the
American descent upon Cuba began.   To use a
military figure, the first of the Americans who hastened
to the island were the scouts, or skirmishers, of a new
force or army — that of commercial occupation.   The
main body of this force did not arrive in Havana until
after the Spanish army had gone home.   It was a motley mass.   There was no coherency or order about this
new army.   It was a case of every man for himself and
the devil take the hindmost.   Without being too literal
in the application, it may be said that the devil not only
took the hindmost, but a good many of the foremost of
the arrivals.   By the 1st of February Havana was filled
with Americans, and there were a good many who wished
they had not come.

It was interesting to study this secondary American
army.   Its members seemed to outnumber the real
American army of occupation — the military.   There
were thousands of men who really had legitimate business on the island; there were hundreds who were mere

adventurers in business, syndicate-chasers, franchise-grabbers, political contractors, and the like. Among the first arrivals after the activities of war had ceased were the newspaper correspondents. Their errand was of the highest rank. Next to them in importance were the

HAVANA'S STEAM-DUMMY STREET-CAR LINE

men who had business interests in the island, vested rights, and other property of various kinds — men who took the first opportunity of reaching the place where their money was at stake. Some of them had been fugitives from the island, and some were Americans who had

investments to be safeguarded. Then came the representatives of business houses whose trade with the island
had been interrupted by the war, and who desired to re-
establish business connections. Then came emissaries
from business men who had never had any dealings in
Cuba, but who thought that the new conditions presented a legitimate opportunity for the extension of trade.

Soon there arrived the franchise-seekers, the contractors, the adventurers in business, willing to take hold of
"any old thing" for the sake of selling out again ; a few
gamblers and crooks ; men of limited means, hoping to
get profitable jobs in the work of regenerating the place
on American ideas ; some office-seekers with more or
less hazy "pulls" in Washington and elsewhere ; tourists
of all sorts ; merchants of small capital intending to
open retail shops ; and, by no means least of all, the
agents of American breweries, who plastered Havana
from one end to the other with lithographed advertise-
ments of American beer, giving the Cubans warped and
exaggerated ideas of Americans as a nation of hard
drinkers.

This second army of American occupation was always
seen to the best advantage at night, in and around Central Park in Havana. Its members filled the cafés,
crowded the sidewalks, patronized the cabs extensively,
filled the theatres that were running, and caused a babel
of voices in the centre of town, in which more English
words than Spanish could be heard as one passed along.
Most of these Americans had serious faces. Their money
was being used up every day, and there was little certainty that any adequate return would result from their

work. They saluted one another at night, and asked how they were getting on, and the commonest expression to be heard was:

"I think I'll go home next week."

A great many did go home after a few days' visit, but there were some who could not, as the Collector of Customs, Colonel Tasker H. Bliss, and the Director of Posts, Mr. E. G. Rathbone, could testify, for men descended upon them in swarms with applications for jobs ; and the lot of the applicants was like unto that of the office-seeker who goes to Washington when an administration changes, and who finally jumps a board bill, or else takes to sweeping out some place for a livelihood.

The real men of power in this army, however, were seldom seen. They had little time for drinking in public places. They were fighting for position in the future, and they played a great game. This competition became so fierce over one business enterprise that there were resultant hints and finally open charges of corruption and bribery.

One of the storm centres of American commercial occupation of Cuba was to be found in the effort to secure control of the street-railway system of Havana. The struggle began long before the Spanish army left town, and it was characterized by excitement. A combination of an American and a European syndicate apparently was successful in defeating half a dozen other syndicates in getting hold of this property and its supposed valuable opportunities, but the struggle was transferred to the courts, where the agents of the deal were indicted for bribery.

There were many reasons why the street-car system of Havana seemed to be an excellent field for investment. In the first place, the climate of the place is such that one can rarely walk more than a few blocks in comfort. In the second place, the trolley improvements in recent years have made street-car enterprises most profitable in any city of good size. The street-car system of Havana was antiquated, badly conducted, and yet it is said to have paid excellent dividends upon an investment capitalized at $1,500,000. Although there were said to be 6000 cabs in the city, which gave expeditious service at very reasonable rates, it was seen that a modern trolley system running to the four leading suburbs of the town, and to the ferry to another suburb, would probably not only secure that increase in business which usually follows improvements in street-car service, but would lessen the number of cabs along the lines of the road in the city. This matter of control of the street-car lines of Havana, therefore, came to be regarded as probably the best business opportunity for American capitalists on the island of Cuba. There are four of these railroads in the city. They run to the suburbs known as Vedado, Principe, Cerro, and Jesus del Monte. They were all controlled by one company, known as the Urbano Company, and the entire length of all the systems is about twenty-five miles. The cars of the company were dirty and old. Each car was drawn at a snail's pace by three mules, except on the line to Vedado, where steam-dummies were the propelling power. There had always been stealing on the line by employés, and the usual corruption attendant upon the management of any enterprise, public or semi-public, by

Spanish interests. The Spanish soldiers never pretended to pay fare on any of the lines, and on some of them it was the custom not to charge fare for persons who rode on the platform. The entire system was run down, with miserable rolling-stock and road-bed; and yet, with all these disadvantages, and with the corruption that found a lodging-place there, it managed to pay such dividends that the stock was quoted at par.

There were seven syndicates after the system. One was known popularly as the Harvey syndicate of New York, and that is the one which secured possession. Percival Farquhar, of New York, was the attorney who looked after the legal transfer of the property. There was an English syndicate, represented by McLean and Dickinson, one of whom was superintendent and general manager of the small railroad running from Havana to Marianao. Another syndicate was English and French in origin, and was known as the Ruffel and Todd syndicate, representing foreign banking interests. Still another syndicate was backed by the International Bank of Paris, whose interests were finally pooled with those of the Harvey syndicate, and which was represented in Havana by a lawyer named Castaneda, well known in Madrid and Cuba. Another was the Toronto syndicate, backed by Mr. McKenzie and the Bank of Toronto. Another was the Tom Johnson syndicate of New York and Ohio, represented by a man named R. Guzman; and still another was the American-Indes company, commonly known as the Widener-Elkins syndicate.

The stock of the company was held in such small lots

PICTURESQUE SIDE OF THE CAMP OF THE TENTH REGULARS ON THE PRADO, HAVANA

that it was seen that it would be impossible for any one syndicate to get control by dealing directly with the stockholders. Operations had to be conducted with the board of directors and the officials as the point of attack. One of the syndicates obtained a minor concession, and began constructing branch lines in the hope of getting a foothold in the company's affairs. First one of the combinations and then another seemed to have the advantage in the fierce rivalry. The company that built the branch lines operated under what was known as the Plá concession. It was a legitimate enterprise, but under its franchise the existing company had the right to buy at cost figures any branch lines built under the concession, and so this flanking operation came to naught by the discovery of a clause in the charter which had been overlooked by many who had interests at stake. The rivalry reached such a stage finally that it seemed desirable for combinations among the competitors, and the syndicates represented by Mr. Farquhar and by Mr. Castaneda pooled their interests. Mr. Castaneda had succeeded in having a meeting of the stockholders called at which only one proposition could be considered. That was an authorization for the trustees to sell the railroad system to the interests he represented. The meeting was held on December 14, 1898, and lasted all the afternoon. It was an exciting time. Speeches of such intensity as only Cubans and Spaniards can deliver were made, and the tide surged back and forth. Finally the Castaneda side won, and the sale was authorized. The meeting, under some technical ruling, could not consider any other offer. It might reject the Castaneda proposition, but it could adopt no other. It showed the clever skirmishing that abounded in the fight.

Before the papers could be signed a serious complication arose. Mr. Castaneda was arrested one night— through the influence of rival syndicates, it is charged —and thrown in prison. The Spanish still occupied the main part of the city, and an order is said to have been secured to transport Mr. Castaneda to Spain on a steamer the next morning as a person whose presence was not conducive to the public welfare. Mr. Castaneda was placed incommunicado. He was missed, and an effort was made to get him out of jail, where he had been committed by the civil governor of Havana province. Señor Montoro, Minister of Finance, was aroused, and through his intercession the syndicate lawyer was released. He went straight to the American lines in the suburbs, and also gave a power of attorney in case of any similar trouble.

The control of the system thus passed into the hands of the combined syndicates ; but it was charged that the directors were bribed to sell out at ninety-two cents on the dollar, when another company was willing to pay a premium of eight per cent. on the dollar for the same stock. Some stockholders got together and began operations to have the sale of the road set aside, and to prosecute the directors and agents criminally for bribery. It had the effect of tying up further operations. The men who were behind the prosecution in the courts declared that they had indisputable proof of bribery in the shape of documentary evidence. The managers of the Harvey syndicate declared as positively that there was no truth in the assertion, and said it was an attempt at blackmail by certain stockholders who thought they could make a few thousand dollars in that way. The difference between the price paid for the property and the price said to have been offered was $240,000.

The criminal charges came up before the Judge of the Cathedral, Mr. Ayllon, Marquis of Villalba, of whom *La Lucha*, the leading newspaper of Havana, spoke as enjoying "in this community the reputation of being one of the few judges whose honesty and energy have never been doubted." He, in his capacity as a grand jury, found an indictment against the officials. The case was taken before another judge for review, and the men behind the prosecution said they had good reason to fear that they would lose the case. In some way it was transferred to still another judge, and he decided that the indictment must stand and the case proceed.

It was the intention of the Harvey syndicate to put the system in the best possible condition. About sixty cars were in use under the old régime, and it was intended to increase the number to one hundred at first, and to two hundred ultimately. The double overhead trolley system was decided upon for installation, inasmuch as the heavy rains in the summer made the underground trolley impracticable. It was planned to bring down Italian laborers from the United States, largely because there were no available manual laborers to be had in Cuba, and because Italian labor could be secured which would be familiar with that kind of work.

Among the other syndicates that were planning to, operate in Havana was one seeking to control the gas supply. It was said that the works were bonded to the extent of several times the price that the syndicate wished to pay, and at the time of my visit nothing had been done of a definite nature about the matter. There were other syndicates desiring to erect warehouses and piers, but the outlook was not favorable for the investment of large sums in such enterprises.

In Cienfuegos I ran across the agents of an American enterprise that planned to make money out of investments in Cuba, Puerto Rico, and the Philippines. The prospectus was flowery, and the agents were energetic. They told me that they had secured control of the telephone system in Cienfuegos, and that they hoped to get hold of some valuable concessions. The city was sorely in need of a modern water system, and the contract of installing and operating one was another of the enterprises they hoped to secure. They had also taken steps to install a water plant in Santa Clara, but the amendment to the Army bill, passed just before Congress adjourned, forbidding the United States authorities to grant concessions of this nature, probably put a stop to the prosecution of these enterprises. I remember that in Santa Clara I met an American who was in consultation with a resident of that city. The Cuban held in his hand what appeared to be a piece of coal. He lighted a match and applied the flame to the black substance, and it gave out a series of sparks. I asked what it was, and was told that it was asphalt, and that the American had arrived there to secure an option on the deposit.

The clause in the Army bill to which I have referred reads :

TENTH REGULARS UNLOADING WOOD FOR THE CAMP ON THE PRADO, HAVANA.

And provided further, That no business franchises or concessions of any kind whatever shall be granted by the United States,
or by any military or other authority whatever, in the island of
Cuba during the occupation thereof by the United States.

It is a constitutional question whether Congress has
the right to hamper the executive power in its military
operations in a foreign land by such a clause, but there
can be no doubt that such a provision in the law in no
way interfered with the right of purchase by Americans
of property rights from owners. Even if the prohibi-
tion as to franchises and concessions were to be con-
strued literally, it probably could not be made to apply
to the furthering of plans to improve the health conditions of the cities. There was no doubt that the
clause in the Army bill gave a chill to many of the
Americans who were as busy as bees trying to secure
options of various kinds for future sale. Some of these
options were described to me as "options on air," but
there was no doubt that a lot of men were running
around after them. Street-paving contractors were
thick. "There's going to be a lot of that kind of work,"
one of them told me, "and I guess we can get the contracts in such a tangle that we shall all get a bite of the
cherry."

Many men in Havana looking for business openings
seemed to be inspired by over-zealousness. I remember
one man who was always on the jump, and who was
continually working over a lot of figures whenever he
sat down. I was told that he was from Michigan, and
that he wanted to introduce Grand Rapids furniture in
the island. Any one who studied the ways of the

Cuban people, and observed how devoted they are to the four rocking-chairs that face four other rocking-chairs across a rug in the parlor of every home, could see what a difficult task that American agent had. The Cubans get mahogany for their furniture, and the pieces are of a most solid and substantial nature. There is no such thing as plush or velvet in common use on furniture, and the American agent was somewhat discouraged towards the end of his stay. There were climatic influences of a forbidding nature against the introduction of ordinary American furniture.

I remember meeting two men in Pinar del Rio who were looking for good grazing land, so as to go into the cattle business. They took mules and went over the mountain range to the north. A few days later I ran across one of them in Matanzas province. The Pinar del Rio hunt had been without profit, but, to his amazement, he found beautiful grass much closer to Havana, and in such quantities that hundreds of thousands of cattle could be fed there. Then there were the men looking for chances to grow fruits ; the men who had agricultural machinery to sell; the men who had come from Louisiana to restore the sugar-mills that had been destroyed in the war ; the men who wanted to buy or to sell lumber, as the case might be ; and lots of other men on practical or impracticable errands.

There were two discouraging features, however, for most of those who were in earnest in seeking investments. The Cubans were holding property and other purchasable things at rates that were too high, and the unsettled conditions as to the future government of the island made investors wary. For these reasons I could not learn that there were many new enterprises which the Americans had taken hold of, and it was altogether likely that what new business they had engaged in was simply the buying and selling that grew from the ordinary law of supply and demand in commerce. The Cubans are extremely keen and clever bargainers. They expected a horde of American capitalists as soon as the war was over, and they were prepared for them. Real estate, especially tobacco - producing tracts, went up to double the prices that were quoted before the war ; and so, with the clause in the Army bill, the high prices for everything of real value, and the unsettled problem of the future of the country, hundreds and probably thousands of Americans who went to the island in the hope of securing such riches as generally come with the upbuilding of a country made desolate by war, went home disappointed and discouraged.

There was one kind of American visitor to the island, however, concerning the beneficial effects of whose mission there could be no doubt. He was the practical missionary, who not only held religious exercises, but established schools. I met one of these men in Santa Clara. He was a Rev. Dr. Powell, secretary of a college in Tennessee, and he had been sent to Cuba on what might be called a scouting trip for the Southern Baptist Missionary Society. He had formerly been a missionary in Mexico, and he spoke Spanish fluently. Before the Spanish forces evacuated Santa Clara there were twenty-two priests in the city. After they had gone only two priests remained. The people were practically without religious instruction, and the children were clamoring for schools and school-books. In three days Dr. Powell had congregations of from six hundred to eight hundred at his preaching services. The people were actually turned away. But what impressed me more was to see the children flocking to his hotel to be enrolled in the school he arranged to open. They came singly and in twos and threes, and frequently the mothers came along, and, with tears in their eyes, thanked the missionary for opening a school. Dr. Powell was not the only man in Cuba on such a mission, and it is pleasant to record that invariably their efforts to establish schools were meeting with success.

CHAPTER X

CONDITIONS IN PINAR DEL RIO

WHEN one wishes to leave Havana by rail to see something of the real Cuba—say, to take a trip to Pinar del Rio or to Cienfuegos—he must get up very early. The through trains leave at six o'clock in the morning. I asked a high official of the railroad to Pinar del Rio why so early a start was made for a town only 109 miles away, and he said it was so as to get back the same day. That sounds ludicrous, but when one went over the road and learned something of the hardships involved to keep the road in running order in the last four years—a struggle against men with torches, who burned down stations; against men with crowbars, who tore up mile after mile of rails and twisted them out of shape or hid them; against armed bands of revolutionists, and on more than one occasion with Maceo's army of several thousand men, the railroad officials shooting from armored cars; against dynamite explosions, and the practical loss of all revenue, with continued confiscations and taxation and reprisals by the Spanish authorities—one wondered how the trains, only a few weeks after the war closed, managed to start out at all, to say nothing of coming back.

The American traveller is not only likely to grumble when he is compelled to hurry to the station in the thick gloom of the early morning, but when he reaches the station and finds that he must pay about five cents a mile in gold, and from seven to eight cents a mile in Spanish silver, to ride in the back-breaking cars known as first-class carriages, and that for an ordinary trunk he must pay about half fare, he is inclined to scoff at the primitive mode of travel, and to long for the luxury of even stage-coach journeying on a Western mountain-road. The amazing amount of computation by the ticket-agent before he sells a ticket, the smoky lamps, the three preliminary tootings by the engine before the train starts, the final ringing of a bell by the baggage-master as a signal that the train really is going, the crowded condition of the aisles, choked with luggage for which the passengers do not care to pay toll, and every man in the train, from the conductor down to the bare-footed brakemen, smoking tobacco of varying degrees of excellence — all this is likely to weary the American traveller used to the luxury of Pullman-cars. One was inclined at the very outset to rail at the crudities of travel by cars in the island of Cuba.

And yet such travel was not really disagreeable. I have ridden on worse road-beds and in cars almost as uncomfortable within 150 miles of New York City, and it may be said with truth that the road-beds of the Cuban railroads only a short time after a devastating war, in which they were continual sufferers, were in much better condition than the average Southern railroad was in our own country ten years ago. I had the

MULE TRAIN COMING INTO PINAR DEL RIO FROM THE MOUNTAINS

pleasure of travelling several hundred miles in Cuba with Mr. W. F. Allen, the editor of the *Travellers' Official Railroad Guide*, an authority in the matter, and here is what he wrote on the subject of Cuban railroads after his return :

The railways are not far behind the times, when the conditions by which they have been surrounded and the traffic they have to provide for are carefully considered. The right of way is fenced—if that is the proper term to use for cactus hedges or stone walls. The cactus hedge is admirable for the purpose, being almost impenetrable, and unpleasant to surmount. The roads are laid with steel rails, from fifty to sixty-two pounds to the yard, joined with fish-plates, with rock ballast, and generally well tied and surfaced. Some of the switches are of the stub variety, but split switches are also in use. The couplings are of the old-fashioned link and pin style, but automatic couplers are being introduced. The passenger-trains are equipped with air-brakes. Freight-cars are of smaller dimensions than cars recently built in the United States, and more like those of thirty years ago. Permanent tops are used, not the tarpaulin covers employed on English goods-wagons.

The ticket-agent does not have an enviable time in making change. He now has three currencies to deal with—viz., American money, Spanish gold, and Spanish silver. The Spanish peso, or dollar, is nominally the same as our dollar, but actually is quite different. An American dollar is worth about $1 07 in Spanish gold and about $1 66 in Spanish silver at the published rates. These rates are regulated in part by the government terms of exchange at the Post-office and Custom-house. The actual weight of the gold and the current value of silver, which varies from day to day, affects the rate of exchange, which is announced in the daily papers.

I have rarely had a more enjoyable railroad trip than

the one I took one morning in February to Pinar del
Rio. The cactus hedges; the absence of dust; the first
glimpses of a rolling landscape with the splendid royal
palms, now marking a watercourse or road • and now
grouped ·by the hundreds in some old grove; the red,
black, and gray soils; the return of the people to agricultural pursuits near the towns; the waste places overgrown with weeds; the cattle roaming about, at last in
peace; the crude viaducts bringing water to tobacco
tracts; the enlarged graveyards; the ruins of stations;
the block-houses at almost every mile of the journey;
the ragged and half-starved people; the beggars at
every stopping-place; the Cuban soldiers doing police
duty at all stations; the passengers, from the German
planter, lugging out great bags of silver to pay his
plantation hands, and the officers of the American army
going out to new duties, to the pinched-faced widows
going back to what was once home; the thatch-roofed
villages, where thousands of reconcentrados starved; a
beautiful range of mountains running along the coast
from east to west, protecting the famous Vuelta Abajo
tobacco district from harsh winds, and resembling in
their contours the Catskills, but only about one-half as
high—all these made every rod of the journey interesting and picturesque. The first-class car on the train
had seats with cane bottoms and backs—necessary because of climatic conditions—and one soon forgot to
look at the sickening greenish-yellow decorations of the
car and to notice the small windows with sliding blinds
to keep out the glare of the sun and the heat. When
one had a guide to point out places of interest along the

route, the irregularities of the road-bed and the half-cleaned condition of the cars were forgotten entirely.

On the train that morning I had the good fortune to meet Mr. Alfred P. Livesey, the resident engineer of this railroad, which is known officially as the Western Railway of Habana (limited), and during the war its real superintendent. He is a young Englishman. The road is owned by English capitalists, but, with a protracted strike and the war with which to contend on the one hand and Spanish extortion on the other, it is not surprising that no dividends have been paid for seven years. The story that Mr. Livesey told of the tribulations of the road is practically a duplicate of the experiences on other railroads in Cuba before and during the war, and explains why excessive rates for freight and transportation are charged, and why the systems are in a crude condition. Mr. Livesey said that the import duties on a locomotive during Spanish rule were almost $5000, and that coal cost nearly $6 a ton ; taxation rates were enormous, and Spanish extortion was such that it was almost a wonder that a railroad could do any business at all.

In the western part of the island during the war Antonio Maceo and his men operated. They burned towns and destroyed plantations and roamed apparently at will even to within a few miles of Havana. Their stronghold in the mountains was never attacked. They tore up the tracks of the railroad week after week ; and yet the company, under the constant supervision of Mr. Livesey, managed to operate about sixty miles of the road all the time, in a hit-or-miss fashion. Three locomotives and sixty cars of the small equipment necessary to such a short line were destroyed, nine out of fewer than thirty stations were burned, mile after mile of rails was carried off, and yet the road would not give up. No thorough track-work could be done, and all paying traffic ceased.

CIVIL PRISONERS MADE TO WORK ON THE STREETS OF PINAR DEL RIO

Mr. Livesey built what he called "armored wagons," thirteen of them, at a cost in placing the crude iron plates and strips about them of about $500 each. The iron protection, consisting of any kind of scraps, weighed about 3000 pounds to the car. In all, 180 armed men were employed on these trains, and usually there were forty men to a train. They were sent out daily to repair bridges and culverts, to find stolen rails and replace them.

On one occasion one of these trains was out two weeks. The rails had been taken up behind it, and the crew nearly starved. Day and night the men shot at revolutionists from their cars. One day, just beyond the town of Artemesia, forty-four miles from Havana, they met Maceo and 5000 men. The advance-guard of the insurgents attacked the train. No one was killed on the train, but the railroad men killed eight of the insurgents and captured nine of their horses. On another occasion a train trying to get back to Havana found a gap of 200 feet in the road-bed without rails. All the rails from the sidings and from branch roads running to sugar-plantations had been taken up and used in the effort to get home, and no more could be found. It became necessary to take up the rails from behind the train to piece out the gap.

Mr. Livesey told me that on his various trips he had seen the bodies of fully one hundred men "hanged like dogs on little shrubs" in the cruel warfare practised in that region. These fatalities represented raids at night on plantations or into small villages. The stories he told of the people starving in the larger towns were too horrible for comfortable reading. He said to me that in the town of San Cristóbal, one of the largest on the way to Pinar del Rio, a little over sixty miles from Havana, more than 6000 persons had died during the war. The normal population of the place is about 5000. It was at Candelaria, one station before San Cristóbal is reached, that General Weyler went out to find Maceo and to capture and destroy him. This, in popular language, was one of the few military grand-stand plays that Weyler made. He was to come back to Havana a conquering hero; and Antonio Maceo, dead or alive, was to come back with him. He came back, but Maceo remained in the mountains. The Spanish troops experienced a frightful mortality, and one day Mr. Livesey superintended the removal of 2500 sick soldiers to Havana. It required six special trains. Near by, and almost visible from the railroad station, was the mountain stronghold of Maceo, Cacarajicara, that was never taken by the Spaniards, and the Cuban general almost enjoyed seeing with his own eyes the flight of Weyler back to his guarded palace in the Cuban metropolis.

This was a novel kind of railroading for a mild-mannered gentleman who had been sent from England to help make a railroad pay; and at the time of my visit he said he had not yet got over the surprise of receiving letters occasionally from planters saying some of the rails of the Western Railroad were down their wells, and asking him to please send a force to pull them out, for the sake of improving the water, if for nothing else. Labor was scarce in the island at that time, and although repairs were being made to the road-bed and to trestles and bridges, and although new stations were being erected in the places of those that were burned, it was slow work putting the line in good order. No one rejoiced more than the railroad men at the termination of the war. The excessive Spanish duties on rolling-stock and on rails, and the killing taxes imposed by the Spanish, were at an end. Mr. Livesey said his road would practically have to be rebuilt. He contemplated building modern cars in Havana. New rails, he said, would be laid, and, under the peace that American occupation had brought, he hoped soon to see the day when the railroad would not only be in first-class condition with a modern plant, but when a dividend would be earned and freight and passenger rates reduced to a reasonable figure. Reduced freight rates will mean much to the enormous tobacco business carried on in the western end of the island.

For a little distance after leaving Havana on this railroad one catches glimpses of the one good road in the island—a yellow thread that winds about in the rough green carpet covering the flat country. There are knolls here and there, and, except for the palms and strange people and houses, one might fancy himself in central Ohio, so far as the country is concerned. Track laborers could be seen occasionally, and when one of the passengers saw a solitary ploughman out in the deserted country there was a crowding to windows to catch a look at such a curiosity. The first block-house along the road attracted general attention, and there was a sense of satisfaction in seeing that it was being dismantled. Altogether there were no less than seventy-five of these block-houses along the road to protect its bridges and trestles and rails, but Mr. Livesey told me that they were "utterly useless." The region a few miles out of Havana was so deserted that when a buzzard began a race with the train there was a general exclamation of pleasure that there was at least something alive in the region. We passed over several substantial bridges and culverts, and the eye roamed across the country in vain to find the people at work, in as fertile a region as probably can be found any-where, but there were only shrubs and weeds and grass to be seen. Morning-glories along the track seemed curi-ous in a region that had been devastated.

When the first village was reached, one saw that truly Havana and the other large cities of the island were not representative dwelling-places of the Cubans. In a vil-lage of perhaps one thousand inhabitants probably not more than half a dozen buildings would be of stone. The rest were mere huts of palm leaves or boards with thatched roofs, and all arranged in rows for streets. Naked children swarmed out of the huts, and women in black came to the openings called doors, and they gave the Cuban salute which corresponds to our waving of the hand. They raised a hand with the palm towards the train, and opened and shut their fingers in a rapid move-ment. The red tiles on some of the huts in place of the thatched roofs added picturesqueness to the village. We stopped long enough to be overwhelmed by begging chil-dren, and then the ting-a-ling of the baggage-master's bell was heard, and off we went, to a general salute from the town.

A dozen miles out of Havana one may see, off towards the north, the curious geological formation of the only hill or mountain thereabouts. It is the Hill of the Jesuits, on which the famous Catalan Club was situated. It looks to the traveller like Snake Hill, on the New Jersey mead-ows back of Hoboken, only it seems three times as long and half again as high. It is a beautiful place, and a landmark for a score of miles around. It was near this hill that Antonio Maceo lost his life. Not until one reaches Candelaria, fifty-seven miles from Havana, does he see the chief topographical glory of the province of Pinar del Rio. It is the beautiful mountain range that runs parallel with the northern coast to the western end of the island. The rugged slopes and thick growth of timber on the peaks, with here and there a cliff hundreds of feet high, and almost no broad passes, make the range almost impregnable. It seems as if a hundred thousand men might hide in its recesses with comfort and safety.

TOWN MILKMAN IN PINAR DEL RIO

Deer are said to be plenty there, and so long as Maceo remained in these mountains he was in no more danger from roving Spaniards than he was from the shadows that chased up and down the beautiful flanks of the range.

At every station there was something novel to be seen. At San Cristóbal we saw where the water-works of the town had been blown to pieces by a dynamite bomb placed in the roof. Some of the machinery had been forced four feet into the ground by the explosion. As we left the station we ran by the small-pox hospital of the place. It was close to the town and very dirty. A man stood in the doorway, and it was to be presumed that he was immune to the germs that must have been thick about the place. At Palacios, eighty miles from Havana, we found the railroad company putting in a fine new trestle about three hundred feet long, to take the place of one not destroyed, as we thought at first, by the insurgents, but by a disastrous flood in 1896. There had been no opportunity up to this time to make the repairs. After we left Palacios we found the country open and flat, with the frowning mountain range running parallel to our course, but from five to ten miles away. The smoke of the charcoal-burners arose in black shafts, and made one think of the burnings of towns and villages in the war-time. Palacios itself was burned twice during the war, and there was scarcely a roof left in the place. The town was new so far as the buildings were concerned, and doubtless this fact added to its healthfulness. Little patches of tobacco under cultivation were now numerous, and the palms took on a new shape. They were of the kind known popularly as "belly-palms." Half or two-thirds up the slender trunk they swelled out and resembled the condition of the bodies of the starving children during the reconcentrado period. Many of them had been felled, and as they lay they looked like the swollen bodies of some animal partly hidden in the weeds.

Twenty miles from Pinar del Rio we emerged into a beautiful open country — the best part of the Vuelta Abajo district. Tobacco-plantations under a high state of cultivation came into view. The leaves of the plants

BRIGADIER-GENERAL GEORGE W. DAVIS, U. S. V., AND MEMBERS OF HIS STAFF IN FRONT OF HIS HEADQUARTERS

were so strong and large and so rich in the beautiful deep green color that one felt that Cuba was becoming itself again. Here was the beginning of the return of prosperity, and the land was smiling. Finally, through a landscape dotted with palms irregularly and huts scattered about promiscuously, as if on some Western prairie beginning to fill up rapidly, we saw the outskirts of Pinar del Rio, and then its cathedral and its fine military hospital standing out above the other buildings conspicuously. We stopped at a comfortable and large railroad station, and soon were whirling through the rough streets and up a hill, past substantial buildings, to the centre of the town.

Here we were at last in real Cuban life, far from Havana and the coast. The buildings were one - storied affairs with barred windows. The atmosphere of the place was one of indolence, and the nervous activity of Havana was absent. Block-houses encircled the town of perhaps seven thousand inhabitants, but they were occupied by families of reconcentrados. Sentinels of the American regular army marched up and down the streets, doing police duty in the absence of any regular police force of the town. The shops were empty, and tracts of tobacco were seen almost in the centre of the town. The place had a rural aspect, and the acres upon acres of tobacco showed that in a few weeks at least prosperity of a limited kind was to return to the place. It did one's eyes good to see the city, probably the only place in Cuba at that time where there was evidence of a swift and sure return to the conditions that were almost normal.

There are few cities in Cuba more beautifully situated than Pinar del Rio. It is on the side of a gently sloping hill, with a range of mountains three miles away that give a rugged and picturesque background to it. The scenes in the town were distinctively Cuban. Men were busy playing the gambling game of the island—dominos—in the cafés. At night there was an open-air bowling game going on in a space near the post-office; long trains of mules, tied nose to tail, brought in bananas and wood and vegetables from almost inaccessible plantations among and beyond the mountain range; the town milkmen drove their cows and goats from door to door, and gave their patrons their choice of the kind of milk supplied fresh at one's door; the boys were playing baseball in the streets and on vacant lots, and using American words in the game; double-teamed American army wagons were rumbling through the town to the camp of the regulars out on the plain a mile and a half away; and the widows that came out at sunset told a story of the meaning of war in that region.

Our military governor of Pinar del Rio at that time was Brigadier-General George W. Davis, who has since been assigned to the command of Puerto Rico. A few minutes' conversation showed that General Davis was no ordinary man. He is blunt and direct, kindly but firm, and entirely devoid of any suggestion of vanity or pomp. Out West they would say he has plenty of "horse-sense." With perhaps one or two exceptions he had done the best work in Cuba, and it had attracted little attention. He had made a tour through the larger part of his province, knew the military and political situation thoroughly, had gathered information of great use to this government, had used great tact and patience with the Cubans, had encouraged them to peaceful pursuits, and had impressed upon them, by his clever executive ability, that the Americans were really honest and true friends of the Cuban people. He had not upset the normal functions of government, and he told me that he

COUNTRY NEAR PINAR DEL RIO—AMERICAN MILITARY CAMP IN THE DISTANCE

had had the fullest co-operation of the citizens in his work. He was deservedly popular, and the day that he left, having been summoned to Washington, the railroad station was thronged, and there was a suspicious moistening in many eyes at the thought that he might not come back.

I was surprised to find that not only was General Davis a good military man (that was to be expected) and a good civil administrator, but that he was something of a student, not only of governmental questions, but of natural history. I remember that, coming down to Havana with him on the day he left Pinar del Rio, he pointed out various botanical specimens. He seemed to know all about the trees and shrubs and grasses and flowers. He talked also about the animal life of Cuba, not as one who had heard certain interesting things, but as one who had studied them. He discussed governmental problems and theories—not for publication, of course, but I am sure he will not object if I use his words on one topic. He pointed out a peasant's hut with its thatched roof and palm-leaf sides, its ragged and naked children, its two pigs tied by their legs close to the one door of the hovel, its dog, and its owner sitting on a bench smoking a pipe at his resting-time in the middle of the day. The peasant was little more than a mere animal. He knew nothing, of course, and cared for little except to be let alone in peace. Since the American soldiers had come he had learned that there were other countries in the world besides Spain and Cuba, but that was all. Pointing to him, General Davis said :

" If annexation is to be the outcome of all this trouble, there is the man whom we must make an American citizen. Can we do it ?"

General Davis did not answer the question himself, and the way he put it indicated that it needed no answer in his mind. I do not know his real sentiments on the matter, but I was repeating his remark to another general of high rank, also a military governor, and, with some spirit, that general said to me :

"What does General Davis know of the limitations of American citizenship, and who shall circumscribe its bounds?"

There you are, and rather than begin a controversy upon a delicate question, I hasten back to General Davis. Still talking about the man who lives in a hut

A FIELD OF THE FINEST TOBACCO IN THE WORLD,
NEAR PINAR DEL RIO

in Cuba, and who cares for nothing in his ignorance but to live from day to day, he said:

"The richness of this region almost surpasses belief. I know of no other place in the world where a man can prosper with so little effort as he can here. Take that man out there. Give him a hoe and a machete, and enough beans and potatoes to last for three months, and by cultivating from an acre to two acres of tobacco he can clear, say, $250 in ninety days, having started with nothing but his two tools, his seed, and a few dollars' worth of food. He and his wife may have not more than two garments apiece; his children may have no clothes at all. With his machete he will build himself a hut, and with his hoe he will raise tobacco, and in ninety days he will be well off. In two years he can afford to hire others to work for him, and in three years, if he so chooses, he can be rich for a man in his station. Where else in the world can this be done? I say that it is marvellous."

Speaking still of the problems involved in American occupation, General Davis told me that he had asked a leading member of the bar in Pinar del Rio if he knew what the right of habeas corpus, as it is known in England and the United States, was. The lawyer said he did, and when General Davis asked him to define it, the lawyer became confused and went to pieces. He had no conception of it at all, though a very bright man. General Davis cited this to me to show that only the vaguest ideas were held by the most intelligent of the masses in Cuba as to what free government, as we understand it, really means. He paid a tribute to the thorough and efficient work done by Spanish officials in drawing up papers for official preservation. They were always complete, he said; faultlessly written out, and a misspelled word was a curiosity. As I have said, I do not know General Davis's innermost ideas about the future of Cuba, but I think I am warranted in saying that those of the administration who have that problem to solve would do well to summon the general to a protracted conference, for he has opinions on the subject of value, and he knows how to tell them.

In his investigations into the affairs of his province General Davis found that two censuses had been taken in recent years. One was in 1877, and the other in 1887. The later census showed that there were about 220,000 persons in the province, of whom about 60,000 were blacks.

He estimated that by 1896 there must have been, in the normal increase of the population, from 280,000 to 300,000 persons in the province. Of these, judging from the examinations of various places, and from the records kept, he thought that fully 150,000 persons had died in the province during the war. In a town which had 9000 inhabitants before the war, there were in January last about 4000. One place of 1600 people before the war, had only 250 early in 1899. Towns of 5000 were reduced to from 1600 to 2000. All this reduction in population meant death by disease and famine from the effects of the war. In the city of Pinar del Rio, General Davis said he had records of the deaths of 5800 persons, giving the name, age, and sex of each. He thought that perhaps 2000 others had died there, reconcentrados who had been driven in from the country.

Such was Pinar del Rio during the war and immediately after. As early as February its entire tobacco crop had been sold, and there was money in active circulation in the town.

CHAPTER XI

SO much interest in the reconstruction of Cuba centred in Havana and Santiago that little was heard
from Matanzas in the early days. Events of much
importance occurred there. The American military occupation of Matanzas showed most pointedly that it was
possible for an American military governor to be, in the
truest sense, a statesman as well as a soldier. The administration of General James H. Wilson in that province attracted little attention in the United States, for
the reason that Havana and Santiago were the news
centres, and the correspondents in the island, except in
a few cases, were not brought in direct contact with affairs in Matanzas, although that city is less than sixty
miles east of Havana. The truth is that no more thorough, profitable, energetic, and satisfactory work was
done in our military occupation of Cuba than that in the
province of Matanzas. To one who is familiar with the
facts it is impossible to speak of General Wilson's work
without enthusiasm. Most delicate tact characterized
all his labors, and the result was that in Matanzas and
its province there was probably less friction over our
management of affairs than in any other district of Cuba.

GENERAL JAMES H. WILSON

When one would write about the conditions in the province he must necessarily make the story revolve around James H. Wilson.

General Wilson was one of the most brilliant soldiers of our Civil War. After he left the army, affairs of business, of study, of diplomacy, engaged his attention, and as a result he became one of the best equipped men of affairs, in an all-around sense, in the country. Extensive travel brought a rare polish to his make-up, and contact with men in every degree of life so increased his horizon as to give his active powers of observation unusual scope, and to develop his instincts of sympathy and justice to a rare extent. He is the broadest kind of a man, the best type of an American civilian and an American soldier. He made American military occupation of Matanzas pleasant, and one might almost say delightful, to the people. He harmonized jarring interests. He brought about a condition of peace among the people themselves that they never experienced before, and it was easy for an observer to see that the people of the province almost idolized him.

Here is an illustration of the general's way of doing things: When the Spaniards left the province the Cubans came to him and asked if they might not have a celebration in honor of the event. Similar requests were refused in other places.

"Certainly," said General Wilson. "Move right into town and have a three days' fiesta if you wish. Put up your flags and banners and have your parades and dances, and when you get through I will order out my entire complement of troops to show you what American soldiers are like and to pay honor to you."

And the Cubans did move in. They decorated their streets with massive palms. They built arches in half a dozen places in the town. They strung flags and banners and streamers from house to house and across streets. They made the town look like a fairy abode. They made floats symbolic of liberty because the Americans had come and because they were free from Spain. They paraded and danced and sang, and when they were tired out, and the feast had come to an end, General Wilson moved his troops exactly on the minute, and the populace cheered itself hoarse in its huzzas for the United States and the broad-gauged man who represented this country among them.

Another illustration : I was seated in General Wilson's office, one day in February, when the civil governor of the province came in to tell the general that General Gomez was coming to town, and to ask what should be done about it. I shall always remember General Wilson's action on that morning. He wheeled around, placed his hand on the governor's shoulder, his eyes bright with enthusiasm, and said :

"So the old gentleman is really coming ? I am glad to hear it. Now make him comfortable. Do everything you can to give him pleasure. Turn out all your troops, and find out what he would like to have us do. He can have any kind of escort he wants. If he wants only a battalion, all right ; if he wants a regiment, he shall have it ; if he would like to have our entire forces turn out, we will do that. He can have anything he wants in that line ; and, by-the-way, be sure to say that we will take any place in the line that those in charge of the reception may designate."

THE THREE DAYS' FIESTA AT MATANZAS
Cuban Cavalry passing in Review in Front of the Palace

That governor left the place with smiles, and his eyes moistened. Here is another illustration—a little thing: Every night, from eight to nine o'clock, General Wilson had an American military band play in the plaza for the benefit of the people. In other cities the military bands played once or twice a week; in Matanzas it was every night. If an American would like to feel a thrill of patriotism such as never came to him at home, one of those nightly concerts would have been the place. It stirred the blood to hear "The Star-spangled Banner" played in a foreign land, with the odor of flowers heavy in the air, with royal palms and other tropical vegetation for a background, and with the shouts of hundreds of happy children who had just escaped an awful death of starvation. And when every American—soldier and civilian—rose to his feet and uncovered, it was thrilling to see hundreds of foreigners do the same with reverence and gratitude. I never knew what "The Star-spangled Banner" meant until I heard one of General Wilson's bands play it at night on the public square in Matanzas. Not having a military training, I had listened to it at home seated, and perhaps with my hat on, hundreds of times. I was never taught as a boy to uncover at the sound of its strains, but, if the reader will pardon the introduction of purely personal matters into this story, I should like to say that hereafter I shall always rise and uncover. The natives of Matanzas taught me a lesson—one that I wish could be taught to every American citizen. Our schools now teach that hymn faithfully in their singing exercises; how many of them teach the pupils to rise as they sing it and whenever they hear it?

Let me bring other testimony as to the tact and
ability of General Wilson. Here is an extract from an
article written by Mr. W. F. Allen, editor of the *Travellers' Official Railway Guide*, who visited Cardenas in
February:

When Cardenas was first occupied by our troops there were
forty prisoners in the jail. It is stated that General Wilson released them all, with a warning as to their fate if caught in any
unlawful act. For a month after that there was not a single
occupant in the jail, and the patriotic inhabitants of the city
hoisted a flag over the building in commemoration of the fact.

Every correspondent who has examined into the management of affairs in Matanzas province has had the
same story to tell. It was a story of tact, common-
sense, good judgment, and as a result the people looked
upon us not as conquerors, but as allies, in the island
solely for their benefit and theirs alone. I venture to
say that there was less suspicion of Americans in Matanzas than in any other city in Cuba.

Almost before he got settled in Matanzas General
Wilson was up and doing. One of his first acts was to
take a trip through his entire province by train and on
horseback. He visited every place of importance to be
found. His special train consisted of one day coach,
two passenger-cars with seats removed and supplied
with cots and bedding, one cooking and mess car, one
baggage-car, and two freight-cars for horses. He
learned all there was to learn of the people and their
condition in every city, town, and hamlet. I have never
seen a more thorough bit of investigation—and as a newspaper man I have been used to investigation all my life

DECORATIONS IN MATANZAS DURING THE THREE DAYS' FIESTA

—than that done by General Wilson. He made exhaustive notes, and although they were for his private use, he allowed me to examine them freely. He knew the number of people in every place, their condition physically, morally, and mentally; knew what the condition of agriculture was; who the officials of the place were; how many starving and impoverished persons there were; the state of education and religion; what the needs of the place were in a governmental sense; how many animals, cattle, hogs, and horses, there were—in short, everything of human interest in every town and village under his control. From his rough notes alone I could write a book. Here is a sample on the very first page:

SABANILLA.—Arrived 2.30 P.M. Four thousand two hundred people, one-third of whom are reconcentrados; about 1700 indigent, and need work; have returned about 200 families to their farms. Plantations are not working fully because they are short of cattle; they are growing potatoes and vegetables enough to keep the people going; if they do not have cattle, they cannot begin farming on any scale of importance. Everybody says: "Must have cattle." One hundred and fifty yoke of oxen are necessary. Have about 14 milking cows in the town. Spaniards left on December 15th; people were not permitted to return to their places until the Spaniards were gone. Eight cases of small-pox here; doctor has visited them, and all people are now vaccinated. Fifteen thousand rations have been received to date, and 3300 already distributed; balance will last 18 or 20 days; 10 on the committee of distribution; people all want rations; mayor is giving only to those who are helpless. About 800 widows, girls, and helpless children left without male support. Mayor himself is working plantation with 80 men and 42 oxen. Will have 100,000 arrobas of cane this year, which he will send to Conchita mill for grinding. Four more plantations producing cane. Four or five caballerias is all mayor is working himself; he has 104, but cannot work them for lack of cattle and money. Situation is gradually improving, people are getting to work, are in fairly good condition, and very hopeful.

Here is another extract selected at haphazard:

LAS CABEZAS.—Arrived 9.20 A.M., Tuesday, January 24th. Met at depot by alcalde and ayuntamiento; name of alcalde, Doctor Lino Fumero. Señora Adelaida Perez, the school-mistress, with her school of 64 girls, also at depot. The girls were all well dressed and clean, and Señora Perez made a very intelligent and patriotic address. She has received no pay for three years, and the alcalde was instructed to furnish her with rations if she was needy. The town looks poor, scattered, and very dirty, and yet the alcalde states that in former times they were very prosperous. Visited the church, which had formerly been used by the Spanish troops as a barracks; it was in a filthy condition, and the priest was under the influence of liquor; he was an illiterate Spaniard brought over with the Spanish troops, and evidently not worth taking back. The cemetery (the care of which seems heretofore to have been one of the functions of the priests) was in a horrible condition; skulls and bones lying on top of the ground, and everything unkempt and decaying. Town people advised to secure another priest.

Railroad has been running into the town about four years. Between 5000 and 6000 people in the termino; before the war there were 9700; the difference in numbers represents the people who have died, starved, or been killed. They had in this town 4500 reconcentrados, many of whom died. There are now about 300 widows and their families. Total destitute, from 700 to 1000. Some of the people have left for the sugar estates in other terminos to find employment. They are raising a few vegetables, enough to keep the people from starving. Twenty-six families, some with male members, are waiting to be placed on their plantations and farms. No rations yet received. Some small-pox in December, but none now. Rations have been received at Bermeja in same termino. Alcalde instructed to ration only the helpless, and to use his best endeavors to teach the people to begin to help themselves.

Termino is very rich in agriculture in good times. People are industrious and expect in a couple of years to have recovered from the effects of the war. One man has 20 caballerias of cane; cattle and oxen needed badly. Three hundred and thirty Spanish troops here for two years; after the people had planted and raised crops the Spanish soldiers would not permit them to gather, but took from them, and also stole everything they had, cattle, cows, chickens—everything. Naturally a healthy town; situated at the edge of the plain, near the hill country; hills not to exceed 50 feet in height; have five good wells; plenty of water.

Some of the general information that General Wilson secured in the first days of his administration may be summed up as follows: In 1894 there were 298,391 cattle in the province of Matanzas; in January, 1899, there were only 8800. In 1894 there were 102,000 horses in the province, and at the beginning of 1899 only 3700. Matanzas province had a population of 272,000 in 1894; in the beginning of 1899 the population numbered 191,000. Practically one-third of the people died during the war. The percentage of starvation from the Weyler reconcentration order was greater in Matanzas than in any other city of the island, but in the small towns of the province it was even larger than in Matanzas city. Here is a sample from statistics collected by Captain Thompson of General Wilson's staff, who went to the small town of

Mocha, only eleven miles from Matanzas : In Mocha, in 1894, there were 80 houses and 600 people. By orders of General Weyler 4500 people were concentrated there to starve. In the early part of 1899 there were 1280 people in that village. In the year 1897 alone there were 1214 deaths there. To any one knowing the circumstances of the situation could figures tell a greater story of absolute horror? Fully 70 per cent. of those driven to this village by Spanish soldiers died of starvation. Oh, what stories those enlarged graveyards of Cuba could tell if the dead could speak !

But turn to a pleasanter picture. It was Carnival Week when I reached Matanzas, and for three nights the plaza in the centre of town was a scene of jollity. A blizzard was raging in the eastern part of the United States at the time, and the sharp wind of the cool wave that blasted Florida swept across the Gulf Stream and made light overcoats comfortable in Cuba. The hot moist condition of the atmosphere was gone, and in its place was an air that made romping comfortable. For three nights all the healthful youngsters in town, and many that were not healthful, crowded to the plaza, wearing masks and dominos. They masqueraded in outlandish costumes, and danced and frolicked to the music made by a regimental band from Indiana. A happier lot than these youngsters was never collected. They shouted and screamed, made believe to frighten one another, delivered grandiloquent speeches, imitated all sorts of animals, tossed flowers about, and gave themselves up to a riot of fun. Hundreds of grown folks— chiefly negroes—also masked themselves and went prancing about. There was no spirit of war in that gathering, and even hunger was forgotten until morning, when the poor gathered at the palace to receive the food the army was distributing to those who needed it.

All the clubs in town were lighted up, and in the largest one facing the plaza there was a full-dress ball, to which the *élite* of the city went, and where a score or more of American army officers and their wives were guests. Down a side street there were two or three Cuban balls, or, to be more exact, Cuban negro balls, where the distinctive Cuban dance, puzzling in its short mincing step, its twisting motion of feet and body, curious in its mental if not its moral effect, was danced to the weird combination of music consisting of violins and trumpets and tomtoms that always goes with that dance. The town was gay and happy, and the sombre cathedral in the centre of town, with its jangling bells—there does seem to be a tuneful church-bell in all Cuba—seemed out of place in a setting of so much joy.

Matanzas, like Havana, was being cleaned by the United States authorities. The prisoners were set at cleaning streets, and Cubans were being hired to help in the work. General Wilson made no secret of the fact that he saw no necessity for our government to put in sewers and the like in a foreign city. He believed in cleaning up the place on general principles, but as for installing a system of public works, that he believed was extra-territorial, and not incumbent upon a force sent to the island for the purpose of pacification. He said to me:

"The Federal government in our own country does

not put in sewers, pave streets, and the like. Why should we do it here?"

General Wilson said he believed in the efficacy of ordinary cleanliness, and if that was enforced strictly, he said, he thought there would be no unusual epidemic of yellow-fever in the city. That his views about cleanliness were well founded was shown by the remarkably

GOVERNOR'S PALACE, AND PLAZA DE ARMAS, MATANZAS

good health of our soldiers there. There was no sickness of any account among them in Matanzas, and I was told that the health of the city was better than ever before. It is an attractive place. Many of the streets are well paved, and although the architecture of the city resembles that of all the other cities of Cuba, the city did not have that peculiar Spanish aspect that Havana has. It was a delight to see the inscription on an arch, left over from the festivities when the Cubans celebrated the Spanish evacuation, reading, "Hurrah, the United States," even if it did make one smile. Matanzas, worst scourged of all Cuban cities by hunger and famine and death, was the happiest in the island in carnival days and under the administration of General Wilson. As an American to an American, I give him a cordial salute!

In going from Havana to Matanzas one finds the country slightly different in character from that to the west of Havana, on the way to Pinar del Rio. In places it is rugged and rough. There are gullies and gorges, over which the railroad runs. Huge stones in many places crop out of the soil. There are sharp variations in the color of the earth. In one place it will be reddish, and only a short distance away it will be nearly black. The color of the soil seems to have little to do with its fertility. There is good and bad red soil, and also good and bad black soil. One goes through sharp cuts on the railroad and over several high trestles soon after leaving Havana. In the distance, here and there, low ranges of hills are visible. At almost every station the traces of the torch were visible. The ruins of sugar-factories were in evidence in half a dozen places in this distance of fifty-four miles from Havana to Matanzas. Near the city of Havana, Maceo made frequent dashes into towns and villages, emptying the jails, shooting at the guards in the block-houses, burning houses and factories. Nearer to Matanzas, on the open plain and in the foot-hills about the famous Pan of Matanzas, General Betancourt fought many pitched battles with the Spanish forces that were stationed in and about Matanzas.

It was a pleasure to see some of the sugar-centrals in operation. I remember one that had its tall smoke-stack painted bright red. It seemed like a beacon to all the country round, and it proclaimed a new order of things. There were said to be 105 sugar-centrals in Matanzas province. One-half of them were destroyed in the war, and about thirty-five of them expected to do some grinding this year. Another pleasing sight on the way to Matanzas was the presence here and there of bunches of cattle. I travelled for nearly a day with a cattle-man from the United States. He was amazed at the fine grasses and water in Matanzas province. He declared that the land was not only good for agricultural purposes, but that there was sufficient grass in the province to support a million cattle.

Everywhere that one went in Matanzas province the cry was for cattle. I can probably illustrate the importance of this need by a conversation, taken from General Wilson's notes, between the general and a Mr. Mendoza, owner of a sugar-plantation at Banaguises. The conversation occurred on the plantation during General Wilson's tour.

GENERAL WILSON. "I have been told in the termino of El Roque that they had 30,000 head of cattle before the Spanish soldiers began their depredations, or before they began to lose them through the effects of the war. Is this correct?"

MR. MENDOZA. "I think it is, because I had myself over 2000 cattle, and now I have but one cow. I had 1000 cattle and 700 cows in all; but these cows had calves, and the number had increased to about 2000. I simply lost them all. At first I killed a great many myself, and fed my people fresh meat free. Every day I saw the Spanish soldiers taking them away or killing them, and I thought I might as well make use of them."

GENERAL WILSON. " All of your cattle were destroyed in some way or another. How about your neighbors? Did they fare the same?"

MR. MENDOZA. "So far as I know, they were treated the same way, every one of them. We used to get our cattle from Puerto Principe, where they made a business of breeding them, and we never imported any cattle, not a single head, for the last ten years. I imported four Holstein cows and a bull recently, which cost me $1000, but they are all dead but one cow, and that is dying. Before the war a good cow cost from $60 to $70, and a pair of oxen from $70 to $75. I have bought this year 250 oxen, and have paid about $130 per yoke."

GENERAL WILSON. " Would it not now be profitable to breed and fatten cattle?"

MR. MENDOZA. " I was thinking of that, but am afraid of having many cattle just now. There is so much suffering in the island that, while people would not ordinarily steal, they might do it now; they are none too honest at any time, and the temptation would be too great for them."

Everywhere that General Wilson went it was the same cry. I notice that under the heading "Amarillas" he says, in his notes:

Greatest of all necessities—oxen, oxen, oxen!

In his note on Calimete he says:

Several small colonias near here are cutting cane, but they have no oxen; only the great estates have any oxen this season. Sixty yoke of oxen would greatly aid in re-establishing business, but a far greater number will be needed before normal conditions can be obtained.

And so throughout these valuable and exhaustive notes there was scarcely a place mentioned where General Wilson did not reiterate the need of oxen.

It is worthy of mention that all Americans who were competent to judge agreed that there was a great future for fruit-growing in Cuba. Twenty years ago the Havana orange was one of the commonest fruits in the

VIEW ON THE SAN JUAN RIVER AT MATANZAS

American markets. The Florida and California oranges practically drove it out. Orange-growing has received a severe set-back in Florida from two destructive freezes within the last ten years. Frosts cannot affect the Cuban orange. It is to-day one of the sweetest and richest of fruits. It has not so delicate a flavor as the Florida orange, but it is sweeter than our home product. Transportation to this country is cheap, and when final peace comes to Cuba it would seem to be probable that, in view of the failure of the orange experiment in Florida, a large trade in oranges should spring up from Cuba. In his notes on Ytabo, General Wilson remarked:

This looks like a good place for Americans to come to grow fruit. It is one of the best places in the island for this purpose, more especially for pineapples, which do not require care. Certain lands known here as "dry lands" are particularly good. A fine quality of tobacco is also grown here.

This extract simply illustrates, as I have pointed out, the great thoroughness and mental alertness of General Wilson in his work. When it is considered that he made preparations for taking a census long before any official instructions reached him, that he made a study of labor conditions, gathered statistics of every kind in relation to the province—his material on sugar alone would be sufficient for an exhaustive treatise—and, in addition, governed wisely, meeting the many complicated problems with resource, courage, and frankness, it is impossible to restrain admiration for him. He retained men in the offices they held, unless they were incompetent or guilty of improper conduct. He induced the Cubans even to select former Spanish sympathizers to serve with them in several places on the boards that managed municipal affairs, and he kept reiterating on all proper occasions that the mission of the United States forces in Cuba was for pacification solely. He fed from 20,000 to 30,000 persons daily for a time, sought ways of finding employment for the poor, and encouraged them to take heart. He visited the hospitals, and caused them to be purified; opened homes for orphans; cleaned the streets and pestholes—work in which he had the full co-operation and support of his chief military assistant, Brigadier-General Sanger. He tried to devise means of improving commerce, and so thoroughly was he informed that while talking on this subject I remember he quoted almost offhand figures showing the amount of sugar shipments from Cardenas and Matanzas. In 1894, he said, there were 2,471,000 sacks shipped, and in 1898 the shipments had fallen to 920,000 sacks. He told me that in his investigations he had found that the pay of unskilled labor was forty cents a day, and the cost of living from twenty to twenty-five cents a day—allowing six cents for rice, four cents for meal, seven cents for beans, and the rest for other things. He had gathered full statistics about the 500 miles of railroads in the province and about the shipping interests of the various harbors. The province of Santa Clara was added to his command later.

I might go on at great length about the conditions in Matanzas, but it would amount largely to a reiteration of General Wilson's name. I might add that he did not hesitate to apply the knife where it was necessary, but he was engaged chiefly in binding up wounds. His relations with the priests were cordial—with one exception, perhaps. That was in a small town where General Wilson found a church in a most filthy condition. It was a menace to health. He ordered the priest to have the church cleaned, and rode on. He was out of patience, and finally decided to send General Betancourt back to the priest with imperative orders as to cleanliness. General Betancourt told the man that if his Master should come to this earth again He would not set foot inside of

"OH! HOLY HEAVEN!"

General Betancourt and the Spanish Priest at Cabezas

the priest's church, because it was so dirty. The priest raised his chin, opened his hands, and said, "Oh, holy Heaven!" That priest found it convenient to leave the place.

Perhaps the conditions in Matanzas province can be summed up best in the words of General Wilson to the

WHERE THE FAMOUS MULE WAS KILLED

officials of the town of Colon, a place of about 16,000 people. General Betancourt acted as interpreter at the conference, and General Wilson said :

"Say to them, general, that I have been in every country in the Northern Hemisphere, and I have never seen any portion of the world that presents more evidences of fertility and possible richness than the coun-

271

try from La Union to this place, where you can plant and harvest every day of the year."

The civil governor made this graceful reply :

" If you have found the country fertile and the soil rich, you will also find the Cuban hearts as rich in their gratitude and appreciation ; and as the country grows richer, due entirely to the assistance given to it by the United States, you will find also that the Cuban hearts will grow daily in their appreciation of and love for the great American republic."

General Wilson responded to that, and his response threw light on the actual situation in Cuba :

" I am very much surprised to find the people so deserving and industrious. The impression prevalent in many portions of the world is that the Spanish-American people are not industrious, that they are a light and trivial people ; but any one who entertains this opinion will be compelled to change it if he comes to the island of Cuba."

CHAPTER XII

THE province of Santa Clara is probably the most fertile in Cuba. It has for its chief city and seaport Cienfuegos on the southern coast. Almost directly in the centre of the province and also of the island is the old city of Santa Clara, known commonly in Cuba as Villa Clara, one of the most healthful places in Cuba. The province is the chief centre of the sugar industry in the island, has some of the best tobacco lands in Cuba, has various kinds of minerals, none of which, with the exception of asphaltum, has been found in paying quantities, has rich plains and lofty mountains, and abounds in the best tropical agricultural conditions. There is nothing which will grow in Cuba that will not flourish there. Its agriculture at once began to revive after the war ceased. It was there also that the greatest distrust and active opposition to American rule were manifested in the early days of our military occupation.

Cienfuegos, the metropolis of the province, felt the effects of the war least of all the large cities in Cuba. Its people regard it as the greatest commercial rival of Havana, and they do not hesitate to predict that the time is coming when it will be the chief seaport town in the island. Its harbor is one of the most commodious in the world, and is completely landlocked. Captain Mahan has called attention to its deep water and to its strategic importance in relation to the Caribbean Sea. The city has vast commercial possibilities. Its streets are among the widest in any Cuban city, and few difficulties will be encountered in securing a perfect sanitation system. And yet, at the time of my visit in February, it was the most foul-smelling city probably in Cuba, due largely to almost a total lack of water-supply, and to the fact that the Spanish soldiers had just gone home, and also to the lack of full co-operation of the people with the United States authorities.

In going to Cienfuegos from Matanzas one passed through long stretches of fertile lands as barren of people as the Dakota Bad Lands. Here and there near the towns and villages one saw women working in the fields, and occasionally a few cattle were in evidence, but they were not far away from the towns. There were some bandits abroad in the province, and the people were afraid to go far from settlements. The smoke of charcoal-burners and from numerous sugar-mills was reaching up to the sky in many places, in towering shafts, and as one approached Cienfuegos and saw the lofty Trinidad Mountains in the distance, the evidences of an improved condition of agricultural and commercial activity seemed a fitting accompaniment to the inspiring aspect of nature. Only thirteen miles from Cienfuegos the great sugar plantation at Hormiguero came into view. Its grinding mills are about a mile from one of the prettiest railroad stations in the island, and its smoke and evident business activity formed one of the brightest spots in the island. A large American flag standing out in the brisk breeze from the top of the sugar *central* told a story of the changed conditions and probably of the aspirations of its owner. Before that we had passed the great plantation of Caracas, the largest in the island, also in operation, so that by the time we reached Cienfuegos, after three changes of cars, we were prepared to find a city not utterly prostrate as a result of the war. There had been cable cutting during the war at the entrance to the port, and the destruction of a light-house, with some loss of life among our fearless sailors, but that was practically all of war that the city had experienced, and it also had the distinction—if such it may be called —of being the last place occupied by Spanish troops in the island. The city had the novelty, in addition, of seeing Spanish, Cuban, and American soldiers on guard in its streets at the same time, and it had at that time something of a scare lest there should be bloodshed between the troops.

Before we reached Cienfuegos it became evident that the city was in a state of agitation. When we reached the little town of Palmira, nine miles away, we found the railroad station decorated with palms and banners, and we saw that flags were flying from almost every building in town. One of the banners had this inscription : "Al Illustre Libertador, Maximo Gomez." Then we knew that Gomez had come to town, and, in anticipation of seeing a Cuban city *en fête*, we forgot all about the beggars at the railroad stations, and even omitted to write in our note-books that from San Domingo to

Cruces, a distance of eighteen miles, we had ridden in clean cars, with inlaid hardwood floors, windows free from dirt, comfortable seats, and even a wicker chair in a vestibule of the first-class coach, all furnished by the Sagua la Grande Railroad, the most progressive, from the standpoint of comfort, of any in Cuba. As we rolled into the city, with its beautiful bay spread before us, and with children running along the streets shouting "Good-bye," with the houses decorated with flags and the people beckoning their peculiar salute of welcome. it seemed impossible to fancy any scenes of starvation or of the horrors of war in that place. The railroad station was all a-flutter with flags and streamers and greens, and as we dashed up the street past the plaza we saw where Gomez had spoken from a rostrum the day before. Every building about the square was fluttering with Cuban and American flags. The dingy and picturesque cathedral over in one corner of the plaza seemed out of place in the emancipation that had come with the new-born activities in the old Cuban town.

Gomez had come after his campaigning in lonely hills and woods into a large city. A gay procession had met him at the railroad station, and had escorted him on foot, the women and children leading in the enthusiasm, to the home of Nicolas Acea, a millionaire sugar-planter, who lives in one of the finest houses in Cuba, at one corner of the plaza. The interior of the marble house is gorgeous, and its court-yard one of the most picturesque on the island. In that palatial home Gomez slept in a room the furniture of which was gilded, and where every luxury was at his command. It was a mighty

change for the stern old warrior, who for years had been
sleeping almost anywhere he could lay his head, and who
had faced the perils of starvation and abject misery in
his campaigning. He was ill when he arrived, and his
host secured as much quiet for him as possible. The day
after his arrival he spent most of his time in bed, and
that night there was little for us to do but to go to the
plaza and watch the throng promenade to the music of
an American regimental band. The plaza is probably
the largest and handsomest in Cuba. It was so crowded
that armed American sentries had to keep the crowd
moving constantly. There must have been from three
to four thousand promenaders there that night. The
electric illuminations on various buildings, a mellow
moon shining down, and the ordinary lights of the place,
made the scene extremely bright. The air was balmy,
and the wealth and aristocracy of the place were on
show. It was a beautiful picture. A crowded American
summer resort never presented a handsomer array of
women, the greater part of whom were young. Their
gowns were modish, and their appearance was distinctively smart. If there were any poverty-stricken people
in town—any beggars, any large number of women in
black as the result of the war—they did not show themselves in that brilliant scene. The people were happy
and vivacious, and it was difficult to believe that the
sounds of war had been heard anywhere near such a
lively and contented city. American army officers were
promenading with señoritas, and there was that dexter-
ous use of the fan, and that peculiar way of using the
eyes as aids to conversation that indicated that the

Cuban girl was enjoying herself to the utmost in her favorite way. And when the band played "Yankee Doodle," the new conditions of American unity found voice in shouts from fully a hundred throats for "Dixie." And so the promenading and lively conversation went on until suddenly the strains of "The Star-spangled Banner" were heard, and then a hush fell upon the multitude. Every army officer ceased his attenton to his escort and stood at attention; every American civilian stood still; hundreds of citizens of the place removed their hats, and, when the inspiring tune was finished, the plaza broke into cheers. It simply thrilled the American soul to see and hear it.

The next morning General Gomez paid a formal call upon General Bates, the commander of Santa Clara province. The time fixed was eleven o'clock. Exactly three minutes before the hour General Gomez emerged from his host's door. Mr. Acea's carriage was not on hand. The imposing coachman had something of the mañana spirit in him. It was necessary to call a hack, but exactly on the minute General Gomez and staff reached General Bates's office across the plaza, and fifteen minutes later the belated coachman in his elaborate rig arrived. Soon Gomez came out and got in the carriage of his host, which was probably the most luxuriant he had ever used, and drove to the Liceo Club, next to Mr. Acea's house, where a breakfast was given in his honor, and where, in company with several others, I had been invited to meet him. He seated himself in one of the rocking-chairs of the main room as soon as he arrived. and began talking softly to the man who was next

WATER SUPPLY IN A VILLAGE IN SANTA CLARA PROVINCE

to him. The place was large, and the seventy-five or a hundred men in the room sat or stood about in silence, every eye watching the aged chief. Their manner was a splendid tribute to the general. In another place I have described how he began to talk of the duty of the citizen to the commonwealth, and how gradually his voice raised in intensity until it rang through the room, indisposed as he was, with the resonance of a commander on the field. He was magnetic and fascinating. I could think of no American whose personal manner could be compared favorably with his, except perhaps James G. Blaine. And yet in every motion and tone the military man was pre-eminent. He was a general as well as a statesman and philosopher and adroit politician. After a few minutes he lapsed into silence, and then one of his aids arose and whispered a few words to him, and then came across the room to say that Gomez would be glad to have a few words with me. He arose as I approached, shook hands cordially, but eyed me with evident suspicion lest he should fall into some kind of a trap which an American newspaper man might set for him. I had been warned that he was not prepared to declare himself as to American occupation, and I gathered from his manner and words that it would be many, many months before he would speak frankly upon that subject, if ever he does. He wore large spectacles, there was a slight stoop in his shoulders, he seemed to be weary, mentally and physically, and his thin, yellow face, his pronounced cheek-bones, gave a stern aspect to his otherwise kindly countenance. His voice was deep and clear, and he showed a reserve of vitality that explained why he was able to campaign in the exposure and deprivations he had undergone. He told me frankly that he could not talk for publication, but that he was very glad to see me. I asked him if some time, not too remote, he did not intend to visit the United States. I assured him that the warmest kind of a welcome would be his, and that in a reception by the American people he might find the best kind of a tonic for his shattered health. His face became sad as he shook his head in reply and said:

"No; I do not think I can find an opportunity to visit your great country. I am an old man. My duty to my family and to Cuba is such that I must give whatever of service remains in me to them, and I fear I shall never be able to visit the United States."

Then, with the simplicity of a most unassuming man, he asked permission to sit down, while he continued the conversation for about five minutes. Other men were waiting to be presented, and the interview closed, the general, with the skill of an American used for years to interviewers, having contrived to say nothing on a subject about which he did not care to talk. If Gomez were a citizen of the United States I am convinced that he would be one of the foremost men of the country. He seemed a Tilden in cunning and resource, a McKinley in affability, a Grant in simplicity, a Lee in dignity. He was composite in character, and, like most eminent men, a riddle.

That evening there was a reception at the Liceo Club, which was crowded, handsome women abounding, and Gomez sat for an hour and a half and listened to patriotic speeches, after which he arose and greeted a few friends and some Americans and went next door to his host's home. The next day he went to another city, and his tour of triumph finally culminated in a tremendous demonstration in the city of Havana, the details of which have been made familiar to the readers of the daily newspapers.

I had seen so many persons of apparent prosperity and wealth in the plaza and at the Gomez receptions that I went about Cienfuegos, which is a city of propably 40,000, to find their homes. It was an elusive search. In a most unaccountable way the homes of the rich and those in most moderate circumstances seemed completely mixed. There is no distinctive part of the city where the well-to-do live. Their homes are scattered all about, and are unassuming as to the exterior. The architecture about the plaza, however, is most impressive. It is of the Renaissance type, but arranged in a continuity of finish that one rarely sees in Cuban cities. It seemed as if each building around that extensive plaza was planned and built with due regard for the symmetry and architectural appearance of its neighbor. The Palace, City Hall, and the leading clubs — Spanish, Cuban, Workingmen's — seemed part of a broad scheme of utility and decoration, and the result was that there were few places to look upon in any city of the island so pleasing as the surroundings of that plaza.

When one went about the streets, however, it seemed as if the United States authorities were not so keen in matters of sanitation as in other places. We were told that the officials were having the town cleaned, and the next night we had proof of some of this activity. The air was very oppressive, and about nine o'clock, with a friend, I went to the plaza to sit down and to try to get cool. We leaned back against the iron railing of the stone seats that extend about the plaza on all sides, and stretched our legs. We extended our arms along the railing and noticed that it felt damp. A glance at our hands showed that it had been painted that afternoon, and as we arose hastily we found that our backs contained a very vivid representation of the pattern of the railing in fresh white paint. Why money should have been spent in freshening up an extensive iron railing in a park, and the bad smells in the streets not a hundred yards away allowed to remain, were things we could not understand, and we said things on the spur of the moment that were severe and would have made a Spaniard dance with delight. Nevertheless, the work of cleaning up the town was really going on, and it had been simply a little misdirected effort that had put some fresh paint where it was least needed.

Major-General Bates, who was in command of Santa Clara province, had his headquarters in Cienfuegos. He has since been transferred to Manila. He is a quiet, unassuming soldier, a splendid fighter. He is a silent man, and reminds one something of General Grant. He was working hard, but he did not seem to have qualities of tact and delicacy in dealing with a frivolous, excitable people like the Cubans. He went at his work in the most straightforward fashion. He appointed a new Mayor of Cienfuegos, a former eminent law professor, Dr. José Antonio Frias. He sent for all leading officials in his province, for conferences, and he retained most of them in

TYPICAL CUBAN TOWN AS SEEN FROM THE RAILROAD

office. That caused trouble among the political agitators with whom the province seemed to abound. General Bates, to use an expressive term, did not feel it incumbent upon him to "jolly" them. He at once set a street-cleaning force of 200 men at work, and if little had been accomplished it was because the Spaniards had been gone only about ten days. He had been feeding about 10,000 hungry people a day in the province, mostly in the country. He was forming a police guard and looking after other details of his administration on a broad scale. He had no time for trifles. He was also studying the best problem of securing water for the city. There was a proposition to bring water about twenty miles, at a cost of $1,000,000 or more, and there were other propositions looking towards a supply from artesian wells. Then there were plans for establishing a sewer system and for other municipal improvements, the backers for which were clamoring for recognition by General Bates.

The silent general went on studying and endeavoring to learn what the best interests of the city of Cienfuegos and the province of Santa Clara demanded. He consulted with the best-informed men of all shades of political opinion, moved slowly in any changes of established rules or customs that he made, and, above all, tried to convince the people generally that the supreme duty of the hour was to co-operate most fully with the United States authorities, to the end that a civil government of their own should be set up within the shortest possible time. This was no easy task in the city that had been chastened less by war than any of the other cities of the island, for many of the agitators were spreading the suspicion that the United States was simply manœuvring to get hold of the island of Cuba as its own possession.

General Bates made friends with some of the former Spanish sympathizers, and this did not please some of the extremists of the former revolutionists. They asserted that in several places he had violated the principle of home rule in sending officials there who were residents of other places. There was a constant clamor that the extremists among the Cubans should have all the offices. When it was found that the general would not be moved, all sorts of stories were spread abroad about his inefficiency and indifference. These stories simply illustrate what harm irresponsible and persistent clamor can accomplish if kept up, for many of the rumors were believed. I had a long talk with General Bates about his work. It concerned every feature of the government. I learned that while outwardly he seemed to be slow in bringing about improvements, he was really working with the utmost energy. He did not take the masses into his confidence. He was moving along straight lines, and moving surely. He was always the cautious military man, and if his methods were not adapted to the executive work of government in a foreign land, it was because he was a soldier rather than a politician, using the word politician in its best sense. He was hampered by a lot of irreconcilables, and they would have made as much trouble for almost any other general.

There were some persons who declared that the spirit of discontent in the province was responsible for the outlawry in the country. Several parties of what were called bandits were swooping down from the mountains

and hills and stealing what they could lay their hands
on in small towns. In the Western part of our country
we would have called them simply horse-thieves. In the
East they would have been thieving tramps. In Cuba
they were bandits. Our forces, with natives as guides,
were chasing them. Some they captured, and some they
killed. General Bates was alert in this work, just as he
was in all that pertained to the peaceful government of
the province. He went after the bandits just as he had
gone at once about the establishment of schools, the creation of a guard in the country districts, the restoration
of the functions of civil government, in his own quiet
way, and if there was any fault to be found with him, it
was, as I have said, because he moved in military lines
and had not those qualities for smoothing over persons
who could make trouble, but who really were not worth
serious consideration.

In going from Cienfuegos to the city of Santa Clara,
evidences of the revival of agriculture were seen on every
hand. It is the garden spot of Cuba. One passes through
Esperanza, the centre of the guava jelly making industry. Dozens of men and boys were on the station platform with boxes of the product, and they did a lively business with American travellers. For the rest of the way
to Santa Clara, almost all the land seemed under cultivation. Corn was growing, sweet-potatoes were springing up, ox-carts were seen at the railroad stations with
loads of sugar-cane, patches of tobacco were flourishing,
cattle were grazing, and in scores of places women and
children were in the fields at work.

In going into the city of Santa Clara, however, there

T

was one evidence of what the war in Cuba meant, which probably was not to be seen in any large town as late as February. A barbed-wire barricade, with openings here and there for wagons, was stretched entirely around the city. It consisted of two lines of posts about ten feet apart, and the wire was strung from line to line in criss-cross fashion, a hopeless entanglement. Block-houses were strung about the city, and it gave one a vivid idea of what a trocha in Cuba meant, and of what the obstructions around Santiago were like when our troops had to charge through them. To me it seemed like a cowardly arrangement. It illustrated the character of the warfare of the Spaniards vividly. They seemed possessed of the idea that if they held the cities they were victors in the contest that was going on. They left the country districts open to the insurgents, but so long as they barricaded themselves in block-houses and behind barbed-wire barriers they thought they had the military situation in full control. There must have been eight miles of this barbed-wire barrier around Santa Clara, and it was still intact.

This city of Santa Clara has boasted that it is the most healthful of any in the island. Why it should be so is difficult to imagine. There are the same rough streets as have existed in all Cuban cities. No roads run from the place, worth calling roads. The dwellings are huddled close together, and a glance down any of the thoroughfares makes one think of a series of jails, with the windows of every building barred and shut in. But it was the water supply that seemed to be the source of the greatest danger. A small creek, called by courtesy a river, runs around the city, and out on the edge of the town is a small, dirty building with a pump and a cistern inside, where the water supply of the city is collected. In a tank in that building was a lot of stagnant water, covered with a green scum, and it was from that source that the city was supplied with water. Men with carts would drive up to the tank-house, fill their carts, and then peddle the water about town at so much a barrel or pail. The tank was foul-smelling and the water was impure. How a city dependent for the most part upon such a supply of water could escape epidemics of yellow-fever is a mystery.

To the north and east of Santa Clara city many battles were fought on the plains between the insurgents and the Spaniards. After they were over, the insurgents usually retired to the mountains in the distance, and the Spaniards went back into town with the dead and wounded. Usually neither side won. The fights filled up the military hospitals in town and swelled the size of the burial plots. When the war was over and the time was set for the evacuation by the Spanish troops, the Cuban forces gathered to the north of the town and encamped. As the Spaniards moved out on one side of the city the Cubans moved in on the other side and took possession. The United States forces had not arrived, but the Cubans kept order and preserved peace. Their administration was marked by wholesome restraint, and no reasonable fault could be found with it.

It was in Santa Clara that the Rev. Dr. W. D. Powell, of Jackson, Tennessee, the Secretary of the Southwestern Baptist University, was opening schools and holding religious services. Only two of the twenty-two priests had remained in town after the Spaniards left, and the people were glad to attend the religious services that Dr. Powell started. I do not know what impression was made upon the people by these services, but I do know that the schools did much good. The children flocked to be enrolled by the hundreds.

It was in Santa Clara that the last of the Red Cross provisions, sent to the island as soon as the war was over, were distributed. The agents of the Red Cross found that there was no need of the provisions at the harbor on the northern coast to which the cargo had been consigned, and so they moved into Santa Clara to finish up the distribution. The army officials were distributing food there, but the people seemed to prefer the Red Cross supplies. The agents had been in the island from the first time the Red Cross had sent supplies to Cuba, and they had perfected a system of distribution that seemed to supply the people more effectively than that used by the army officials.

It was a curious commentary on some of the army methods to find that, when I spoke to General Brooke about the work of the Red Cross men in Santa Clara, he did not know they were there. He added, that he supposed that all distribution of food by the Red Cross people in Cuba had ceased. It was evident that some of his subordinates had not thought it worth while to call his attention to that most important feature of the situation in Cuba, and he made no attempt to conceal his surprise over it. I told him that if he would telegraph to Santa Clara he could get full details in an hour or two. It was such incidents as these that brought about the criticism that our military men were not fully informed as to the real situation of affairs in general in Cuba. There was too much waiting for the perfunctory military re-

COURT-YARD IN A HOTEL IN SANTA CLARA—SAID TO BE THE CLEANEST HOTEL ON THE ISLAND

ports on this and that matter. The reports would be considered in the usual routine, military way, and answered and filed away. It required a long time to accomplish things, and this seemed vexatious. I say it in no spirit of criticism, but as a matter worthy of passing attention, that at General Brooke's headquarters in Vedado, as late as February, there was little information to be obtained as to the real condition of the island, except that which was strictly military in character. There was public comment that certain important matters were never brought to the consideration of General Brooke, as Governor-General of the island. The incident of the Red Cross distribution of provisions in Santa Clara seemed to confirm this. And it may have been because of this system, thorough enough for ordinary military procedure, that General Brooke asked me to call on him after I had made a trip through the island, so that, as he said, he might see the situation through eyes that were not military. I found him eager for information, desirous of responding to every need of the island, and, if he was not in direct touch with the details of all that was going on, it was because along the pathway of military red tape certain things were turned aside here and there, where they were blocked completely.

In one respect Santa Clara stands pre-eminent above all the cities in Cuba: it has a hotel that is really clean. It is said to be the only one in Cuba. It certainly was the only one I found, and if it is any advertisement to the establishment to make mention of the fact, it deserves it freely. The place—it is the only hotel of importance in town—was absolutely clean from front to back; there was no second story. I examined every part, and the shocking things that may be found in any public house in Cuba, if one looks far enough, were entirely absent. The court-yard was beautiful, but what was of more importance, the bath-rooms and closets were entirely clean and in a wholesome sanitary condition. Dirt of every kind seemed eliminated from the place, and bad smells simply could not exist there. Such a unique manifestation of cleanliness in Cuba merits wide publicity, and the city of Santa Clara should be proud over this distinguishing characteristic.

CHAPTER XIII

THE United States was fortunate in many of the men it sent to fight the skirmishes and other encounters with the Spanish forces near Santiago in June and July, 1898, and it was even more fortunate in some of the men left there to reconstruct the city and province. The chief one of these men was Leonard Wood, who went to Santiago as colonel of the famous Rough Riders, was made a brigadier and then a major-general of the volunteer army for military services there, and who was appointed military governor of the province. He was unknown to the country when Theodore Roosevelt asked that he be made colonel of the Rough Riders, so that Mr. Roosevelt, who was to go out as lieutenant-colonel of the regiment, might learn more soldiering than he knew at that time under Wood. Up to that time Wood was known among his immediate friends as a modest army surgeon of great strength of character, undaunted courage, excellent executive ability, and towering common - sense. The country soon came to know him as a magnificent fighter, brave as he was modest, and his words, " Don't swear ; shoot," were one of the pithy sayings of the war that will live.

CONDITIONS IN SANTIAGO

Brave as Wood was as a fighter, it was in a semi-civil capacity that he did his greatest work in Cuba and set a standard which will not only be a monument to him and a lasting credit to the United States, but which will be the model, so far as efficiency and results go, for the government by the United States of extra-territorial regions which may come under its jurisdiction. His will be the proud distinction of having set the pace in honest, efficient, economical government by this country in a foreign land. Disregarding "pulls" and politics of every kind, he governed with subordinates selected solely for merit and with the one purpose of benefiting the people of whom he had charge. It was on July 20, 1898, that General Wood was ordered by General Shafter to take command of the city of Santiago, to clean it up, maintain order, feed the people, and start them at work. There were probably 120,000 persons of all kinds, soldiers of two nations included, and of all degrees of health, in the city at that time. Pestilence was stalking about with starvation as a companion. Poverty was on every side and filth was supreme. Courage in soldier or civilian had practically fled. The dead were lying in houses or on the highways by the hundreds, and sick and dying could be found wherever one might turn.

The full military occupation of Cuba as an island and a country by the United States did not occur until nearly six months after General Wood had taken charge of affairs in Santiago. During those six months his work attracted more attention than it would have done, probably, had other men been grappling with similar problems to his in other cities in the island. In a few days the country knew that it had drawn a prize again in General Wood, and he was allowed to go on with his work for several months practically undisturbed by those in authority above him. He cleaned the streets, buried the dead, grappled with sickness and disease germs, fed the poor, set the idle at work, opened the schools, established order, used the money received in customs duties on public works, taught the people something about the rudiments of proper self-government, subordinated the military side of American control, organized a native police force, abolished useless offices, consulted with the representative citizens on all important moves, and, in short, made American occupation of the city and province a blessing to the people.

One of the first things that General Wood did was to establish a Sanitary Department, at the head of which he placed Major George M. Barbour. The work of cleaning the city was begun the day after Wood was made governor. The soldiers rounded up men out of work, and they were set to entering deserted houses, removing the dead from them, and in cleaning out breeding-places of germs. Few men wanted to do that kind of work, but it had to be done. When the natives found that it meant not only food and drink to them, but wages as well, it soon became easy to get them to work. Houses were broken into wherever there was a smell to justify it. In 68 days Major Barbour removed 1161 dead persons and animals. Most of them were burned. It was necessary to use fire to destroy fever germs. The bodies of men and beasts and the heaps of garbage,

GENERAL LEONARD WOOD

which could not be buried for lack of time or for other reasons, were soaked with crude petroleum and burned slowly. One day, when there were 216 deaths in the city, the Sanitary Board burned more than 100 bodies, and buried the rest. It was made a criminal offence not to report deaths. Every available cart in town was impressed into the sanitary service, and Major Barbour grappled with the filth of 400 years. What he accomplished may be judged best by the fact that yellow-fever was practically eliminated from the town in the early part of 1899, and General Wood declared over his own signature that the city was "as healthy as any city of its size in the United States, excepting, perhaps, for the constant presence of malaria." In a letter written by Major Barbour to a friend in Washington and printed in May, 1899, there was the corroboration of statistics to these words of General Wood. Major Barbour said that for the month of April, 1899, there were "nine days with but one death," an unheard-of thing in Santiago. To show the changed conditions, Major Barbour took the date April 12th and compared the death-rate for several years with this result: April 12, 1893, 11 deaths; 1894, 17; 1895, not given; 1896, 9; 1897, 32; 1898, 41; 1899 (American control), none. In the latter part of June, however, while General Wood was in the United States for a conference with the President, yellow-fever appeared again and there was danger of a serious epidemic. General Wood hastened back and soon had the situation practically under control.

In April, 1899, after the sanitary system had been established thoroughly, Major Barbour was employing about thirty-five teams a day about the city. These removed about 200 loads of refuse a day. Two carts were kept busy all the time scattering disinfectants about the streets. The entire force was composed of Cubans, except Major Barbour and two assistants, one of whom was an interpreter. All the men of the corps were uniformed and organized in a semi - military fashion. They were made to give the military salute, and their retention at the work depended solely on their records. The foremen had absolute control over the selection and dismissal of the men. Under this system the mob of 600 men with which Major Barbour started soon became an orderly and efficient force, and there are hundreds, if not thousands, of persons alive to-day in Santiago in consequence of this work who would have been in their graves had the old methods prevailed. In Santiago, early in the year, it was seen that the matter of American military occupation could be reduced to a basis of statistics with the reduced death-roll as the first exhibit.

After having started the sanitary work, General Wood began a general overhauling of affairs. He found, as all the other of our military commanders in Cuba found after him, that there were no official records of any value, that the public treasury was empty, that there was no government anywhere, and that the people were in a state of helplessness — starving, sick, or idle. General Wood began to appoint officials, consulting the people first as to the best men for the places. He appointed mayors here and there, and, not to make a too violent change in the orderly procedure, put certain minor

MORRO CASTLE—THE CELL IN WHICH LIEUT. HOBSON WAS IMPRISONED

officials in power when there might have been some question as to their strict utility. The people were used to them, and it was thought best to keep up the old machinery to some extent. All the officials had to accept lower pay and to give a full return in service for their salaries.

Probably the most important improvement of a permanent character in the public works of Santiago, next to the cleaning of the houses and the laying of new pavements in the streets, was the repair of the water-supply system. In the early days of American military control water was as necessary as fire in the cleansing process. The water system in Santiago had been established in 1839, and through neglect and mismanagement it was in a deplorable condition. There were thousands of leaks in the pipes. Gradually these leaks were stopped to a large extent, and then a moderate supply of water became available in every part of town. The men who had food to sell at that time held it at enormous prices, and it became necessary for General Wood to issue an order . regulating food prices. To this order, with the improvement in sanitary conditions and a better supply of water, could be attributed at once a change in the physical condition of the people. The establishment of a yellow-fever hospital on an island in the harbor, and of detention hospitals at the water's edge, soon brought about a great change in the matter of infectious diseases.

It was necessary to open the courts as soon as possible and get them going once more. General Wood went through the prisons and administered justice off-hand himself for a time. It was not long before he made some radical changes in the matter of rights of citizens. After proper consideration of the matter he established a Bill of Rights, which included the freedom of the press, the right of peaceable assembly, the right of habeas corpus, and the right to give bail for all offences not capital. It was there that a most important part of General Wood's plan of reconstruction was put in force. He wanted to impress upon the people that the civil law must be supreme, and that such a thing as self-government could not be established unless there should be respect for law. He showed that there were to be no privileged classes in the province in the future, and he made it plain that militarism was to be avoided in every possible way.

General Wood quickly turned his attention to the schools of the province. In nearly every place in the province he soon had them in operation. The teachers were willing to work for less than their former salaries, where it was found that the cities and towns could not raise sufficient money to pay them, and would have to rely upon help from the customs duties of the province to make both ends meet. In the city of Santiago nearly thirty kindergartens were established for children under seven years of age, and the other schools were started up once more. General Wood has said that he has never seen a more enthusiastic set of youngsters than those in these schools. A broad scheme of school reform has been studied out, and in the evolution of self-government which must be started by the United States, doubtless this will be one of the most important steps. It will mean good school-houses and progressive methods of

A MULE-TRAIN IN SANTIAGO

teaching—methods especially adapted to the changed condition of affairs in Cuba.

With all the confusion when General Wood took hold of affairs in Santiago, there was one really attractive phase of the situation—there was plenty of work to be done. Another pleasing phase of the situation was that through the customs receipts there was money available to a limited extent to pay for the work. The first work in all the towns of the province, as well as in the city of Santiago itself, was to clean up. Then came work on street improvements and on bridges. General Wood set apart every dollar that he could spare of the customs receipts for this kind of work. He paid a daily wage of seventy-five cents, or of fifty cents and a ration of food, for labor on public works. Some of his workmen took three rations of food instead of money. Where men were able to work, no food would be given unless they gave labor in exchange. Of course, in the early occupation of the place, food was given to the hungry and no questions were asked. Rations were issued at that time to from 18,000 to 25,000 a day, and on one day the issue is said to have run as high as 50,000. Early in 1899 the issue of free rations practically ended, and after October, 1898, the province practically became self-sustaining. The revenues were sufficient to pay for all salaries, to support schools, keep the light-houses in operation, and to pay for the sanitary and police measures that were in force. In addition to all this, General Wood noted with pride that he had been able to accumulate nearly a quarter of a million dollars as a surplus for sanitary and harbor work.

At first General Wood had complete control over the revenue receipts of the province, but after the occupation of Cuba had become general by the United States the money was turned into the general treasury of the island, from which appropriations were made for work in Santiago. General Wood noted with satisfaction that most of the larger towns in his province became self-supporting in a short time from their own municipal taxes. Those which were not self-sustaining he helped out from the general funds. It was found that by economy and by the abolition of useless offices the municipalities could sustain themselves upon a very much reduced income. The wholesome lesson of living within one's income was thus taught to the people.

In writing of the matter of taxation and the use of public revenues, General Wood has said in his reports and other papers that he believes that all the public revenues of the island must be used, for a time at least, in establishing courts, schools, opening highways, maintaining a rural police, and in making various other improvements, so as to give employment to large numbers of men. He has said that in a short time a modified system of taxation can be put in force, and the condition of the people be improved through that time-honored and well-proved remedy for trouble—plenty of work. To tax the people in the interior of the island directly, he declared, would be simply the extortion of blood-money.

General Wood made several trips throughout the province, and soon had encouraging progress to report on every side. As an illustration of the cleansing process in other places than Santiago, it may be mentioned

THE CUSTOM-HOUSE.

that there were no less than 3000 cases of small-pox in the town of Holguin when Colonel Duncan N. Hood took charge there, with instructions from General Wood to stamp out the pestilence. Hood did stamp it out, but every house in the place had to be almost literally scraped from top to bottom. Early in June, 1899, the War Department made public a report from General Wood, telling of a trip he had made along the north coast of the province. He had taken a trip to other places in the province only a few days before. He reported that the people were all at work, and that not once was he approached by a beggar or asked to give assistance. He visited Santa Lucia, where it was reported that there had been some brigandage. General Wood's words in regard to this side of Cuban life reveal not only an excellent glimpse into the Cuban situation in the country districts, but show his own methods so well that they are worth quoting. He said :

I visited Santa Lucia, near Sama, and the estates of the Boston Fruit Company near Banes. Everything at these places was quiet, and there was no brigandage there. The reports which had alarmed them were, as far as I could learn, circulated by an old scoundrel called Feria. He has spent his time, apparently, in circulating reports of brigandage, and actually inciting some ignorant men to committing some lawless acts in order to give color to his reports, and following up this work with telegrams to Havana requesting that he be authorized to pursue the bandits, and incidentally be given a command and big pay. I took him off quietly and told him that my orders to my officers and to the Guardia Rural were to give all men of his description a short shrift if they were caught engaged in any work of this sort ;

that he was a marked individual, was closely watched, and would be summarily dealt with. Most of these reports that have reached you have been gotten up in this way, and they mean nothing. Now and then there is a case of stealing or robbery, just as there is in all our Western States, but nothing more.

The whole problem to-day in Cuba is work. Put the idle people who are now reading the incendiary press to work, relegate to a back seat the politicians, whose present importance rests solely on the attentions they are receiving from our people, and they will not have followers enough left to give them the slightest importance or weight in the community. Agitators have tried to stir up the people of this province, but they cannot do it, simply because we have given the people something to do and put them in a condition so good that they will not leave it for a lawless life unless absolutely forced to. The people who are creating the disturbances to-day in Cuba do not represent two per cent. of the population.

There are no Cuban troops in arms in this province, absolutely not a man, and yet we have here more than two-fifths of the entire Cuban army and most of its desperate officers. It is impossible for them to take their men from their fields and homes. In short, the whole question is a question of labor, not of politics, and the factions warring in the press would be immediately without support could their idle followers become engaged in any kind of work. I believe there is money enough, with the revenues, to accomplish this end, not to the detriment of our administration, but to its everlasting benefit.

General Wood has made no secret of the fact that he does not agree with those who assert that the Cubans are not capable of self-government. He thinks that they can be taught to control their emotional tendencies, and has declared with pride that he has not had occasion to re-

A TYPICAL CUBAN WOMAN

move one of the officials picked out for him by the Cuban people. All the officials have been competent and trustworthy. To inexperience, and to that alone, can any just cause for complaint be charged. General Wood, in June, 1899, summed up his policy in Santiago by saying that, on the one hand, it was one of good schools, good courts, and good municipal government along simple lines, with the use of public revenues for public works, so as to improve the sanitary conditions of the people, and, on the other hand, of the abolition of useless offices, of high salaries, of heavy taxation, and of neglect of industry and commerce. He also has urged with repetition that the process of giving self-government to Cuba shall be made one of evolution, and that, above all things else, militarism be banished. He has declared that regeneration will come through setting the people at work, instead of through proclamations and orders declaring that the Cubans are, and henceforth shall be, a free and independent people. Put them to work, and the free and independent part of their existence will come naturally and of itself, has been General Wood's theory, and on that theory he has based his work.

General Wood has also said in reference to Cuba that "everything is in the future." Not everything; that is one mistake that this modest and useful man, representing so fully and faithfully the highest type of American manhood—the kind that blossoms out in our national history so unexpectedly and so effectively at times—has made. The work that he has done, while it may find its best exemplification in the future, is already of the past. Valuable beyond the matter of price as it has been to

Santiago, and to Cuba as well, and monumental in the upbuilding of reputation as it has been to General Wood, it has been even of greater service to the United States, for, disregarding political spoils, it has shown the true way, the only way, for this government to rule a foreign land with honor and lasting credit.

CHAPTER XIV

AMERICAN SOLDIERS IN CUBA

ONE of the first things that the average American visitor to Havana did in the early days of our military occupation was to stop the first private soldier he met off duty in the streets of Havana and ask how the boys were getting along, and how they liked duty in Cuba. There was intense interest by American civilians in the welfare of the troops, and an earnest desire to learn if they were conducting themselves in a way to reflect credit upon the United States. The attitude of the Cuban people showed that the troops were respected everywhere, and it was a pleasure to note that, on the whole, the soldiers realized that to a great extent the repute of our country was in their keeping. The soldiers invariably said, in answer to the questions, that they were getting food that was satisfactory in the main, that their commanders were zealous in caring for them, and that there was little cause for complaint, except that they wished they were back in the United States once more. They rebelled inwardly against doing police duty in the streets of the city, but they went about the work cheerfully and vigorously enough.

I can best illustrate what the presence of the American soldier meant to the masses of Havana by telling an anecdote or two. I made friends with two artillery-men off duty on the first Sunday of the Carnival. We were seated on a bench on the Prado promenade watching the show. Suddenly one of the soldiers leaped from the bench, sprang out into the street, and rescued a child from under an uncontrollable horse's feet. Five minutes later he dashed away again. An old man had fallen in a dizzy spell and had fractured his skull. The soldier carried the man out of the crowd in his arms and saw that he received medical attention. He was gone half an hour. Later in the day I met him nearly exhausted and mopping his brow.

"You see, it was this way," he explained. "Just after you left us, a little boy was run over. He was unconscious. I picked him up and learned that his home was only a block away down a side street. I carried him home, and when his mother saw the boy she fainted. The boy's father was useless. I put the boy down, and by motions told the father to loosen his wife's dress at the neck and dash some water in her face. He went almost into hysterics. He paid no attention to the boy, but knelt beside his wife, began to caress her, pray over her, and lament things generally. You would have thought she was dead or dying. Again I told him to loosen her dress, and showed him what I wanted. I called for water. He just kept on bellowing. I told him to get out. He wouldn't move. What do you suppose I did? I just took him by the collar and the trousers and pitched him clear into the middle of the street, and shut the door and locked it. I loosened the woman's dress myself, got some water, and brought her around. In ten minutes she was caring for the boy. I don't think he'll live. When I came out I saw that whelp of a father, and I simply chased him out of sight. I should like to have given him a thrashing. I have been having a lively time, considering that I am off duty."

That man was simply an ordinary American soldier who did things whenever he saw that it was necessary for some one to jump in and do them. His companion told me of an episode in which he had figured only the day before. The soldiers had orders to prevent cruelty to animals, and especially to the little mules that draw the immense drays about the streets of Havana. The sight of one of those little animals struggling with a load which in our own country would require at least two horses to pull is about the most irritating sight in Havana, barring the cruel way the ox-teams are yoked. This soldier saw a driver of one of these carts goading a little mule that could scarcely stand up, into trying to pull eight large casks of molasses through the streets. The soldier stopped the driver and told him to take off part of his load. The driver pretended not to understand. The soldier made motions that could not be misunderstood. The driver refused to obey and declined to get off his cart. The exasperated soldier pulled him from his seat. The driver climbed back, and again he was pulled down. Again he climbed back, and was pulled down, and then he came at the soldier in a furious rage and struck at him. That was enough; the butt of a musket whisked through the air and the driver lay prostrate on the ground with a gash in his head. The sol-

dier was at his side in an instant and to his relief found
that the driver was not hurt badly. The man was cowed
completely and stood by meekly as the soldier climbed
into the cart and began rolling the casks out. One of
them was splintered in the fall and most of the molasses
was lost. The soldier went on until all the casks were
on the ground but two, and then he told the driver to go
on. He made that man come back and take two hogs-
heads each time until the load was all carted away, and
then he reported to his superior officer and received
commendation.

In their police duty the soldiers were constantly settling brawls. They went into many dangerous fights, settled petty problems on the streets in a common-sense way,
and the result was that everywhere they went they were
respected. There was no drawing of skirts by women
as they passed the soldiers, as I have pointed out before,
and no insults were hurled at them by any one. On the
other hand, there was nothing of the air of the conqueror
in their behavior, and soon the utmost good feeling prevailed between men wearing the United States army
uniform and the citizens. On all sides it was recognized
that our troops, in the parlance of the day, meant business.
When the First North Carolina Volunteers landed in
Havana and marched through the streets, their band
playing the Cuban national hymn, the Spanish soldiers
glared in anger at them and the people were sullen.
More than one of those Tar Heel soldiers took a long
breath, felt to see if his ammunition belt was all right,
threw his head back, and marched along as if he were the
personal representative of the entire nation of the United

CAMP OF THE TENTH REGULARS ON THE PRADO

States. The tension lessened in a few days, and soon the people began to look upon the soldiers as really true friends.

It was down in Cienfuegos that an Ohio regiment was under probably the severest stress of any that occupied a Cuban city before the Spaniards went home. Cienfuegos was the last place evacuated by Spanish troops. There were 30,000 of them in that town when the Ohio men arrived. The Cuban troops moved in also, and Spaniards, Cubans, and the United States forces each established a patrol in the streets, and the lines lapped over. Every Spanish soldier had his cartridge-belt filled and he carried a Mauser. The Ohio men had about a dozen cartridges to a man, and they had Springfields. For the first twenty-four hours our soldiers were in a desperate frame of mind. Their officers could not persuade them that there would be no conflict. They made up their minds that if a fight came they would sell their lives dearly.

Finally the tension became too severe for one of the Ohio boys. In some mysterious way he had secured a quantity of liquid that was not good for him. His steps did not show what he had swallowed, and he went on his patrol with a determination to whip the entire Spanish army if necessary. He was simply spoiling for a fight. The Spanish soldiers did not commit any overt act in his presence, and he was at a loss how to teach them a lesson. Finally he decided that it had to be done, and that the credit and reputation of the American army as a fighting force rested on him. He swaggered around and put on airs. The Spaniards refused to be insulted, and when he could endure the situation no longer his eye lighted on a glass insulator at the top of a telephone pole. He raised his rifle to his shoulder. The Spaniards tightened their grips on their weapons. He pointed his gun at the insulator and fired. There was a commotion on the street, but the insulator was broken into bits. The Ohio man tossed his head to one side, raised his gun, and fired again. Another insulator went to bits. The volunteer was in high feather, and brought down a third insulator. He had done his duty, and he went on about his patrol, relieved and proud that he had shown the Spaniards what a United States soldier could do.

The effect upon the Spanish soldiers was electric. After they were sure that there was no danger of being shot, they dashed to the foot of the pole, picked up the pieces of broken glass, and kept them as mementoes. They even took the pieces to Spain with them as souvenirs of the marvellous shooting of an American soldier. The news spread rapidly, and although it is not over-creditable in all its aspects to our troops, that incident was powerful in relieving the tension in Cienfuegos. Our troops were without food. The Spanish soldiers, respecting men who could shoot like that drunken soldier, generously offered part of their food to our lads, and soon they were fast friends, and so remained until the transports sailed away to Spain with the last of their forces ever to serve on Cuban soil. The Ohio volunteer took his punishment like a man, satisfied, as also were most of his fellow-soldiers, that he had played an important part at a critical time in international affairs.

Although the soldier, whether volunteer or regular, ac-

quitted himself creditably in Cuba, it must not be inferred that there were no exceptions. The list of court-
martials, published in the English edition of *La Lucha*,
made an American wince a little as he read the charges
and the sentences. Most of the soldiers on trial were
accused of drunkenness. Occasionally one was punished
for impudence or assault, and now and then one was sen-
tenced heavily for stealing. Most of the troops in the
island in the first months of military occupation were
volunteers, and in the haste of securing them there were
a few undesirable men among them. Most of these,
however, were whipped into shape, but there was not
that strict submission to discipline on the part of the
volunteers that characterizes the regulars. The percentage of men punished for unmilitary conduct, however, was small, and the fact that they were punished
severely was of itself a tribute to our military thoroughness.

It was when one visited the American camps on the
island that he felt proud of the service. There was one
military exercise in Havana every morning that invariably attracted attention. It was guard-mount by the
Tenth Regular Infantry in their camp at the head of the
Prado. Just before nine o'clock every morning the bugle
calls would ring through the camp, and the band would
take up its position in a broad street that was roped off
in front of a park, with the trumpeters standing behind
on the sidewalk. With a flourish of trumpets and the
band playing a march the sergeants and their details
would come swinging up into place to report to the sergeant-major. The men of the new guard would be

placed in the line, and the sergeants with a salute would drop to the rear. The sergeant-major would report to the regimental adjutant, and then the band would play light music while the adjutant made an inspection. The colonel's orderly would be picked out, and the adjutant would report to the officer of the day, after which the

WATCHING THE GUARD-MOUNT

trumpeters would rush to the front and march off with the new guard, while the band played a march and wound up occasionally with "The Star-spangled Banner." If was no different from guard-mount at home, but with a setting of royal palms in the background, a motley crowd of citizens to watch the ceremony in a foreign land, it filled the Americans who watched the performance with a pride and satisfaction that always manifested themselves in numerous proud nods of the head.

The camp of the Tenth Regulars on the Prado was somewhat pinched for room, but served a good purpose. The people of Havana could walk past the tents that backed up on the sidewalk, look into them, and observe closely the American soldier at work and at rest. The same was true down at the foot of the Prado, at the Punta, and directly opposite Morro Castle. Across the bay, and behind the heights of old Cabañas, two or three batteries of artillery were encamped on the open sloping ground towards the sea, and there were the same order and neatness to be observed as in the camps in town. The soldiers over there complained a little of the dampness at night, and some admitted that they would prefer the life in town, even if it did call for police duty. Down in front of the governor-general's palace two or three companies were encamped, and out at Vedado, three miles to the west, there were more artillerymen and the Seventh Cavalry, Custer's old regiment.

The great camp of American soldiers in Cuba was at Buena Vista, about eight miles to the west of Havana, on a beautiful ridge overlooking the Atlantic. It was there that General Fitzhugh Lee had his entire Seventh Corps, made up of volunteers. Although General Lee was governor of the province of Havana, his duties were chiefly military. Probably there was never a better conducted military camp than that at Buena Vista. Out of nearly 17,000 men there were only about 230 on the sick-list on the day of my visit. The camps of the regiments stretched along a railroad track on either side for a dis-

tance of fully two miles. The men went through their
daily duties with a snap. A mile away was the ocean,
and there they went for their bathing and their frolick-
ing. The streets of the camp were of double width, and
the spaces between the tents were unusually large. Twice
a day every company turned out for police duty, and
the result was that the place was scrupulously clean.
The men beautified the streets by setting out palms, by
making sidewalks, and by making fancy designs from
coral and stones and white sand at company headquarters to designate their names. The American eagle with
wings spread wide, made with sand and coral and colored
stones, was a favorite device to mark a company street.
The 161st Indiana boys, however, decided that they
would leave a permanent memento of their encampment.
They erected a monument with two bases, the lower sixteen feet square. The shaft was pyramidical in shape
and was twenty feet high. It was made of large pieces of
gray coral, collected by the soldiers at the sea-shore, and
cemented to a frame. The corners of the bases were orna-
mented by old cannon-balls obtained from the old Spanish
forts near by, and on the sides of the bases were cut the
name and hailing-place of the regiment. It was a pleasing object, although at first glance it had somewhat the
appearance of a graveyard memorial. It was symmetri-
cal in design and well finished, and served its purpose
admirably.

General Lee was the easiest of the major-generals in
the army to approach. Although his family occupied a
fine house near by he remained in camp at night, sleeping in a tent. As one entered the house where his official

quarters were situated, he could walk almost directly into the general's presence. He greeted me:

"Down here to look over the camps and other things, eh?"

"Yes."

"Been on any marches yet?"

"No."

"Haven't drank any muddy water, eh?"

"No."

"Oh, then you don't know what it is to be a soldier. Why weren't you here yesterday, when I sent a regiment out on a ten days' marching trip? You could have gone along, and you might have come back at least half a soldier."

Then the general laughed heartily and told me about camp-life. He was especially proud of the small sick-list. He had had the camp watered with the same supply used in Havana, and it was interesting to observe the extension of the system by the engineer corps. There was a sewer system being put in for every street, and preparations were being made for a healthful stay of the troops during the rainy season. The volunteers who were in that camp are now back in the United States, but their sojourn in that beautiful camping-ground just outside the city doubtless will linger long in their memories as a delight rather than a hardship of war.

The camp was busy at all times. There were scores of army-wagons moving about on various errands. The large freight yards were the scenes of constant activity. At every available moment some of the soldiers were out playing baseball. Others were engaged in beautifying the tents or company streets. There were the usual regimental drills and occasional brigade or corps review. The gospel-tents always had large attendances at services. The troops published a weekly corps newspaper, called *Cuban Camp Clippings*, giving all the gossip and news of the day in the camps. Perhaps no better idea of what military life meant in Camp Columbia under Lee can be given than by printing an extract from this newspaper of the date of February 11, 1899, under the heading, "First North Carolina":

Of course, you have heard of the six-days march our first battalion made recently. Well, we had both a good time and a bad time of it—that is, some of us did. We left here Sunday morning, the 22d ult., and marched about fourteen miles, going through Havana. The next day we made about fifteen miles, and camped at a place by the name of Bejucal, in the centre of which is situated one of the prettiest little parks imaginable. Here passes were issued, and a great many of us visited the city that night and enjoyed ourselves in different ways.

After marching the next day about ten miles over a very rough road, we pitched tents just outside a little town by the name of San Antonio. It was but a short time until we had dinner. Every soldier was full of life, although decidedly foot-sore. Some had worn the bottoms clear off their shoes. After dinner we lay around on the grass for an hour or two enjoying a good rest, and then we were ordered to get ready for dress-parade. This was unlooked-for, and was met with general disapproval. The boys were tired, stiff, and sore, and very much disinclined to do anything for the rest of the day, but at the sound of the bugle all was astir, and soon the battalion was formed.

The Sixth Missouri was camped here also, and we borrowed their band, behind which we marched out and passed in review

GENERAL FITZ-HUGH LEE

before Major Smith. The guard-lines were amply looked after that night, and no passes were issued. The next day the boys were given passes, and they took in the town. The citizens were very kind and sociable, and did all they could to show they appreciated Uncle Sam's intervention in their behalf.

That extract, written by a private soldier, shows something of what soldiering under Lee meant. If there were room, other extracts that might be given from this little newspaper would cover the entire round of camp-life. Lee was as popular with his troops as with the civilians in Cuba. He regarded his position in the transformation that was going on as merely that of a soldier. There may have been a game of politics behind this assignment of Lee, but the general would not even hint that he was not entirely satisfied with his work. He had made a trip through the province of Havana, and had been over to the Isle of Pines, which he found to be largely a waste place. He had made changes here and there of the alcaldes of towns, but he was going slowly in the matter, his aim being to make the civil branch of his administration rest as lightly upon the people as possible. Whenever he appeared in town, however, he received cheers at almost every step, and if there is any satisfaction in popular approval of one's course, that emphatically was Fitzhugh Lee's reward for his work in Cuba, a reward which is the lot of few public men to receive in unbounded measure. Later, in the military changes that were made, he was assigned to the command of the province of Pinar del Rio in addition to that of the province of Havana.

When one went through the island on railroad trains

he was sure to meet military men on various errands. I travelled one entire day with a paymaster and a detail of soldiers protecting nearly $100,000, packed in great chests. On another occasion I travelled with a brigadier-general and his entire staff. On still another I had the pleasure of nearly a day's journey with Inspector-General Breckinridge. Another day I travelled with Brigadier-General George W. Davis, and was delighted as he talked about the botany of Cuba and indulged in philosophical comment upon various topics of more or less abstract nature. His accomplishments were unusual for a soldier. It was in Pinar del Rio that General Davis had command before he was sent to Puerto Rico. His military force in the city of Pinar del Rio consisted of regulars, under the command in camp of Lieutenant-Colonel Bisbee, of the First Regular Infantry, General Shafter's old regiment. The camp was on an open, sunny plain, between the town and the mountains, and was unusually healthful. The hospital arrangements were in accordance with the best scientific principles. The water was filtered by a most elaborate system. The company kitchens would have delighted a Yankee housewife. Even the men in the guard-house were contented, and I remember that several of them asked me to take their pictures for print, although they were in disgrace. Colonel Bisbee gave his men just sufficient exercise to keep them up to a thorough military standard and no more, because of the climatic conditions. Through the camp there passed daily cavalcades of men from behind the mountains, their mules carrying fruits and vegetables to market in Pinar del Rio, forming one of the most picturesque sights in the island. General Davis was having the big military hospital in the town cleaned for use of the troops as barracks. The soldiers amused themselves with games, and scores of them had parrots as tent companions. Twice a week the regimental band played in the town plaza for the people. Altogether the camp was one of the most attractive in Cuba.

Attached to the headquarters of General Davis was Captain Ambrose Higgins of the Signal Corps. To illustrate the thorough character of our military work in Cuba mention should be made of a trip over beyond the mountains and around the coast-line of the western end of Cuba by Captain Higgins and a party to learn the nature of the country and people. He went to the north and south coasts, a distance of 105 miles in one direction and 125 in another. He found evidences of destruction of towns at every hand. There was little in the way of government, although every place had an alcalde or head man of some kind. The most interesting place he came across was a settlement of Congo negroes, brought to Cuba as slaves in 1842. They still spoke their native language and knew almost nothing of Spanish. They were in a sad plight, suffering from a war which they could not understand and into which they had been dragged indirectly to a greater or less extent. It was difficult to impress upon them that the United States was now in charge of the island, and Captain Higgins left there conscious of having accomplished little in the way of good teaching as to the pacific intentions of this country.

In every part of the island the Signal Corps was erect-
ing telegraph and telephone lines so as to establish com-
munication with the various military camps. That branch
of the service also had charge of the commercial telegraph
systems of the island, and these were soon placed in a
satisfactory condition.

I have referred in other chapters to the satisfactory
military conditions in the province of Matanzas. Coming from Havana and approaching the city of Matanzas
one saw across the valley and about two miles from the
city a camp of regular cavalry. The white tents and
rows of tethered bay horses brought out exclamations of
admiration over the picturesque effect from the train
passengers who crowded to the windows. Down on the
bay in Matanzas harbor, in the immediate neighborhood
of Fort San Severino, where the famous mule was killed,
was a large infantry camp. The ocean breezes swept
through the tents and there was abundant salt-water
bathing for the soldiers. The aspects of nature in and
around Matanzas are among the most pleasing in Cuba,
and if one's surroundings can have a beneficial effect upon
one's health, perhaps that may account for the wonderful
condition of the troops under General Wilson and General
Sanger, for there was practically no serious sickness there.
To show the care that was taken in the selection of camp-
ing grounds let me quote from the notes, to which I have
referred frequently, taken by General Wilson on his visit
to Cardenas, where later some of his soldiers went into
camp. General Wilson inspected the site for the camp
and dictated off-hand the following to the stenographer
who acted as his secretary :

AMERICAN MILITARY CAMP AT MATANZAS

The encampment selected for the troops at the ball-grounds is very good. It is level, smooth, sloping off gradually towards the north, and is in every way suitable for a battalion of infantry. The water is perhaps half a mile distant, and will have to be hauled. Of course in time of wet weather the ground will be more or less moist, but the soil is smooth and will probably shed water as fast as any other point so level. The tents should be floored, and the flooring raised off the ground one foot, if practicable.

The highway to the land or ridge back of the city is direct, with but few turns, though very rough in spots. It is composed either of heavy paving or of natural rough stone, which, lying undisturbed, has been worn into ruts, and will require some work of improvement; but the materials are at hand, and the work could be done rapidly, if necessary. The site chosen for a large encampment is on top of a ridge, which appears to be between 50 and 100 feet above the sea-level; the slopes are beautiful, even, and smooth, and an admirable encampment could be made for any number of troops up to 10,000. Wells are from 175 to 250 feet in depth, and, while somewhat scattered, it is said they have been used for plantation purposes, and are believed to be inexhaustible. It will be necessary to raise the water by steam. The distance from the camp to the city is between five and six miles. The ground is covered with stone fences, and the fields are 70 or 80 acres in extent; grazing is excellent, and there is sufficient shade for all proper purposes. The view from the top of the hill is quite extended, and the ships beyond the harbor can be seen for twelve or fifteen miles at sea. However, as there seems to be no use for this site at present, it need not be further considered.

The soldiers had their vicissitudes in camp, and one of the most serious occurred in the camp of the Sixth Ohio, about six miles out from Cienfuegos, on the line of the railroad reaching the place from the north. There was evident confusion in the camp as our train came along. We stopped, and Colonel McMahen hurried down to the track to greet General Breckinridge, who was on his tour of inspection. "We are not very well to-day," said the colonel to the general's inquiry as to the conditions in camp. "You see, we had a tornado here night before last. It was a terrible twister. About half the camp was blown down. Half a dozen of the biggest palms were uprooted, and one of them wrecked the hospital tent where there were fifty patients. No one was killed, but we had several men injured seriously, and it was a lively time. However, we'll try to be in good shape for you, sir, when you come out to inspect us."

That was a trying time for the volunteers, but I do not think the men in that camp were in a more deplorable condition than those of a battalion of the same regiment at Santa Clara. The camp there was on bad, marshy ground, with poor water-supply and inadequate drainage. There was no shelter from the scorching sun. I remember that one night about eight o'clock I found nearly a dozen soldiers from the battalion sitting in the plaza of Santa Clara, mopping their brows and in a state of semi-exhaustion. I asked what was the trouble, and they said that the major in command had given them an extra drill that afternoon in the broiling sun, and at the end had put them through nearly twenty minutes of double-quick work. They did not recover for several hours. I did not have opportunity to see the major and get his side of the story, but on the face of things it looked like an evidence of the greatest drawback to the efficiency of the volunteer soldiers during the war—namely, officers lacking military training and the true military instinct.

And so the story of the camps in Cuba might be continued at great length. As a rule, the men were contented and well fed. Measles seemed to be the prevailing sickness of serious character, although on several occasions there were deaths from yellow - fever. The officers were diligent, with only a few exceptions, in looking after the health of their men, and discipline was maintained at every place. The soldiers were intelligent and physically fine-looking men. They were creditable representatives of the American people, and I did not meet an American visitor who was not satisfied with their appearance and general behavior.

The navy has its sea-lawyers, and the army has also its profound legal minds among the high privates, but not to such a degree as the navy. The army lawyers, however, were using up some of their spare intellectual activity in discussing the food problem in Cuba. About one in ten of the soldiers would tell you that the food given to the men was execrable — some of them used that word. There were many outcries against Alger and Eagan, and even against the administration. While confessing to no unbounded admiration on my part for General Alger, it may be well to give some figures showing what a thorough inspection of the food - supply in Havana disclosed, according to a report made by General Ernst, of General Brooke's staff. In February, a whole ship-load of canned meat, according to the newspaper correspondents—and it was pretty near that amount, for the ship was small — had been taken out to sea and thrown away. It seemed like a terrible thing, until the little matter of percentage was considered. An exhaustive inspection of the canned-beef was made with this result: total number of cans, 106,994; total number of pounds of meat, 213,988; number of cases opened, 513; number of cans examined minutely, 10,692 (one-tenth of the whole); number of bad cans, 198; number of pounds of bad meat, 396; percentage of bad meat to entire lot, 1.85—or less than 4000 pounds out of 213,000.

General Brooke gave me these figures for use, and made no secret of his satisfaction over them. He even ventured to say that in one's household domestic economy such a small percentage of spoiled groceries would not excite serious comment, but some correspondents and many of the devotees of yellow journalism made the most of the opportunity when the bad meat was sent out to sea from Havana. I examined minutely the system of inspection in Havana under Lieutenant-Colonel Philip Reade, and can assert with positiveness that not an ounce of food came into that city for the army's use which could not be traced step by step from abattoir to the storehouses in Havana. Under such a system it was impossible that bad food should be anything but an exception, although it was undeniable that some was to be found there.

CHAPTER XV

THE prostration of commerce in Cuba during the war with Spain was caused in large part by the almost complete ruin of the sugar industry of the island. Cuba has been called an immense sugar-producing plant. That industry has been, and undoubtedly will continue to be, the chief one in the island's commerce. With the exception of the tobacco industry, every other form of business is subservient practically to sugar. The cane is not native in the island, but there is no place in all the world where it thrives better or produces more satisfactory results. When the island became a theatre of war, the conflict was largely an effort on the one side to save the sugar-plantations and keep them going, and on the other to destroy them.

The most deplorable sights in Cuba after the war closed, barring the starving widows and children, were the burned sugar-mills. A destroyed village could be rebuilt easily, nature being prodigal with raw material for huts. The twisted machinery in the charred ruins of a sugar *central* told a story that meant a far more complicated problem. Not only was there the question of the ability to secure capital involved, but the political

problems of the future were wrapped up in it. You
could see the ruins from railroad trains on every side,
and when you considered how much the sugar industry
meant to Cuba, the outlook for prosperity was gloomy.
On the other hand, many sugar *centrals* were in operation in March and April, and some of them had fresh
paint on them. These were mills that had immense
capital behind them, and had survived the dangers of
the torch at a most costly outlay. It was estimated
that about one-half of the sugar *centrals* in the island
were destroyed. Those that survived were the larger
and more important ones. So when the war was over,
the sugar industrial situation was not so bad as it
seemed at first, for there was a good foundation upon
which to start afresh.

But the production of sugar is dependent upon other
factors than mills. The matter of securing the cane is
the chief thing. The cane-fields were laid waste as far
as possible. When one recalls that a single large sugar-
mill in Cuba often draws part of its supply of cane from
fields as far distant as fifty miles, the complications in
the production of sugar during such a war as raged in
Cuba are obvious. A field of sugar-cane lasts from five
to seven years, and then it is worn out, and a new stock
is planted. The cane does not propagate itself. After
it is planted one gets a crop in twelve or eighteen
months, according as the planting season varies from
the cutting season. The fields have to be renewed constantly and systematically.

The production of sugar to-day in Cuba, as elsewhere,
is chiefly an agricultural problem. The opinion has

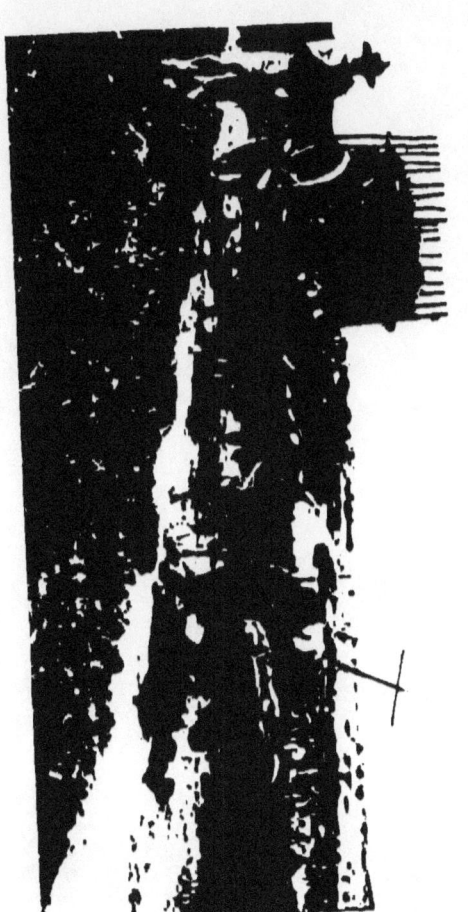

BRINGING IN THE CANE FROM THE FIELDS

been general that the most important side of sugar-making lies in the sugar-mill. A few years ago that might have been true, but, owing to competition and the perfection of manufacturing methods, a change has come over the industry. It is open to any man who has the capital to set up a sugar-mill, and by the use of ordinary business methods to make as much money as his neighbor in the sugar-manufacturing business. Whatever improvements and economies are to be made henceforth in the manufacturing side of sugar production must be of a minor character. The point is to secure the cane, which involves the control of the cane-producing land. Sugar-cane being a vegetable product, many persons have thought that, having the vegetable supplied by nature, the problem of securing sugar remained exclusively with the manufacture of it, and that the chief economy involved was to get every bit of sugar out of the cane that was possible. The problem is far deeper than that. The key to it is a constant and steady supply of cane delivered to a mill at a minimum cost for growing and cutting and hauling, to which is added a minimum cost of shipping to the refinery after the raw sugar has been made. A sugar-refinery, no matter how scientifically equipped, is likely to be a most expensive toy, unless there is complete co-ordination between the manufacturing and agricultural sides of the industry.

There are few more complicated and more delicate business operations than running one of the immense sugar estates in Cuba. The value of the plant, if the company owns its own lands, is usually from three to five millions of dollars. On some of the plantations there are towns of from 1500 to 2000 inhabitants. There must be a working capital of from $500,000 to $1,000,000 to operate the plant. Some of the plantations own and operate as much as from fifty to sixty miles of private railroad. There are immense repair and machine shops on the estates. Not only must several thousand men be employed and cared for, but they must be kept at work systematically. To supply certain mills with cane during the grinding season, from fifty to seventy acres of cane must be cut every day, and hauled from fields to trains, and then carried miles away to the mills. The slightest break in the supply of cane means great waste of resources, for after the saccharine matter is squeezed from cane the fibre is used for fuel to run the plant. The use of coal and wood, owing to their cost in Cuba, for such purposes for any decided length of time would ruin the plant. Then the matter of shipping the product after the sugar is crystallized, the purchase of food for men, women, and children on the place, the financial operations involved in always having money on hand for wages and other operating expenses, and the thousand and one details of business life affecting directly the daily life of thousands of persons—all must be studied and worked out.

To understand what the problems in the conduct of such an estate were I spent some time on the well-known Constancia sugar estate, ten or a dozen miles up a small river from the city of Cienfuegos. It is a picturesque journey up this river, bordered as it is with royal palms and a thick undergrowth of shrubbery here

and there. Great numbers of pelicans were flying about
or dozing on trees or shrubs. Far away one might see
the tall smoke-stack of the *central* standing out on a
sloping hill-side, a beacon of industry to all the country
roundabout. One of the little cars drawn by a mule,
such as one sees at many railroad stations where there
is a *central* near by, waited at the steamboat-landing to
carry one up to the plant, half a mile inland, and just
beyond a beautiful grove of palm-trees. A dozen or
more large buildings make up the plant at the *central*,
and the many railroad sidings, the locomotives and cars
belonging to the place, the large number of men employed, form a scene of activity, such as is seen only in
very large plants in cities devoted to manufacture rather
than in countries where agriculture is the chief pursuit.

A short time before the insurrection started, Marques
de Apezteguia, the owner of Constancia, formed a company to operate the plant, most of the capital being
secured in this country. It really became an American
corporation, the president of the company being Mr. Os-
good Welsh, of New York City. Marques de Apezteguia
remained in active charge of the enterprise to direct its
fortunes. The war had an almost blighting effect upon
the place. It was necessary to equip about eight hundred men with arms to protect it. Block-houses were
built about it, and there were fully forty skirmishes with
the Cuban insurgents, who tried many times to destroy
the plant. There was some bloodshed in these fights,
and a constant state of fear and agitation, but Constancia was saved. Before the war ended, the provisions ran
low, and almost all the cattle had been used up for food.

The women and children worked in the fields to a large extent, and, by the most careful and persistent effort, labor of some character was carried on all the time. The owners assert with pride that they never paid a cent to either side for protection, and there are many men conversant with the sugar situation in Cuba who declare that it is probably the only plantation in Cuba of which this can be said.

Constancia, although second in rank of the sugar plants in Cuba, has one advantage over the others in that it is on tide-water and can send its sugar on lighters at minimum cost, direct from its mill to vessels in the harbor of Cienfuegos, only a few miles away, there to be loaded for shipment to this country. The other factories, almost without exception, have to send their sugar to some port by rail, and any one who knows what the ruinous rates of freight in Cuba are can understand what an advantage Constancia possesses. It means that it can produce raw sugar a margin of a cent cheaper than any plant of large size in the island. That margin may mean the difference between a profit and a loss. What a plant of this size consists of may be conjectured from a few statistics.

There are 66,000 acres owned by the company. There are nearly fifty miles of private railroad under operation to bring the cane from the fields to the factory. Six good-sized locomotives are used in this work, with fully 200 cars of various kinds. About 1200 men are employed in the fields and 300 in and about the yards and buildings of the *central*. The capacity of the land is sufficient to produce 80,000 tons of sugar a year, and

RIVER STEAMBOAT, TUG, AND SUGAR-LIGHTER AT THE LANDING, CONSTANCIA PLANTATION

the capacity of the mill is equal to about 30,000. The mill uses up about 3,000,000 pounds of sugar-cane a day, and has produced as high as 21,000 tons of sugar in one grinding season. In the yard of the *central* there are sixteen acres of land, with nearly six miles of railroad sidings. Among the main buildings are the sugar factory, a distillery, machine-shop, lime-kilns, foundry, and carpenter-shop, electric-light plant, an extensive trolley system for moving the cars which bring in the cane about the yard, an elaborate telephone central office, by which a train-despatcher moves his cars miles and miles away — just as the train-despatcher on many a railroad operates his cars. The machine-shop of the place is the most extensive private plant of the kind in Cuba. Then there are tugs and lighters used for taking the sugar to steamships in the harbor.

It is most interesting to watch the plant at work. The great loads of cane are taken to the crushers, and then the juice goes one way to be boiled and cooked, until the crystals are whirled about in centrifugals and the sugar is packed and shipped. The fibre goes another way, to be used in the great fires which keep the plant going. There is a great bustle in unloading and shifting the cars in the yard, and a constant economy to prevent waste that to an ordinary observer would seem of little importance, but that to the initiated is known to be vital to the prosperity of the place. If one is growing sugar-cane and making sugar from it, no false moves must be made. When more than a thousand men are at work in the fields, principally cutting the cane; when scores of ox-carts are drawing the cane to the cars, and a half-dozen trains are hauling it to the mill miles and miles away; when provision must be made so that night and day for, say, four months, there must be no lack of fuel and no cessation in the flow of the cane-juice, or else a ruinous expense follows; when 200 tons of sugar must be

LOCOMOTIVE IN CENTRAL RAILROAD YARD, CONSTANCIA SUGAR-
PLANTATION

made and shipped daily, one realizes the importance of entire business harmony in every part of the plant.

To emphasize the fact that the production of sugar is chiefly an agricultural question, it should be remembered that it costs about one cent and a half to produce a pound of sugar in Cuba, and of this almost exactly one cent is the cost of the agricultural side. The cost of manufacture having been reduced practically to a minimum, it is on the agricultural side that further economies must be made in the reduction of cost. It is to this end that the trolley system is being introduced in the yards of many *centrals* to shift the cane after it arrives from the fields. It is also to this end that constant experiments are being made to cheapen the cost of cutting and hauling the cane to the *central*. From ten to twelve per cent. of the weight of the cane is expressed in juice at the factory, but only from seventy-five to eighty per cent. of the sugar in the cane is squeezed out under present methods. The problem of getting all the sugar out of the cane has not yet been solved, nor are all the matters of conserving labor in the fields settled. A plantation the size of Constancia requires 1000 oxen, 250 horses, and 100 mules, as well as its other equipment, to operate it successfully. When one also considers that there are several thousands of persons upon a plantation, with probably three or four good-sized towns, the question of government plays an important part, and the moral responsibility to give the people as much work as possible, as well as to prevent them from being discontented, becomes a matter of grave import.

Sugar plants in Cuba which produce their own cane and make their own sugar are known as ingenios. Those which grow the cane but do not make the sugar are known as colonias. There are thousands of colonias in the island. These suffered greatly from the war. The owners of these deliver their cane to the factories within easy reach, and the custom is to pay them for six per cent. of the weight of the sugar-cane. In other words, the purely agricultural producer of the cane goes half-shares with the manufacturer, the total amount of the sugar secured from the cane being about twelve per cent. On most of the colonias cane-cutting is done by contract. The contractor cuts the cane at the rate of $1 50 for 100 arrobas—a weight of 2500 pounds. He pays his workmen from forty to fifty cents for the actual cutting, and the rest of his expense is in loading the cane on the cars by the use of his ox-carts and delivering it to the factory. Some of the laborers, however, prefer to work for themselves and not for a contractor. Three of them usually combine, two doing the cutting and one doing the hauling with his ox-cart. These ox-carts may be seen at almost any railroad station in the sugar-growing districts of the island. They are picturesque, and the old Roman way of yoking the oxen by the horns gives an insight to the indifference of the Cubans to suffering by any one or by anything except themselves. It is lack of oxen that will cause serious delay in the restoration of prosperity to the island. Trained oxen cannot be procured right away. The island was swept almost bare of them. Cattle were being shipped in from Mexico and Venezuela and other places early in the year, but the Marques de Apezteguia told me that the island needed several hundred thousand cattle before normal conditions on the plantations would prevail. The pay of the laborer in the fields runs from forty to fifty cents a day, but if the employer has to feed his men meat at a high price for cattle, the problem of the cost of producing sugar is enhanced to an alarming extent. The cost of meat before the war in Cuba was about four and one-half cents a pound. In the early months after peace came the cost of meat was fully twenty-five cents a pound.

An excellent idea of the condition of the sugar industry in Cuba at the close of the war may be obtained from the notes, to which I have referred frequently, taken

CUTTING SUGAR-CANE, SHOWING THE CANE STRIPPED FOR CARTING
IN THE FOREGROUND

by General Wilson on his trip in January through the province of Matanzas. General Wilson visited the large sugar-*central* Santa Gertrudes, two miles from Banaguises, and as he was looking over the plant he made inquiries as to opportunities for Americans to grow sugar-cane in Cuba, and asked about the the cost of land. Mr. Mendoza, the proprietor, said :

" I have bought caballerias [a caballeria is thirty-three acres] at $100. Americans would have to pay for good land, say, $150 a caballeria, or about five dollars an acre. One of these caballerias will turn off about 70,000 or 80,-000 arrobas ; the next year twenty per cent. less, and the following year twenty per cent. less. I used to replant about forty or fifty caballerias every year to replace the cane that was wearing out. I am free to say that I think the future of Cuba will be better under American rule."

While visiting the Conchita estate, near Union, José Antonio Freyre, the manager, told General Wilson that he had spent $50,000 last year for oxen, and that this year he would spend the same amount. He said the sugar estate needed at least 900 more working-cattle. He was buying cattle from Mexico, and thought the age of five years the best. After the oxen are secured they have to be trained. The Conchita ingenio has a tributary area of sugar-growing lands twenty miles long and ten miles wide. This area is said to be among the best in Cuba.

Among other sugar estates also visited by General Wilson was that of Occitania, owned by the Himely family of New York. The manager is Mr. William Himely, part owner of the estate. He told General Wilson that he had plenty of cane for his capacity in grinding. One great difficulty was to get sufficient ready money for use. He had only about thirty yoke of oxen, but was employing about six hundred men. The ingenio was started in 1847, and had missed grinding only one year. He said that capitalists were timid about making advances on sugar estates during the war because they feared that the properties would be destroyed. After the war was over, they still were reluctant to put out their money in loans for the working capital of the estates, because of uncertainty as to the island's political future.

An illustration of Spanish indifference and almost treachery towards the sugar-refining industry of the island was noted by General Wilson in his visit to Cardenas. Here is what he jotted down in his rough notes:

"Visited large sugar-refinery, the third in size in the island. It was not in operation. Formerly turned out 200 bags of sugar a day, the bulk of their product going to Spain. Being ambitious, they increased the capacity of the plant to 1000 bags a day, and increased the capital stock from $200,000 to $1,000,000. Just when they had commenced to reap the benefit of their increased business, the Spanish government, in order to protect the sugar interests of Malaga, placed a prohibitive tariff on sugar, and this concern was forced to close."

Few persons understand the necessity of running the sugar-mills night and day during the grinding season in the spring of the year, from four to five months. It is because the raw material deteriorates if kept for any length of time. The sugar in the cane dries up if the cane is not crushed promptly. After being harvested it cannot be kept like cereals. Grain and cotton may be kept for a long time before they are transformed into the finished product. It is not so with sugar. The most expeditious action is necessary if the full available strength is to be procured from the cane.

All sugar is produced from two sources—the sugar-

cane and the sugar-beet. The cane grows in tropical
countries almost entirely, the fields in Louisiana, in our
own country, being a small and almost inconsiderable
part in the vast output. The beets grow in the temper-
ate zone. It has not been proved that raw sugar made
from the beet can be produced and landed at the refinery
at two cents a pound, and hence one can see what an advantage Cuba has in her great industry. It is for that
reason that the question of the ultimate annexation of
Cuba to this country may play an important part in our
national life. We all remember what a row was caused
by the beet-sugar men and the cane-growers of Louisiana
over the tariff a few years ago, when it became necessary,
because of the McKinley tariff law, to pay a bounty for
sugar produced in this country in competition with free
sugar from other countries. The sugar problem always
complicated the relation of Hawaii to the United States
before annexation. Should Cuba become an integral part
of the United States, another tariff row will undoubtedly
result. It is for that reason that the probabilities that
Cuba will ever become more than a colony of this country are remote. It is only fair, however, to the Cuban
sugar-producers to say that while for business reasons
they would prefer annexation to this country, they all
declared, so far as I was able to get their personal sentiments, that they would be satisfied with an American
protectorate or a colonial government. All they wanted,
they said, was a settled condition of the politics of Cuba.
They declared that under the present tariff conditions
they could make money, and that if the time of the
mortgages were extended, which has been done, they

saw a profitable future ahead of the industry in the island.

Such, in a general way, was the condition of the sugar industry directly after the war ceased. The future of the industry was summed up for me in these words by probably the best-informed man in Cuba on the subject :

" Prosperity in the sugar industry in the future in Cuba lies along a very simple line. It is the ownership or control of the lands suitable for growing the cane, and so situated that the expense of transporting both the cane and the sugar made from it is at the minimum."

CHAPTER XVI

SECOND only in importance to the sugar industry in Cuba is that of tobacco. Its output amounts to many millions of dollars a year, and fully 100,-000 persons, and perhaps more, are dependent upon it for a livelihood. Owing to a peculiar combination of soil and climate, Cuba has a primacy among tobacco-growing countries, which undoubtedly will be retained always, because the flavor of the tobacco raised cannot be, or has not been, equalled anywhere else.

The tobacco industry went through the same vicissitudes during the war as the sugar industry; plantations were destroyed, first by the insurgents and later by the Spanish forces, unless the owners paid for their protection; drying-houses were burned, and the tobacco seedlings destroyed; but as soon as peace came it began to recover swiftly. About half of a normal crop was raised in 1899, and it had the advantage of being of unusually fine flavor and texture. Prices were very high at the beginning of the year, but they came down to a practical business basis soon after the crop was harvested in February and March, and as soon as there were undoubted indications that by the year 1900 a full crop would be raised.

TOBACCO IN CUBA

Large quantities of tobacco had been husbanded, and so when peace came the cigar-making industry in the one hundred or more factories of Havana jumped at once into a really flourishing condition. Every factory was running early in the year, and the wages ranged from four dollars upward a day. To that industry alone prob-

TOBACCO DRYING IN THE SUN

ably could be ascribed the apparent prosperous condition of the people in the city almost as soon as peace came.

In 1897 General Weyler prohibited the exportation of tobacco from Cuba, except to Spain. During the blockade in the war it was necessary to send tobacco to distant ports of the island that were not blockaded, for shipment to foreign lands. The peasants, who are expert in the growing of the staple, were driven from their homes, but the factories in Havana were not entirely shut down. Their owners kept them running at a loss rather than have certain well-known brands of cigars fail their customers in foreign lands, and they sent money to the planters to pay the military factions not to destroy the bases of supply entirely. What might be called tricks of the trade were used in some cases to keep up the supply of raw material, through the importation of tobacco from Puerto Rico and other places. Thousands of cigar-makers went to Florida, where the cigar-making industry flourished as never before, to supply the market in this country.

The war ceased at a most fortunate time for the tobacco industry. The plants are placed in the ground in October, November, and December, and the harvest begins within three months. The harvest in the sugar industry cannot be reaped until from twelve to eighteen months. One can understand at once the immense advantage over sugar that tobacco had in the recuperation of agriculture in the island. Although tobacco is grown almost in every part of Cuba, it is on the western end of the island, in a district about eighty miles long and twenty-five wide, that the most delicate flavors are produced. There is a sheltering mountain-range running from east to west along the Atlantic coast. In the shade on this range the seedlings are propagated. It is through the situation of these mountains that the peculiar climatic effects are secured to the plant's great advantage. The secret of the soil properties has not yet been fathomed. Seedlings from the Vuelta Abajo district do not give the same flavor when raised in other soils.

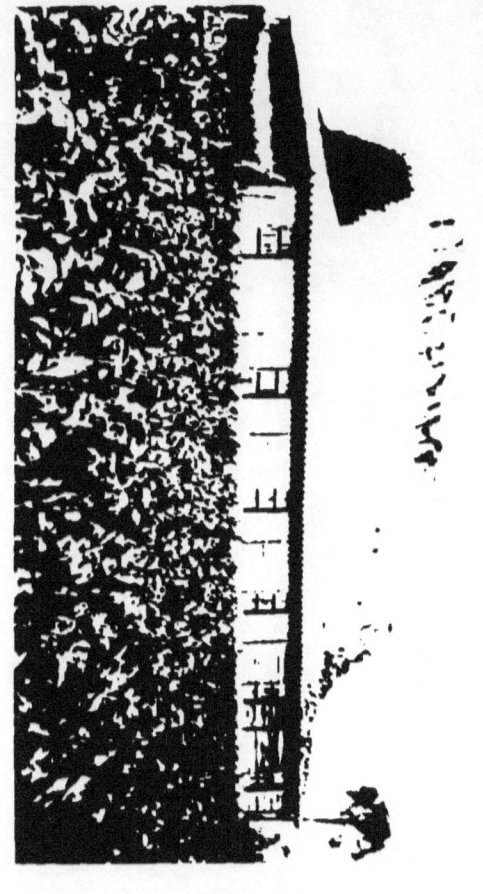

DRYING-HOUSE IN A TOBACCO-FIELD

Not all the Vuelta Abajo district is adapted to tobacco-raising. The plant is grown in patches of from five to thirty acres, and it requires expert labor to produce it. The field-workers are men and women of delicate touch and perception. Every plant is handled and guarded with the utmost care and vigilance. The plants are watched with the closest fidelity, to protect them from insects. When the plant reaches a certain stage all the leaves but about ten or a dozen are stripped off and the head of the plant is taken away. This is to develop the full strength of the plant in the finest and largest kind of leaves. At just the right time the leaves are picked from each plant, with the exception of two or three. The picked leaves are strung across poles in large drying-houses with thatched roofs. The leaves are kept there from two to three months, until they become yellow and dry. They remain in the houses until the rainy season, when they may be packed in bales of about one hundred pounds without danger of crumpling. Some of these bales are worth almost their weight in gold; and, indeed, it may be said of the very finest qualities produced that such a comparison is literally true.

There is immense profit in a well-conducted tobacco-plantation. Many of the owners used to count on a yearly profit of fully fifty per cent. of the actual value of the plantation. The owners of some of the largest factories in Havana either own the fields from which they draw the supply of tobacco for their various brands of cigars, or control them through a working arrangement with their real owners. Many of the growers are tenant farmers, and share equally the profit received from the output with the real owners. Owing to the difficulty of transferring real-estate titles in Cuba, many of the manufacturers of cigars prefer to make an arrangement to control the crop on certain lands.

Recently there has been an attempt on the part of the capitalists interested in the manufacture of Cuban cigars to get control of the agricultural side of the industry, but with what success has not been revealed fully. There has been a combination formed undoubtedly among the manufacturers in Havana, and capital to the value of fully $100,000,000 has been ready to form the so-called trust, but the task of getting the tenant-farmers to pool their interests with those of the combination is not easy, for it runs against the traditions of centuries in this branch of agriculture in Cuba, and might reduce the actual grower to the plane of a mere workman on the lowest possible wages.

It is agreed that one man with an ordinary-sized family may care for from three to four acres of tobacco-plants, and produce in three months about $1000 worth of leaves at about a cost of $175 to $250. To a man who is ignorant; who has few desires for luxuries, as we know them; who is content to live in a hut out in the country with his half-naked family, his pigs and his dogs and his gun; who neither reads nor writes, and who desires to gamble, with dominoes chiefly—such an existence produces a state of happiness that is little short of ideal. Thousands upon thousands of men lead such lives in Cuba, and they welcomed the cessation of war because it restored them to their former life of entire comfort. Free Cuba was a matter to which they were profoundly indifferent politically so long as they were free Cubans.

Some of these tenant farmers hire field laborers. The price for the most expert cultivators was as high as three dollars a day this year, probably owing to the scarcity of laborers, but the price of ordinary labor was about one dollar a day.

So active was the demand for tobacco this year that the entire crop was sold practically before it was harvested. There was no lack in getting money advances, and so a measure of prosperity was quickly restored to the Vuelta Abajo district, the largest part of which is in the province of Pinar del Rio. There was no person of thrift who did not profit by it. It was easy to get land to till, and there was a demand for laborers greater than the supply. The contrast between the fresh and beautiful fields of green tobacco in Pinar del Rio early in the year and the grass-grown districts of the other parts of the island was most marked. I spent part of one day on a plantation on the outskirts of the city of Pinar del Rio, and found an interesting illustration of what thrift in growing tobacco meant. There was a little batch of tobacco leaves set apart for drying in the large drying-house on the plantation, and I asked if they were of a peculiar kind.

"No," said the planter, laughing. "Those do not belong to me. Whose do you suppose they are?"

I said I could not guess, and he replied:

"There is nearly $300 worth of tobacco there, and it all belongs to our cook. He grew it in his spare moments on land near the house, and it is one of the perquisites of his place. You see, there are worse jobs in the world than being a cook in Cuba, if, in addition to your work, you can make what is known in your country as 'velvet,' to the extent of $300."

That planter informed me that a man owning thirty acres of tobacco-growing land in that region could clear

EXPERT FIELD-HANDS AT WORK

from $3000 to $4000 a year easily. He said he knew of one planter who had about 4000 acres, from which his clear profit was fully $40,000 a year before the war. A man named Diaz, in San Luis, was said to reap a profit of $122,000 a year from his estate, one of the largest in Cuba. The largest cigar manufacturer in Cuba, Gustav Bock, who manufactures nearly one-half of the cigars made in Havana, is one of the few manufacturers owning large tracts of tobacco-growing lands. He planted no less than 7,000,000 plants this year. His experience with the agricultural side of the industry had been such that he became the leading spirit in the attempt to transform the industry into the trust already spoken of. There can be no doubt that the agricultural side of the industry is therefore profitable to all growers, large or small.

Throughout the Vuelta Abajo district in March one could see numerous new drying-houses in process of erection. One of the drying-houses that I visited was packed full from ground to roof. There were no less than thirteen stories, or layers, of tobacco leaves hung up in it.

The manufacturing side of this industry, like the agricultural side, has its traditions and well-established customs. The war interfered with one of the most interesting of these customs, but only war could stop it, for as soon as peace came it was resumed. That was the custom of the cigar-makers to hire men to read aloud to them during certain hours of the day. There is not a cigar factory of any size in Havana that does not have its "reader." He comes twice a day and reads aloud to cigar-makers, usually an hour and a half at each session. Each reading is divided into two parts, one part being given to newspaper reading and the other to purely literary reading. The cigar-makers each contribute ten cents a week to the reader's support, and when there are from three to four hundred operatives in one room it may be seen that the reader makes a handy sum for three hours' work a day.

The custom of employing these readers is practically as old as the cigar-making industry in Havana. The manufacturers have tried several times to stop it for one reason or another, but it has invariably brought on a strike, and the workmen have won. When the war came General Weyler stopped the reading in the factories because there was so much of what he thought was seditious in the newspapers, and because he also thought that the readings fomented trouble in the city. As soon as the war was over, the reading was resumed. I attended one of these readings at the factory of J. Vales & Co. The reader sat in a high chair, where he could be seen by all the workers. The president of the labor union rang a bell for silence; and then, with a rasping voice that carried the words sharply into every part of the room, the reader began his literary selection for the day. It was a Spanish translation of *Les Misérables*. Later he read the daily newspaper. The reader is always selected by competition. Trials are held, and then the workmen vote as to a choice. A committee in charge selects the works to be read. Sometimes a vote is taken among the workmen when there is divided opinion as to a programme. Usually a very high grade of fiction is selected. Travel, history, and humor also play a part in the readings, and the result is that the average cigar-maker in Havana has an acquaintance with literature that few persons in his grade of life possess.

The cigar factories in Havana are found in most cases in buildings the exteriors of which resemble stores and dwellings. There are few plain buildings, such as are built for factories in the United States. Some old mansion or building that could be adapted to any of a half-dozen purposes is used. There is a larger percentage of loss in the making up of the raw material than in the United States. It is customary to allow each workman in Cuba to make from five to ten cigars a day for his personal consumption out of the material on which he is working. When that material is of the very finest quality, a leaf that is made into cigars selling for from thirty cents to a dollar each in this country, one can see that the perquisites of cigar-makers are costly to their employers. It is a custom, and that is above all questions of profit and loss, especially when the boss loses.

The wages of the men run from $20 to as high as $35 a week. There is an apprenticeship system. Extensive use is also made of the labor of women and girls. The women and girls make from one dollar to one dollar and a half a day, and are employed in a variety of tasks. They select and grade wrappers, and many of them are employed in the cigarette departments of the factories. They also do some of the packing work, prepare boxes, and place labels on the cigars. The women are of all ages. As a rule, they work in rooms by themselves.

Before the war the annual crop of Cuban tobacco was about 600,000 bales of 100 pounds each. About two-fifths of it was used in Havana in cigar and cigarette making, and the other three-fifths was exported. The crop for 1899 probably ran close to 300,000 bales, despite the scarcity of labor.

The pathway of returning prosperity to Cuba ran through the tobacco-plantations first. It was through the revival of the tobacco industry that the people of the island knew what the blessing of peace meant in a commercial sense.

CHAPTER XVII

JOHN McCULLAGH, former chief of police of New York city, strolled down the Prado in Havana one day in February, 1899, and cast a critical eye over eight hundred men drawn up in double rank in companies and battalions. The men were in citizens' dress, and they stood at attention. They were the men who had been selected from twenty - four hundred applicants for membership in Havana's new and first real police force. They ranged from 5 feet 6½ inches to 6 feet 4½ inches in height. Every eye was towards the front and every man was alert. They were nervous, but keenly intelligent; nearly one - half were well dressed. The rest had made an effort to hide deficiencies in personal appearance. Nine-tenths were in excellent physical condition. Here and there thin and drawn features told a story of the hardships of campaigning or of illness. Most of them had been advocates of Cuba's freedom, and probably one-half of them had served in jungles in the starved so-called Cuban army. It was plain, as McCullagh went down the ranks, that there was an *esprit de corps*. Pride in the work and an eagerness to show efficiency were stamped on every face. Except for their

376

ages, they looked like West Point "plebes" after being
lined up for the fourth or fifth time.

Several American army officers, detailed to give instruction in drilling, were within call as McCullagh
sauntered to the right of the line.

RAW MATERIAL FOR HAVANA'S NEW POLICE DRAWN UP FOR DRILL

He called an interpreter, who summoned the battalion's chiefs and captains.

"I want the men to move by fours right," he said,
"and then form company front and march up the
Prado."

The interpreter told the assembled officers what the
order was; the army officers gave a word of explana-

tion, and then a great jabbering and gesticulation began. The officers all talked at once. They shrieked at one another; they threw their hands this way and that; they took measured steps here and there; then they cooled down into an animated jabbering, and finally one after another ceased talking and assumed an air of calm. In a flash the storm broke again. McCullagh had been standing, half-amused, but with cold exterior, off at one side. His brow now became wrinkled, he bit his lower lip, opened his mouth to speak, checked himself, clinched his hands, and then blurted out in a sharp order:

"Interpreter, tell those men to quit talking, and go and *do it!*"

The officers gave a searching glance at the former New York chief of police. He smiled, and they started off with animation. Shrill commands in Spanish rang down the lines. At last "Forward, march" was given, and the entire body of men moved off at a quick pace. Then they formed company front, and at last John Mc-Cullagh was happy.

"Good! good!" he shouted. "Very good! *Bueno!*"

It had all been done in ten days. It was a show well worth seeing, and it was a worthy source of pride. Only ten days before had the first man in the parade passed his physical and mental examination. If John McCullagh has had one superior quality of excellence as a police-man, it has been as a disciplinarian, a drill-master, and he has always showed it in controlling a large body of men. Raw and crude as was his material in this case, from a military standpoint, his skill—one might almost say his genius—showed itself as those men marched up

Havana's great show street. The drill lasted half an hour. The men were dismissed, and ordered to appear again for the usual morning and afternoon drills. The officers were told to come to police headquarters in the evening for instruction.

Twice a day McCullagh went through the work of drilling his policemen, of putting spirit and pride into

JOHN McCULLAGH
Organizer of the Police Force

them, of instructing their officers in what real police duty means. That alone was a tremendous task, but it was a mere trifle of the work McCullagh had to do in an advisory capacity for the creation and equipment of the Havana police force.

It was on December 14, 1898, that McCullagh arrived in Havana. General Greene, the first military governor of the city under the United States, had asked President

McKinley to send him. Colonel Moulton of the Second Illinois Volunteers had been appointed Chief of Police.

MAJOR EVANS, U. S. V.
Organizer of the Criminal Court

Colonel Moulton and Mr. McCullagh at once plunged into work. For three days they drove about the city. They studied the police system in force. It was a farce. About 1800 men were on duty. Of these, 300 were municipal police, appointed by the City Council to enforce the city ordinances; 300 were government police, appointed by authorities of the province; 1200 belonged to the *orden publico*. The 1200 were really soldiers. They and the city police, in cases of arrest for felony, had to turn prisoners over to the government police. There were no station-houses. All the prisoners were taken to the *vivac*, or city jail. A record was made of the arrest, and that was as far as all police records went. There was no record of criminals kept, and after a man was sent to jail, all sight of him was lost so far as the police were concerned.

The policeman, after an arrest, took his prisoner to his captain, whose office was in his residence. The captain committed him to jail and sent the case to a magistrate. There were twelve magistrates, six of whom were "judges of the first instance." The salary of these was $5000 each, and they adjudicated felonies. The other six judges received no salaries, and they sat in misdemeanor cases. They simply lived on blackmail and robbery. Those prisoners who had money never went to jail to stay. Only a Tammany official in the old days could thoroughly "size-up" such a situation. It would probably appal him at the start as a "magnificent graft." After from one to three days the prisoners' cases were heard, and then came jail or a fine. The police knew no more about the cases, except as an unusually intelli-

THE MOUNTED POLICE

gent policeman kept a record for himself. The man who went to jail got out afterwards as best he could, either from expiration of sentence or through corruption. The system was thoroughly Spanish in its operation, and corruption was its corner-stone.

Four days after his arrival McCullagh reported to General Greene, and laid before him a full and complete reorganization plan. He divided the city into six inspection districts and twelve precincts. He recommended that 360 night posts and 180 day posts be established. He divided the force which was necessary in his judgment as follows: 1 chief, 1 deputy-chief, 8 inspectors, 12 captains, 48 lieutenants, 834 patrolmen, 10 detective sergeants, 14 detectives, 12 precinct detectives, and 12 doormen. Of the patrolmen, 100 were to be mounted for duty in the suburbs. The force was to consist of about 1000 men.

The same day that this report was made applications for membership on the force began. The word was simply passed around. General Greene approved the report, and then McCullagh went to work on equipments. He sent orders to New York for shields, belts, day and night sticks, tassels, wreaths, numbers, and other paraphernalia. The United States government agreed to furnish pistols. General Greene co-operated instantly with McCullagh. A design for a uniform and buttons was agreed upon. There was not sufficient cloth in Havana to make the blue uniforms. The contractor had to sail for New York to get it. For the buttons and shields special dies had to be cast. They had to bear the coat of arms of Havana. This occupied a month.

McCullagh then started to get up his printing. These were desk blotters, arrest-books, force-books, oath-books, returns of various kinds, complaint - books against the force, transfer-books, and other kinds of stationery. He drew up a set of 180 rules and regulations, and instructions in the school of the soldier and of the company— all to be printed in English and Spanish. Bids were asked for the printing, and a contract given. A printers' strike delayed matters in the work for an entire week.

GENERAL MARIO MENOCAL
First Chief of Police of Havana

General Greene went home on December 24th, and General Ludlow took his place as governor of the city. Naturally General Ludlow went all over the ground again with McCullagh. Everything was explained, and General Ludlow approved the plans. There was some delay about the selection of station-houses and their fittings. There also developed some friction in the actual control of the police. Finally Colonel Moulton was deposed as chief and sent back to his regiment, and General Menocal, formerly of the insurgent army, was appointed chief. Practically nothing had been accomplished from December 16th to January 12th. McCullagh grew impatient and wanted to go home. He told General Ludlow so, and it is no secret that General Ludlow refused to let him go. McCullagh asked if anybody was to stand between him and the general in creating the force, and the general said there was not. McCullagh went to work again with renewed vigor, and on January 16th the first applicants were examined. Two surgeons were employed. The men had to be at least 5 feet 6½ inches tall, and to be in good physical condition, or able to be put in that condition soon. They had to read and write. No distinction was made as to religion or past political sympathies. Quite a number of former Spaniards were accepted. Those who stood the test were presented to McCullagh. He took the best and placed them to one side as finally accepted. The others were placed on a reserve list. He did not reject them, because he feared he might run short of men. Day after day the examination went on, until 2700 men had been passed upon, and 800 accepted. Drills began at once; measurements of every man were taken for uniforms, and officers were appointed. Everything was done systematically.

Many of the officers were former Cuban officers. One inspector was General Menocal's brother. A captain was a nephew of Henry Clews; another captain was Roosevelt's bugler, Cassi, who had seen service in Dahomey, in Tonquin, in the Chinese navy, and in the American army. The deputy-chief was General Cardenas of the

Cuban army. Most of the patrolmen were members of the best Cuban families. Some of them had been wealthy, some looked like former prosperous business men. Even in citizen's dress, some of them half-ragged, they presented an unusually intelligent appearance.

McCullagh's hard work was in full swing. He found that there was no accurate map of distances in Havana A civil engineer who was recommended to him from New York as competent—a man who once had surveyed part of Havana — was appointed a lieutenant of police, and ordered to measure every street in the city. Several days were occupied in this, and finally the posts were laid out for the entire city by feet. It was a tremendous undertaking, but Havana distances were soon known to the exact foot.

It was decided to fix their salaries — chief of police, $4000; deputy-chief, $2000; inspectors, $1800; captains, $115 a month; lieutenants (sergeants in New York), $90 a month; sergeants (roundsmen in New York), $65 a month; patrolmen and doormen, $50 a month. Each man had to pay for his equipment in deductions from his salary.

I went with McCullagh to one of his drills. It all had to be done through interpreters. Commands were given in English and Spanish, so as to accustom the men to the Americanizing of affairs. There were many mistakes. McCullagh frequently dashed into the lines and set some officer or man in the right path. He was patient, but severe and stern, and a wave of discipline seemed to run through the ranks at his first approach. Nevertheless, he was kindly at all times, and discouraged no man. It was

a terrific trial. He muttered criticisms in confidence to
me as the men passed before him, pointed out this and
that man as especially adapted to police duty, tried in
vain to repress the jabberings and gesticulations of his
officers, and in an undertone once said, regarding the
display of a piece of annoying stupidity :

"Now wouldn't that drive a New York police official
crazy ?"

Marked progress was made, however, and finally, after
a hard attempt to make the men break ranks in proper
form, he jumped into a carriage half exhausted, but really proud.

"It's hard work," he exclaimed, "but I'll have those
men in as fine shape as any police force in the world before I finish."

Then he dashed to his printers. It was the old mañana story again. Certain blanks would surely be ready
to-morrow.

"What time ?" asked the outwardly imperturbable
McCullagh.

"Two o'clock."

McCullagh sent a look into his contractor's eyes that
would have made a man in New York sink into a chair
in fright. He paused a long time.

"I'll give you until four o'clock," he said, "and if you
don't deliver them you'll not get paid for them."

Then he jumped into his carriage again. He said he
expected to go through with the same thing every day
for a week with his printers. Off he raced to the clothing contractor. Some of the patrolmen were trying on
their uniforms. Here was apparent progress, but it was

THE DRILL OF THE FOURTH BATTALION—" PRESENT ARMS."

only apparent. The force was nearly a week behind time. I have never seen a more excited and gesticulating crowd of men than in that tailoring establishment. From the proprietor down to porters all were crying mañana, and McCullagh finally fled.

Gradually McCullagh perfected his work, and in the latter part of February the force went to work. At first the people refused to take the policemen seriously. There were numerous riots, and several policemen were killed in them. There were several clashes, also, between them and United States soldiers off duty. General Menocal's course failed to secure public approval, and in a few weeks he resigned. Gradually the police force secured public respect. The desire to use fire-arms too freely was repressed, and by mid-summer the force was in satisfactory working order, considering the lack of experience in police-work on the part of the men and the absence of all proper police traditions in Havana. The result was a tribute to McCullagh's ability.

THE END